Dear Reader,

I so enjoy libraries and old houses, so it's been fun to take part in Secrets of the Blue Hill Library. I'm glad you've joined us as we've gotten to know Anne and her family, as well as discover the village of Blue Hill. I hope you've had as much fun with the series as I have had.

I'm a huge fan of Edgar Allan Poe, so it was a pleasure to weave this plot to include one of my all-time favorite authors. Learning the value of some of his early works was fascinating. I hope you enjoy a glimpse into rare literary valuations.

As an avid reader, I love to connect with other readers. Visit me on my Web site robincaroll.com and sign up for my newsletter. You can connect with at facebook.com/robincaroll or write to me via snail mail at PO Box 242091, Little Rock, Arkansas 72223. I can't wait to hear from you!

Blessings,
Robin Caroll
writing as Emily Thomas

Secrets of the Blue Hill Library

Nowhere to Be Found
Shadows of the Past
Unlocking the Truth
Theft and Thanksgiving
The Christmas Key
Off the Shelf
Gone in a Flash
All Sewn Up
If Walls Could Talk

The Rightful Owner

Secrets of the
BLUE HILL LIBRARY

EMILY THOMAS

Guideposts
New York

Secrets of the Blue Hill Library is a trademark of Guideposts.

Published by Guideposts Books & Inspirational Media
110 William Street
New York, New York 10038
Guideposts.org

Copyright © 2014 by Guideposts. All rights reserved.

This book, or parts thereof, may not be reproduced, stored in a retrieval system, or transmitted in any form or by any means, electronic, mechanical, photocopying, recording, or otherwise, without the written permission of the publisher.

The characters and events in this book are fictional, and any resemblance to actual persons or events is coincidental.

Every attempt has been made to credit the sources of copyrighted material used in this book. If any such acknowledgment has been inadvertently omitted or miscredited, receipt of such information would be appreciated.

Scripture references are from the following sources: The Holy Bible, King James Version (KJV). The Holy Bible, New International Version®, NIV®. Copyright © 1973, 1978, 1984 by International Bible Society. Used by permission of Zondervan.

"From the Guideposts Archives" is reprinted with permission from *Guideposts* magazine. Copyright © 2005 by Guideposts. All rights reserved.

Cover and interior design by Müllerhaus
Cover illustration by Rob Fiore, represented by Artworks Illustration
Typeset by Aptara, Inc.

Printed and bound in the United States of America
10 9 8 7 6 5 4 3 2 1

The Rightful Owner

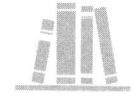

Chapter One

"We may not finish sorting all these by next weekend." Anne Gibson pushed her glasses back up the bridge of her nose and stared at the boxes of books covering every surface—even the floor—in the Reference Room of Blue Hill Library.

The task felt a little overwhelming at the moment.

"I thought the same thing myself," said Grace Hawkins. The editor of the *Blue Hill Gazette* rolled her shoulders as she stood and stretched.

Anne grinned. "I know you didn't come by to volunteer, but when you saw how overwhelmed I was, you offered to help, so thank you."

"No problem. Happy to help a friend in need, but tell me again how Wendy got you to agree to this sale." Grace's blonde hair, blue eyes, and skin so flawless and pale it almost looked translucent fit her beautiful personality to a T.

"Well..." Anne tugged a disinfectant towelette from its tub and wiped the grime from her hands. Some of these books were really old and quite dusty. "I mentioned that I needed to think about a fundraiser for the library, and Wendy...well, she went Wendy on me."

Wendy Pyle had become Anne's close friend and confidante since Anne had returned to town, but sometimes, just sometimes,

Wendy's extreme take-charge manner left others trembling in her wake, feeling as if they'd been run over by a steamroller.

For the most part, however, Anne's and Wendy's individual personalities and strengths truly complemented each other, and Anne was always grateful for Wendy's dedication to the library.

Grace chuckled. "Which means she just plowed on ahead and put the used-book sale in motion."

Anne smiled. "You have to admit, it should bring in quite a bit of money. Especially holding it next weekend in conjunction with the annual town history celebration."

Blue Hill, Pennsylvania, was a charming town tucked into rolling hills that reached out to the mountains in the western part of the state. The landscape captured attention, especially around this time of year when foliage was at its brightest.

Soon, pumpkin patches would be bursting, pulling in more tourists to the area. Even now, the hint of fall seasoned the air with the rustle of leaves and the crispness in the morning breeze.

It was an amazing place to raise a family, Anne knew. She'd grown up in Blue Hill, playing in this very house as a child. Aunt Edie had moved here with her parents, Anne's great-grandparents, after they'd sold their family farm. When Anne's great-grandparents grew frail with age, Aunt Edie reset her life to stay put in Blue Hill so she could care for her parents. They'd left this house to Aunt Edie in their will.

Anne had gone to New York City more than a decade and a half ago, following the career path Aunt Edie had encouraged her to take—the career path that had allowed Anne to follow her dream and her love of reading. It was there that she'd met Eric, an editor at a big publishing house. The fact that he was a dozen years her senior hadn't stopped Anne from falling in love and marrying him. They'd welcomed two beautiful children into their lives—Ben and Liddie—before a sudden heart attack had taken Eric away. That was over three years ago.

And now Anne was back in Blue Hill, following Aunt Edie's bequest to turn her old Victorian house into a library.

Everything always seemed to come back to Aunt Edie, Anne's beloved great-aunt, who seemed to have more layers than a fully ripe onion.

"I sure hope it brings in some money," Grace mumbled, "after all the hours we've spent sorting and pricing these books." She lifted her hand and studied her fingernails. "I'm pretty certain I've ruined this manicure."

"I'll be thanking Wendy when the money from this book sale lets us afford those new audio/video systems for the Children's Room." Anne chuckled. "And I thank you again for giving up your Friday night to help me."

"It wasn't as if I had any other plans," Grace said. She pulled another box toward her and reached for a book. "I guess I could have gone over to the football field and covered the high school game, but the student reporter would have been disappointed. He's hoping to pursue a career in journalism, so I want to teach him all the good stuff he won't learn in college."

The late evening breeze blew over the rolling hills and in through the open window of the second-floor landing. The house-turned-library sat atop Blue Hill, named so because of the fields of bluebells surrounding it. During late spring, beautiful blue flowers covered the entire hill. But this time of year brought its own beauty in the vivid colors of the leaves adorning the stately old trees surrounding Blue Hill.

"So why isn't Wendy here helping us sort?" Grace asked. "With Chad coaching the high school football team, I would have thought she'd use the free time to come over here to help."

Anne shook her head. "Wendy's the best coach's wife. She doesn't miss a game if she can help it. But tonight, I bet she wishes she was here instead. The twins have come down with sore throats, and she wants to make sure she doesn't have a strep outbreak on her hands." Wendy had seven children, ranging from age fourteen down to four-year-old twins. How she found the time to read as much as she did, Anne couldn't guess, but the woman went through books almost as quickly as Anne herself.

"Strep? Ugh." Grace frowned. "Poor Wendy. I hope no one else gets it. I detest being sick."

"Me too. And when kids are sick, it's even worse." Anne hated when Ben or Liddie were under the weather. Even at nine and five, respectively, when they were sick, they were as helpless as toddlers.

"Here's another damaged book." Grace handed a tattered-covered hardback across the table to Anne.

The spine had been cracked and pages drifted to the floor as Anne took the book. She recovered the pages and stared at the title: *Eight Cousins* by Louisa May Alcott. Anne opened the cover and perused the copyright information. It wasn't a particularly old copy of the book, but it had obviously been read many times and apparently carted many places.

Anne smiled to herself. Had some girl, much like herself at a younger age, carried around a favorite book, diving into it like visiting with a best friend? The memory took her back to her childhood when she'd spent many summer days lazing on the creaky porch of this very house, immersed in a book right alongside her aunt until the sun had long disappeared. How many times had she and Aunt Edie come out from under the spell of a book to realize dinnertime had passed them smoothly by? Anne loved those memories. Loved those special times shared with her beloved aunt.

Sometimes Anne really, really missed Aunt Edie. Especially when she was surrounded by stacks and stacks of old books.

Anne loved the feel and smell of books, even the old dusty ones like this copy of *Eight Cousins*. She always had. And she missed having Aunt Edie to share book adventures with. However, in recent days, she'd learned quite a bit about her beloved aunt that she hadn't known before her passing.

"Can you save it?" Grace asked.

Anne returned her attention to the book in her hand. "I don't think so." She set it inside the box under the large reference table. She'd been sorting the damaged books into two boxes: one held books that she could repair with a little time and attention, and in the other she placed books that couldn't be repaired.

It nearly broke her heart to know the books would need to be recycled into something else, but she'd seen a couple of ideas on the DIY channel about how to turn old books into things like lampshades, or how to embroider book pages and frame them. She couldn't wait to try her hand at some of the crafts. The kids would love helping her too. Maybe they could make some Christmas presents for their teachers.

She couldn't believe the holidays were just around the corner. Where had summer gone?

"Here are some more hardback mysteries. Where do you want them, again?" Grace asked.

"There." Anne pointed at the table where she'd sorted all the mystery/suspense/thriller titles.

"This table's getting pretty full too," Grace said, setting a romance novel on the table adjacent to her. The romance table had filled up so quickly that Anne had pushed one of the folding tables beside it to accommodate more titles.

"I know." Anne had no more space available. Maybe she should start pricing and putting books in bins. Alex could help her transport them downstairs in the elevator tomorrow morning so she could store them away until next weekend.

Alex Ochs. He'd been her best friend before they were high school sweethearts. When she'd accepted Aunt Edie's bequest and returned to Blue Hill, she'd hired Alex as the contractor for the library renovations. Since then, they'd reestablished their acquaintance. It was nice to have her friend back.

Actually, it was nice to be back in Blue Hill, period. She'd come home. And it was no longer Aunt Edie's house—it was hers and the kids'. And the town's library.

Anne stood and glanced at her watch: 9:25. "Maybe we should call it a night." They had ordered pizza for supper, then she'd tucked Liddie into bed at eight, but she had let Ben stay up until nine. Anne hated to admit it, but she was exhausted. Getting back into the swing of school after summer break was hard enough, but add to that the chore of getting the library ready for the town's celebration and now this prep work for the sale? Anne was ready to drop.

"Just let me finish this box," Grace said.

Anne grinned. Grace always liked to finish what she started, even if it was sorting a box of used books.

She wiped her hand with another towelette. Maybe tomorrow Wendy and some of her kids could come help finish up the initial sorting. If they didn't have strep. At least the Miller twins, Remi and Bella, the part-time employees of the library, would both be in tomorrow. And Grace had said she would come by to help again tomorrow afternoon after she finished up at work.

"Wow, this is an old one," Grace said.

"What?" Anne moved to stand beside her friend and look over her shoulder.

Grace slowly handed the book to Anne. "It looks pretty unique to me."

Anne's fingers caressed the well-worn and smooth brown-faded-to-yellow cover. The pages snapped brittle as she turned to the title and copyright page and read:

Tales of the Grotesque and Arabesque.

By Edgar A. Poe.

Seltsamen tochter Jovis

Seinem schosskinde

Der *Phantasic*.

Goethe

In Two Volumes.
Vol. I.
Philadelphia:
Lea and Blanchard.
1840.

Anne's heart caught in her throat. Was she *really* holding in her hands a first edition of this rare and valuable book?

Where did it come from? More importantly, who did it belong to?

Chapter Two

"Twelve to forty thousand dollars!"

Wendy and Grace stared at Anne as if she'd just announced she was running off and joining the circus.

Anne was shocked too. "Twelve to forty thousand dollars, depending on the condition of the book, is what this edition is worth. If it's really a first edition." She touched the book she'd carefully slipped into a protective acid/lignin-free sleeve last night.

"That's insane," Wendy said.

"It's not as valuable as one of Poe's other works. One set the record for the highest amount received at auction for American literature back in 2009," Anne explained.

"How much?" Wendy asked.

Anne grinned. She couldn't wait to see Wendy's face on this little tidbit. "The details first," she teased, determined to draw out the suspense. "Poe's first published work, *Tamerlane and Other Poems* is like a forty-page pamphlet. There are only twelve known copies of the publication in existence today. Experts estimate only fifty copies were originally printed, and the twelve known copies were only uncovered eleven years after Poe died."

"Okay, okay...you've got us interested. How much?" Grace urged.

"Six hundred, sixty-two thousand, five hundred dollars."

Wendy's eyes bugged out. Grace's jaw dropped. Literally—her mouth really hung open.

Anne chuckled.

"You have got to be pulling our legs!" Wendy exclaimed.

"Nope. It's the truth. You can look it up. In December of 2009, Christie's Auction in New York City sold it."

"Who has that kind of money?" Grace asked.

Anne shrugged. "Of the twelve known copies, only two are reported to be owned privately to even be put up for auction. The other ten are owned by institutions."

"I can't even write that amount, much less have it to spend. On a skimpy little pamphlet at that," Wendy said.

Anne laughed again. "Well, our Poe book here isn't worth a fraction of that amount. From all the expert sites I could find, these two volumes were the first collections of Edgar Allan Poe's short fiction. These volumes mark the culmination of his efforts that began back in 1833 to see his stories in book form."

Grace, hunched over one of the other library's computers, read out loud: "The publisher, Lea and Blanchard, published approximately 750 copies of the volumes, at their own risk and expense, and Poe only received twenty copies of the book as payment. No royalties were paid."

"Now *that's* crazy," Anne said. "No royalties paid on a book now worth thousands for a single issue."

"What stories are in the book?" Wendy asked. She'd made no apologies for not being a Poe fan when she'd arrived at the library early on this Saturday morning.

"Um, probably the only one you've heard of would be 'The Fall of the House of Usher,'" Anne answered. "Maybe 'The Devil in the Belfry'?"

Wendy shook her head. "I know about the House of Usher one. That one was popular. Oh, and 'The Tell-Tale Heart' and 'The Pit and the Pendulum.' I've heard of those as well."

Anne smiled. "Those came out a few years later, in magazines."

"So do you think that's a first edition?" Grace asked, pointing at the book.

Chewing her lip, Anne carefully removed the book from its protection and evaluated it using the criteria she had found on the Web site. "Well, the publisher's purple muslin with printed paper spine label is cracked, and so are the rear inner hinges." She cautiously inspected the book even more. "It lacks the rear endpaper. The text has darkened with the patina of years. Mild age darkening to the paper, even discoloration to pages, as typical with books of this vintage. It has moderate foxing."

"Okay, I'll bite," Wendy said. "What's foxing?"

Anne slipped the book back into the sleeve. "Foxing is the chemical reaction of the book's paper to the environment. It's the discoloration variance you notice."

"Ah. Now I see," Wendy said. "But, even with the cracks, missing stuff, and darkening and foxing, it's still worth that much?"

Anne looked back at the computer monitor before her. "According to this rare-book site, starting selling price is twelve thousand, five hundred dollars for the same book in similar condition."

"That'll bring in quite a bit of money for the library's audio/visual equipment," Wendy said.

Anne shook her head. "We can't sell it, Wendy. Someone had to have donated it in error. No one would give away something worth so much."

"Are you sure?" Grace asked. "I mean, it wasn't set aside or anything. I found it in the bottom of one of the boxes. It wasn't even in a sleeve like you put it in. Maybe the person didn't know its worth and gave it away."

"Could be, but we still need to find out who the owner is and return it to them," Anne said. "I wouldn't feel right otherwise. It's not really the library's to sell."

"So who accepted donations of the books?" Grace asked.

"Let's see…Wendy and I, and Remi and Bella, of course." Anne wrinkled her nose under her glasses, thinking. "I think Mildred and Coraline were helping out when some boxes were brought in as well. Oh, and Betty Bultman. I know she helped when Reverend Tom brought some boxes of books from the church's garage sale that were left over."

"Did you keep a list of who donated what?" Grace asked.

"No way." Wendy frowned. "You've seen how many boxes of books have been donated. It would have been a huge task to try to keep track of that."

"Much like Goodwill and other groups, we provided blank donation forms to people for tax purposes," Anne said softly. "We helped them fill out the forms by just listing something along the lines of 'twenty used softcover books' or 'twenty hardback used books' under 'items donated.' Just stuff like that."

"Did you keep a copy of those? At least you'd have the names of who made donations at all," Grace said.

Anne shook her head. "We didn't. The library's CPA said we weren't required to keep a copy."

"Maybe you can show the book to everyone who's been here and see if anyone can remember it. That would be a starting point, at least," Grace said.

Wendy nodded. "You and I both don't remember seeing it come in, so that's two down. Remi and Bella are coming in today, right?"

Anne checked the time. "They should be here any minute. Maybe one of them was here when the book came in. They both have amazing memories." No surprise—the twins had graduated high school with honors and 4.0 grade point averages and were in the top five percent of their class. Fraternal twins, the girls looked as opposite as their personalities. They had started out as volunteers before becoming part-time employees. Now they were a huge asset to the library, and personal blessings to Anne.

"Yes, the benefits of youth," Grace said. As if she had anything to complain about. Grace was only in her early thirties, a couple of years younger than Anne herself, but was much accomplished as the town paper's editor-in-chief.

"I think Mrs. Bultman mentioned she had some blank price stickers she would bring by later this afternoon," Wendy said.

"She already did," Anne replied. "Mildred is out of town visiting family, but I think I'll call and invite Coraline to drop by. Maybe if I show her the book, it'll ring a bell or something."

"You have to love the woman, but seriously, she is more of a busybody than the birdwatcher she claims to be," Wendy said.

"That's not nice," Anne admonished. Even if the accusation was true.

"I didn't mean it in a bad way. I've just heard from the lifers of the town that ever since Coraline moved here over a dozen years ago, she's kept up with most everybody's history. If it's ever been public knowledge about this Poe book, Coraline Watson would be the one who'd know," Wendy said.

Very true.

"Didn't you get some of these books from the attic?" Grace asked.

Anne nodded. "Four boxes." But if the Poe title had been Aunt Edie's, why wouldn't Aunt Edie have safeguarded such a valuable edition? Surely she had to have known of its approximate worth. Or maybe she hadn't? Maybe someone had given her the book and she hadn't had any time to research its origin or value.

"So the book might legitimately belong to the library anyway," Wendy said.

"We have to know for sure," Anne answered. She couldn't remember what books were in the boxes from the attic. She couldn't even remember what the boxes she'd brought down had looked like. She must be more tired than she'd assumed. "Maybe between Remi and Bella, Coraline and Betty, someone will have an idea who donated the book."

"If not, how about I run a story in the *Gazette* about the book?" Grace asked. "Surely if the owner of the book reads it, they'll come forward."

"That's a great idea, Grace," Anne said.

"And it'll also give more publicity to the sale," Wendy added.

Anne grinned—Wendy was always thinking of ways to make her projects bigger and better. Her endless energy often tired Anne, but she was so grateful for their friendship—and grateful for how much Wendy did for the library and Anne and the kids.

"Mom, Ben won't let me play fetch with him and Hershey," Liddie whined as she appeared in the checkout area. Sometimes with her deep, brown eyes, Liddie looked so much like her father that it tugged on Anne's heart. Hard.

"Sweetheart, Ben and the dog play really rough together. Why don't you get one of your dolls and play?"

"Can I take Cleopatra outside?" Liddie asked.

"You know you can't take her outside. Why don't you take Betsy instead?" Cleopatra was a special gift given to her by Eric on one of his rare business trips, and she'd received a recent makeover at Minnie's Doll Hospital. Betsy, on the other hand, was a ragdoll Anne had bought Liddie at the local flea market.

"Okay, Mommy." Liddie turned and skipped toward the stairs up to the private living area for the Gibsons.

Lidde sure loved her dolls, and lately she'd developed another hobby—collecting costume jewelry and feather boas she could use in her favorite new game with her best friends, sisters Cindy and Becca. They called it Trading Treasures, and it was popular with most of the lower elementary girls. They traded costume jewelry, purses, boas, tiaras, and the like with their friends. Liddie's pink room had become quite messy with her stock from which to trade.

"Mrs. Gibson?" Remi's voice rang out from the front door.

"Back here." Anne stood as both Remi and Bella approached the checkout area.

"Good morning," Remi said. She was the older of the girls by a full three minutes and stood an inch taller than Anne's five-foot-seven-inches. Remi's brown hair was woven into a fishbone style that was as thick as a three-ply rope. Her eyes were as deep brown as Liddie's, and as unguarded.

"Good morning," Bella echoed. Shorter than her sister by at least six inches or so, Bella's hair was much lighter than Remi's and hung in loose, wavy curls down past her shoulders. Her eyes were an intense blue.

Anne smiled. "Good morning, girls."

"Where would you like us to start?" Remi asked.

"Before you get started with anything, I'd like to show you something," Anne said. She lifted the sleeve with the book. "Do either of you recognize this?"

Remi took it, slowly flipping the book over. The space between her eyebrows creased as she shook her head and handed the book to her twin.

Bella's eyes widened as she read the spine. "This is a rare Poe, isn't it?" she asked Anne with her eyes twinkling. As Anne recognized the look yet again—the one Eric had worn many, many times—she knew Bella was destined for things in the literary industry beyond Blue Hill.

"It is. I think it's a first edition," Anne answered.

"It's wonderful," Bella breathed. "Where'd you get it?"

"We were hoping one of you might have an idea," Anne said. "Grace found it in one of the boxes of donated books."

"Do either of you remember seeing the book, and if so, who might have donated it?" Wendy asked.

Remi shook her head, her braid flipping from one shoulder to the other. "I don't even remember seeing the book."

"Me either," Bella said. "And I would remember seeing this Poe." She ran her hand slowly down the sleeve covering the book, as if stroking a beloved pet.

Anne swallowed the sting of disappointment. "It was a long shot anyway."

Bella handed the book back to Anne. "I'm sorry we couldn't be more help, Mrs. Gibson," she said. "Have you checked with Mrs. Bultman? I know she helped Reverend Tom with all the boxes from the church."

"Thanks. I'll ask her." Anne went on to instruct the Miller twins as to where they should begin with the remaining boxes, then she turned back to Grace and Wendy.

Grace pulled her cell phone from her purse. "It's early enough that I can run an article in this week's paper where everybody in town is sure to see. We'll keep it vague so that we don't give away too much information for people to falsely claim it." She slipped off the stool and moved to a corner, her phone pressed to her ear.

"We'll figure out who the book belongs to," Wendy tried to assure her, but Anne's mind wouldn't stop racing with the thoughts that had haunted her during the night.

Sure, the book had to be donated in error, but who on earth wouldn't have kept such a rare and valuable book in a safe place?

* * *

Several hours later, Anne called Ben and Liddie into the library. They'd been so good about playing and staying out of the way while Anne and the other adults got things ready for the book sale that Anne wanted to give them a little treat. "Come on kids, hop into the car. I have a surprise for you."

They both peppered Anne with questions about where they were going until she pulled into the parking lot for the flea market. Ben grinned and Liddie bounced in her car seat, clapping.

The Saturday flea market on Main Street attracted residents from surrounding towns with its many antiques, crafts, fresh produce, and the honey canned from the nearby honey farms. Ben and Liddie considered it a treat to visit the flea market—Ben always on the lookout for an addition to his Lionel train set and Liddie always eyeing the dolls and doll clothes. Anne had instituted a ten-dollar limit, and the kids knew not to even ask for an item if it was more than ten dollars. Ben usually experienced some disappointment since most items for the Lionel set were expensive.

To take advantage of the cooler weather, the flea market's sliding doors on either end of the long building stood wide open, allowing the breeze to flow through. Inside, the booths were filled with new and different treasures every week, so it was always an adventure. One that Anne, Ben, and Liddie enjoyed together as a family.

In the fourth booth they walked through, Ben found a car for his Lionel train that was under the ten-dollar limit. Ben carefully counted out his money, thanked the lady who handed him the bag, and then handed Anne his change. "I can't believe I found a tank car for less than ten bucks!" His excitement carried in his voice. "I'll need to tighten the back wheel, but it's a steal. I can't wait to show Ryan," he said, gripping the bag tightly.

"Shall we find one of the doll booths, Liddie?" Anne asked.

Liddie shook her head. "I want to find stuff for Trading Treasures with Cindy and Becca. Their mom gave them lots of cool stuff."

"Really?" Anne smiled at her daughter. The trading game these girls played was a benefit to the parents too, in that Anne hadn't had to buy any tiaras, boas, or costume jewelry for Liddie in quite some time. Playing dress up had gotten even more fun for the girls, even if it did put Liddie's room into a permanent state of disarray. But, that could be remedied.

"I have an idea. Let's find a special place to put all your treasures," Anne said.

Liddie's eyes widened. "Like a treasure chest?"

Anne nodded. "Just like that." She gave Ben a gentle nudge. "You're good at finding things, Ben. You can help us find a treasure chest for Liddie."

Ben nodded, his chest puffing out just a little as he darted into the next booth, intent on completing his mission.

But it was Anne who found the perfect treasure chest for Liddie, three booths later. It was an old wooden domed trunk that was small enough to sit perfectly atop Liddie's dresser. Liddie squealed with delight over it, while Anne negotiated the seller's cost down to ten dollars even.

Once Anne paid for the trunk, the threesome made their way back to the car. Both kids were happy, not just with their purchases, but with having spent another fun family afternoon.

Despite the responsibilities of the library and her other obligations to church and community, Anne loved being able to spend quality time with her kids. They were, after all, the greatest blessings in her life.

Chapter Three

*I*f you have any information regarding this book's origin, you are urged to contact the Blue Hill Librarian, Anne Gibson, at the library as soon as possible.

Anne read the article again. Grace had done a great job of describing the book, without giving the title. They'd decided they would allow that it was a book by Edgar Allan Poe but not release the title. The real owner of the book would have to provide that. It was one way Anne could think of to field all the claims she knew would be coming soon.

They had debated whether or not to put in information about the book's worth. Anne had finally decided if someone knew the value and had donated it in error, they would contact her.

"Mom, are you about ready? I don't want to be late to church." Ben's voice snatched Anne's attention. She recognized the tone well as it was almost an exact replica of her own impatience. Ben not only resembled her more than he did Eric, with his brown hair and hazel eyes so similar to hers, but he'd also inherited her stubborn streak and tenacity to details.

"Why the rush today?" Anne asked. She set down the Sunday paper and reached for the brush to run through Liddie's hair.

"I told you, Ryan is going to tell me all about football tryouts." Ben hurriedly placed their breakfast dishes in the dishwasher.

Anne paused in brushing Liddie's hair as her heart stuttered at the word *football*. Didn't she read about players getting concussions all the time? Football was dangerous.

"Ouch, Mommy." Liddie pulled away from Anne's grip and took the hairbrush and set it on the counter.

"Sorry, baby."

"It's okay, Mommy." Liddie hopped from one foot to the other. "I'm ready. I want to talk to Cindy and Becca about our big trade." She suddenly sounded much older than her five years.

Football...big trades...Anne pinched her lips together. Her children were growing up so fast. Too fast.

"Mom, I've finished making my bed, so I'm going to wait in the car." Ben opened the door to their private-entrance staircase. Liddie followed him out into the crisp morning.

Anne snapped out of her melancholy mood, grabbed her purse, and followed the kids. She double-checked Liddie's seat belt, then started the car and blew on her hands. The early October Pennsylvania air held much lower temperatures than just a few days ago. She glanced at the trees, the leaves decorated in exquisite shades of red and yellow, then back to Aunt Edie's old home. Anne always loved the grand Queen Anne Victorian house with its white clapboard and slate blue shingles. Many times, she'd played along the winding footpath down to the base of the hill. She was so glad she'd moved back home, where she belonged.

She steered the car toward the community church as the children talked nonstop, almost over one another.

"...and Ryan says I have a good chance at making the team. If I practice hard enough," Ben was saying as they drove past the

Blue Hill Inn. Anne's attention was caught by a middle-aged woman wearing a familiar oversized gray sweater coming out of the inn and rushing to her car. Rachel Winn. She spent an awful lot of time on her laptop in the library's History Room. Hours every day. Anne had tried to talk to her a couple of times, but Rachel always rushed away. She did that any time someone approached her and tried to start up a conversation.

It was most peculiar, almost like she was a hermit, and yet she came to the library regularly.

"But me and Becca traded so I got the crown, until I traded Cindy for the purse with all the diamonds," Liddie chattered.

"It's *Becca and I*, sweetie," Anne corrected automatically, her mind thinking about how often Rachel had been at the library last week. The front table in the History Room, where she worked on her laptop, had a clear view of the front entry where the boxes of books were dropped off for donation. It was very possible Rachel Winn might have seen someone with the book. Anne would have to ask her tomorrow.

"And Ryan says Alex could probably help me with some moves since he loves to play football," Ben said.

That got Anne's attention. She remembered Alex playing football just as clearly as she remembered his constant complaining about all the practices. She also remembered the time their friend Michael got hit in football and broke a rib. Surely Alex wouldn't be encouraging her son to play the game?

"I'm going to ask Mr. Pyle to give me some pointers too, since he's the high school coach," Ben said.

"I don't know if that's such a good idea, honey," Anne answered.

"Why? I want to make the team." Ben's forehead wrinkled and his nose crinkled up just a little bit in the middle.

It was almost scary how much he looked like her when she got her own mind set on something.

Anne turned into the church's parking lot. "Why don't we talk about it later, honey?"

Ben didn't argue as he barely waited until the silver Impala was parked before clicking off his seat belt and bolting from the car.

Anne sighed and helped Liddie out of her seat. She took her daughter's hand and headed toward the church. The morning sun climbed toward the center of the sky as they slipped in the front door under the beautiful stained glass window. The raw beauty of the setting never failed to steal Anne's breath. The original church bell still hung above the steeple.

The sun's bright rays caught the reds and blues of the stained glass, causing them to glitter and flash. Once inside, she relaxed her shoulders. Something about just being in the church filled her with peace and comfort. She sent up a small prayer of gratitude for all her blessings and made her way down to her regular pew. Anne had grown up in this church. So many Vacation Bible School weeks...Sunday school time and making crafts out of surplus items...accepting Jesus as her Lord and Savior and the whole church praying with and over her...The memories of the church wrapped around her like a welcoming warm shawl.

The church still spoke to her heart and soul.

"Mommy, can I go sit with Cindy and Becca until we go to children's church?" Liddie asked.

"It's *may I,* honey," Anne said as she turned. Yvette, Cindy and Becca's mom, waved and nodded toward Liddie. "Okay, honey. But you mind your manners, understand?"

"Yes, Mommy." Liddie skipped down the aisle, then giggled as she slid into the row and sat between her best friends.

Anne caught sight of Ben scurrying in alongside Ryan. Behind them, at a much more dignified pace, strolled in Alex, looking dashing in dress jeans and a starched button-down shirt. Alex stood just a bit over six feet tall, with strong shoulders and chin. His blue eyes always seemed to twinkle, but it was his personality that really made him shine. He caught sight of Anne and smiled, then moved into the seat behind her.

Alex's nephew, Ryan, slid beside Alex, and Ben sat beside him. For the last several years, Alex had been raising Ryan, following a car accident that took the lives of his sister and brother-in-law. It was clear to see how much Alex loved his nephew and how much he doted on the boy.

Within minutes, Reverend Tom Sloan stood at the pulpit and began the morning's sermon. Anne tried to pay close attention, she really did, but her focus kept straying. She glanced around the church's congregation. It was possible someone here owned the valuable Poe title.

But who?

* * *

Anne sat upstairs in her living area at home with Liddie, Cindy, and Becca. She had invited Cindy and Becca, who were, as Liddie would say, her "bestest friends ever" to come over and play with

Liddie and keep her entertained so Anne could do a little reading on Edgar Allan Poe. Finding a rare title made Anne more curious than ever about the author. Anne watched the girls, sprawled out on the floor playing their Trading Treasures game.

She opened the hardback biography on Poe and started the next chapter. What? Poe had been in the army? How had she missed that little tidbit? She reread that paragraph. Not only had Poe served in the army, he'd done quite well and attained the rank of sergeant major.

"Liddie, I'll give you this pink anklet if you'll give me that blue bracelet," Cindy said.

Anne watched as Liddie seemed to think about the possible trade. After two beats, she nodded, handing over the blue bracelet she'd won from a game machine at Stella's Pizza.

Anne watched the three girls for a few minutes as they continued trading. It was a creative little game. Anne liked that they traded their old things to get things that were brand new to them.

"Becca, I'll give you a green ring for your purple beads," Liddie offered.

"Okay," Becca agreed.

Anne wiggled in her chair to get more comfortable. She started reading her book again. She flipped toward the end of the book, skipping the facts about Poe's writing career. She wanted to know about him as a person.

"Liddie, I'll give you a purple tiara for your yellow duck hair clip," Cindy said.

"Do you have a pink tiara instead?" Liddie asked.

Cindy sifted through her stuff and then pulled out a pink tiara.

"Let's trade," Liddie said.

The girls giggled as they exchanged items.

Anne continued reading through Poe's adult years and his heartbreaks along the path of life. Anne especially ached for all of Poe's failed loves. His first taste of heartbreak came when he'd had to leave the University of Virginia because he was destitute and couldn't afford to even eat. Poe returned to Richmond to visit his fiancée Elmira Royster, only to discover that she had become engaged to another man in his absence.

Suddenly the three girls got quiet, which pulled Anne out of Poe's life and back into her living room.

Cindy held up a pretty purple heart necklace with sparkles that glistened in the lamp's light. It was a cute little thing. Anne smiled at the girls' wonder and awe.

"Wow, Cindy, that's really pretty," Becca said.

"I will give you another blue bracelet with glitter on it if you'll give me that necklace," Liddie said.

"Deal! I love blue," Cindy said, smiling.

Many things were traded: rings, bracelets, necklaces, and more. Anne went back to her reading, this time learning about Edgar Allan Poe's death. Well, the mystery surrounding it.

What was certain was that on October 3, 1849, Poe was found at Ryan's 4th Ward Polls, also known as Gunner's Hall, in Baltimore. Some rumors said he was drunk and in a gutter, but there was no proof of that. He was, however, taken to Washington College Hospital, where he died four days later.

Many noted that in place of his own customary suit of black wool, he instead wore one made of cheap gabardine, with a palm leaf hat. Some described his clothes as being stained, faded, ripped more or less at several seams, soiled, and his pants as half-worn and badly fitting, if they could be said to fit at all. He was found wearing neither vest nor neckcloth, and the bosom of his shirt was both crumpled and badly soiled. That left many to speculate that he'd either been drunk or mugged, although there was no solid evidence of either in all accounts.

The only contemporary public reference to a specific cause of death for Poe was printed in the *Baltimore Clipper*: "congestion of the brain." Death certificates weren't required back then and none was ever known to have been filed for him.

Anne shut the book, sad for the man who'd obviously walked a hard road. She couldn't imagine dying under such miserable and mysterious conditions. When it was time for her to be called Home, she wanted to pass just like Aunt Edie had—peacefully, in her sleep, with a favorite book nearby. No long illness. No pain. No drawn-out burden to family or friends. Just close her eyes and wake up in Paradise.

"Mommy, show Becca how to braid my hair like a fishtail. Please, please, please!" Liddie begged, bouncing up and down in front of Anne.

That was one way to put aside the melancholy—have three active little girls in the living room.

"It's fish*bone*, sweetheart, not fish*tail*." Anne laughed. "Come on, I'll show you."

Anne got down onto the floor and sat cross-legged with the girls. She patiently instructed them and demonstrated how to do the popular braid, then she helped Becca braid Liddie's hair. Then she helped Liddie braid Cindy's hair. Then Anne and Cindy braided Becca's hair.

"Mommy, can I have some of your jewelry to trade?" Liddie asked.

Anne laughed. "Uh, no you may not. You girls trade with your own treasures. Not Mommy's treasures."

The horn honked outside. Anne jumped up from the couch. "Girls, that's your mom. Get your stuff together."

A few moments later, a buzzer sounded at the back door.

Anne opened the door for Yvette. "You didn't have to climb all those stairs. I would have brought them down to you."

Yvette smiled. "Oh, no problem. Were they good?"

"Good as gold, like they always are," Anne answered. "They just played their trading game and did each other's hair and dressed up."

"That's about their normal lately," Yvette said, laughing.

"Yeah, I only had to remind Liddie once that they could only trade their treasures and not mommy's treasures."

Just then, Cindy and Becca ran into the room. "We got new jewelry, Mommy," Becca said.

Not to be outdone, Cindy held out her arm. "I got a new blue sparkly bracelet. See?"

"Beautiful. Just beautiful." Yvette ushered her daughters out the door. She turned to Anne. "Thank you for watching them this afternoon."

"It's no problem," Anne replied. "I enjoyed having them."

Anne shut the door behind them and turned back around. Liddie was nowhere to be seen, but Anne could hear her little voice down the hall. She figured Liddie must be playing in her room.

Anne cuddled back up on the couch and this time grabbed a book from her to-be-read pile. She'd had enough dark and somber tales for one day.

Chapter Four

"Have a good day at school. I love you both," Anne said as she waved to Ben and Liddie. She waited until they were safely inside the school before she steered the car back toward the library.

She'd originally planned to set aside her preparations for the used-book sale and get caught up on new book orders for the library, but after the messages she'd discovered left on the library's phone, she decided she'd better not try to get into such a detailed task. A number of people had left messages about the book sale this weekend, and two unknown callers claimed the Poe book belonged to them. They promised to stop by the library bright and early on Monday. So Anne doubted she'd have the focus needed for the tedious job of filling out book orders.

She drove past the library's parking lot, where three cars sat, and pulled around to the private parking space in back of the large house-turned-library. She recognized one of the cars out front as belonging to Rachel Winn. At least Anne would get the chance to ask her if she noticed anything about the Poe book.

Walking through the quiet library when the only lights were the sunbeams that snuck in through the windows was one of Anne's favorite moments every day. There was just something so peaceful about the subtle light and the comfort of being all alone, surrounded by books. Anne smiled as she crossed into the entry and unlocked the front door.

Rachel Winn was the first one out of her car. She walked with intense purpose into the library, wearing her gray sweater, with her laptop clutched against her chest. She nodded at Anne as she turned toward the History Room.

Anne followed her into the room. "Ms. Winn?"

The taciturn woman turned and faced Anne.

"I don't know if you read the paper Sunday morning, but we had a valuable Edgar Allan Poe book that got mixed in with the books donated for the sale. Since you've been in the History Room so often and have a clear view of the front, I wondered if perhaps you noticed someone setting the book down with others, or anything out of the ordinary."

"I haven't seen anything," Rachel answered.

"Would you like to see the book to see if you recognize it?" Anne asked.

"I don't need to see it. I don't pay attention to anything." Rachel shook her head and hurried along to *her* table in the front of the History Room.

"I'd like to see the book," a woman's voice carried through the library.

Anne shifted behind the desk. "I'm sorry, who are you?"

The tall, lithe, red-haired lady looked about fifty or so. She held out her hand to Anne. "Forgive me. I'm Jenna Coleman."

Anne shook her hand. "Nice to meet you, Ms. Coleman."

"Please, call me Jenna."

Anne smiled. "How may I help you, Jenna?"

"I'm here about the Poe book, of course. It's mine."

"I see." Anne motioned Jenna toward the little sitting area near the checkout area. "Why don't we sit down and you can tell me about yourself and how the book got to the library?"

Jenna sat with a flourish, positioning herself in the chair. "I'm a collector of rare books. Perhaps you've heard of me in the industry? I go by Jenna's Jewels on all the online groups and meetings."

"No, I'm sorry. I don't have much time to join groups, online or in person," Anne said.

"Oh. Well. Anyway," Jenna continued, "I own several first editions, you understand, so I know the value of the Poe book. I pride myself on keeping my rare finds in as pristine condition as when I acquired them."

"I'm a little confused. With you taking such good care of your valuable books, how did this edition get to the library?" Anne asked.

"Several years ago, I owned a small rare bookstore. This was back before alarm systems were so common, you understand. I had some of my Poe materials, including the first edition book, in the display window of my store. Tragically, someone broke in and stole everything from the display window, as well as all the cash from the register and from the lockbox in the office." Jenna fluffed her hair. "I filed a police report, of course."

"Do you have a copy of the report?" Anne asked.

"Somewhere in some of my papers. I have a copy of the original appraisal for all my rare books in my papers as well."

"Great. If you could bring copies of those papers—the police report and the appraisal, then there would be no question of ownership and I'd be delighted to return your property to you," Anne said.

Jenna frowned. "I don't have them with me."

"I understand," Anne said. "I don't mind waiting until you get them and bring them here, and then you can have the book."

"Those papers are in with the documents from my store and they're all in storage. As I said, it's been years since I had the store."

While this was a reasonable and understandable excuse, something didn't sit right with Anne about Jenna's story.

"Is there any marking you recall in the book that you could identify that would prove your ownership?" Anne asked.

Jenna shook her head. "It's been so long ago, you understand."

Something else rang out in Anne's mind. "Let's start with the title." She held her breath.

"I told you, it's been a long time," Jenna said.

Anne stood. "I'm sorry, Jenna, but without any proof of ownership, I can't just hand the book over to you."

Jenna stood as well. "But it's my book. I just explained how it was stolen," she said, her voice rising.

"I'm sorry, but I've received many calls from people who claim to own the book," Anne said. "I'm going to have to require proof. Your appraisal of this particular title and the police report of it being stolen would definitely be all the proof needed." She gently led Jenna toward the entry. "You just bring copies of those, and I'll be more than happy to give you the book."

"It's my book! I demand to at least see it, to make sure it's safe," Jenna hollered and stopped walking. She stomped a heeled foot for good measure.

Anne was thankful there weren't any patrons in the library for Jenna to disturb. Only Rachel Winn, who, by her own admission paid no attention to what was happening around her.

"I'm sure you understand I can't do that, but I assure you the book is very safe," Anne said. Once again, she attempted to lead Jenna to the door.

Jenna refused to budge. "I must insist you at least let me see the book. It's *mine*."

Anne swallowed, holding her ground. She didn't want to have to physically remove the woman from the library, but she would call the police if she had no other choice. "I'm sorry, Jenna, but you need to leave," Anne said. She crossed her arms over her chest and set her jaw. "You're welcome to return when you have the papers that prove you own the book."

The redheaded woman narrowed her eyes, piercing Anne with her hard stare. "You don't think I own the book, do you?" she accused. "You think I'm making it up?"

"I never said that. I'm just asking for proof, which is the responsible thing to do." Anne took a step to block Jenna from the rest of the library. "Now, if you'd please leave…"

The front door opened with a whoosh, causing both women to turn. Donald Bell skidded to a stop in front of Anne. "G—Good morning," he stammered.

"Good morning, Mr. Bell," Anne greeted him. She turned back to Jenna. "Please bring those papers along to clear up any question of ownership."

Mr. Bell lingered at the checkout desk, as if waiting for Anne.

Jenna scowled. "I'll find those papers and prove to you I'm not lying."

The woman would apparently continue to argue for as long as Anne would rise to the bait. "I look forward to then," Anne said before turning and heading to the checkout desk.

"May I help you find something?" Anne asked Mr. Bell as she approached him.

"No. No, ma'am." He hesitated, glancing around the near-empty library. "I was wondering if you would like me to do some volunteer work around here."

"Oh." Anne took her time moving behind the desk. Stalling, she knew, but something about Donald Bell made Anne a little uncomfortable. It wasn't anything he'd done, per se, although he'd been hanging around the library a lot lately, never saying much.

That wasn't necessarily a reason to cause discomfort, but he had never, ever even checked out a library book. Like Rachel Winn, he just seemed to... well, just *be* there.

Sometimes Anne would glance up from shelving books to find him staring at her. *That's* what made her feel uncomfortable.

"Anne?" he asked, pulling her attention back to the here and now.

"I don't need any volunteers at the present," she said.

His face fell.

She felt guilty. He'd never done anything wrong, just stared at her and made her uncomfortable. "But I'm sure I'll need some help soon. I'll let you know when I do, okay?" Anne gave him the brightest smile she could muster.

He smiled back. "Sure. That would be great."

Anne nodded, then brought up the computer system. He continued standing at the checkout desk.

"Is there something else, Mr. Bell?" she asked.

He shifted his weight from one foot to the other, then back again. "I saw the write-up in the paper about the book."

It was entirely possible that as much lingering in the library as he'd done of late, he might have seen someone with the Poe book.

"Yes? Do you know something about the book?" she asked.

"Does that woman who just left here own it?" he asked, avoiding her own question.

Anne shrugged. "Maybe."

"Is the book worth a lot of money? The paper didn't say, but I figured it probably is because you're trying to find out who owns it."

"Every book is worth money, Mr. Bell." Anne believed that, but this whole turn of conversation was making her more than a little uncomfortable.

"Are you keeping it here, at the library?" he asked.

Anne shook her head. It wasn't a lie, exactly, because the book wasn't actually in the *library*, but it was in the building. What had she been thinking to leave a book of such value in her unsecured bedroom? Especially after letting Grace print the article about it in the paper.

"Well, good. You can't be too safe," Mr. Bell said.

"Exactly." Which is why, as soon as Remi and Bella reported for work, Anne planned to take the book to the bank and place it in her safety deposit box.

He gave her a nod, then shuffled off toward the Nonfiction Room.

Anne let out a slow breath and gathered her thoughts. Jenna Coleman was a real piece of work, but Anne had no concrete reason to doubt her story. However, Anne couldn't imagine owning a book worth so much money and not even being able to recall the title. It seemed a little fishy, but if Jenna returned with proof, Anne would hand over the book.

That didn't explain the other callers who'd left messages that they owned the book. Anne took off her glasses and pinched the bridge of her nose. Finding out the book's rightful owner just might prove to be more of a task than she'd imagined.

* * *

"Hi, Mrs. Gibson," Sherri Deveraeux called out as Anne made her way down the grand staircase after hastily retrieving the Poe book from her third-floor bedroom in their personal quarters.

Anne smiled as she approached the checkout desk where Sherri stood. Sherri, one of the most recent volunteers to the Blue Hill Library, was a girl a year younger than Remi and Bella. A recent illness had caused her to miss so much of her senior year of high school that she hadn't been able to graduate with her class. Even though Sherri had recovered, she was still a little weak — and yet fiercely determined to succeed.

And the girl loved New York. Loved everything about the city life.

"Hi, Sherri. How are you today?" Anne asked.

"Great. What do you need me to do this morning?"

Anne couldn't help noticing that the cart of books to be shelved was quite full. "How about shelving some books?"

"Sounds great to me." Sherri ran her finger over the books' spine markings, namely their call numbers. "Did you know that the Dewey Decimal classification system is the most widely used method for classifying books and it is named after Melvil Dewey, an American librarian who developed it in 1876?"

Anne chuckled. The girl had obviously been doing some research on the subject. "Yes, I did know that. Did you know the system is a general knowledge organization tool that is continuously revised to keep pace with knowledge?"

Sherri stopped, her hand on the cart. "Seriously? They revise it a lot?"

Anne nodded. "I know it's a bit surprising, considering how most everyone just does an Internet search for whatever they want these days, but they do update systems in all libraries."

"Well, I bet you did that back in New York, but here in Blue Hill…," Sherri said.

"Everywhere," Anne corrected.

"Oh."

Anne stood. "Listen, I need to run to the bank this morning. Can you hold down the library until Remi and Bella get here? They should be here any minute now."

"Sure. Go ahead."

Anne tucked the book against her chest. She'd feel so much better once the book was out of the library and safe.

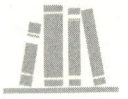

Chapter Five

Goodness, but autumn had arrived overnight.

Anne stepped out of her car, lifted her shoulders to keep the cold fingers of the breeze from slipping down the back of her neck, and headed toward the library. Maybe it was just cooler on the hill than it was down in the town below, but Anne hadn't been nearly as chilled when she'd gotten out of the car at the bank to put the book in her safety deposit box.

She slipped in the back of the library, stowed her purse, then headed to the front. Remi stood behind the checkout desk, handing books to Betty Bultman.

The mayor's wife looked up as Anne approached. "Good morning, Anne. How are you this brisk day?"

"Enjoying the cooler weather, I think," Anne replied with a smile. "I think it's cooler out now than when I took the kids to school."

"Forecast says to expect the temperatures to keep dropping today. I heard on the news this morning that the low tonight will be in the high thirties." Betty hugged herself. "*Brr.*"

"I love the cooler weather," Remi said. She handed the bag of books across the desk to Mrs. Bultman. "You can stay in, curl up under a comfy blanket, and read a couple of good books."

The Rightful Owner | 41

Mrs. Bultman smiled. "That's exactly what I plan to do, Remi. Thank you." She took the bag of books. "Anne, I saw the write-up in the paper about that Poe book. Has someone come forward to claim it yet?"

Anne shook her head. "Not anyone with proof of ownership. That reminds me, Betty, do you recall seeing an old Poe book when you helped Reverend Tom with the books donated from the church?"

"Not that I can remember," Betty said. "The reverend and I sorted the books for the garage sale. Whatever was left over, we boxed up and put in storage until we heard about the used-book sale for the library. I don't think we even opened the boxes up before we brought them over."

Anne shrugged. "It was a long shot anyway."

"I do hope you find the book's owner." Betty gave a finger wave to Remi. "I'll see you ladies next week."

Anne plopped down behind the computer. With Jenna Coleman's appearance, Anne realized she should do more research on rare books, Poe's in particular. The best place to start was the Internet.

She did a search, first, on their book. Volume one appeared to have fourteen stories: "Morella," "Lionizing," "William Wilson," "The Man That Was Used Up—A Tale of the Late Bugaboo and Kickapoo Campaign," "The Fall of the House of Usher," "The Duc de L'Omelette," "MS. Found in a Bottle," "Bon-Bon," "Shadow—A Fable," "The Devil in the Belfry," "Ligeia," "King Pest—A Tale Containing an Allegory," "The Signoria Zenobia," and "The Scythe of Time." Well, that didn't tell her an awful lot.

She continued her Internet search. According to everything Anne read, the publisher, Lea & Blanchard, was willing to print the two-volume anthology based on the rave reviews of Poe's most recent magazine-published piece, "The Fall of the House of Usher." The collection was dedicated to Colonel William Drayton, a former member of Congress who later became a judge.

The publisher didn't pay Poe any royalties, only twenty free copies of the published book. Anne shook her head. Her husband, Eric, had loved working for a publisher, loved working with authors. He loved stories and the ability they had to change lives. Anne couldn't imagine a publisher who wouldn't even pay royalties. Times surely had changed in the industry in the last one hundred and seventy-five plus years.

In the preface to the book, Edgar Allan Poe wrote, "If in many of my productions terror has been the thesis, I maintain that terror is not of Germany but of the soul." He wrote the words, supposedly, in defense of the criticism that many of his tales were part "Germanism."

Interesting reading, for sure, especially one other little tidbit she found on the Internet about this particular volume: Edgar Allan Poe had written to Washington Irving, requesting that Irving endorse the book.

Anne shifted on her stool and kept reading off the vast Internet pages about the American poet who was also a literary critic, and considered part of the American Romantic Movement. He died just nine years after his book was published. Anne hadn't known that. Sad, but at least he'd seen his dream become reality.

What would he think about the popularity of his work today?

Anne moved on to his biography. There was something about the man that seemed to call Anne to pay closer attention.

Poe was one of the earliest American writers of short stories. Many sites credited him as the inventor of the detective fiction genre. He was further credited with contributing to the science fiction genre.

But what Anne found most interesting in his biography was that he was the first well-known American writer to try to earn a living through writing alone. Because of his attempts, Poe experienced a financially difficult life and career.

Anne felt sorry for him. As a true lover of words, her heart ached for his failed attempts. If he could only see his success now.

Having been married to an editor for a New York publishing house, Anne understood the delicacies of the business—having to blend with the personal side of authors. Eric had had such a heart for the writer that every time Anne finished a book, she thought about the author and how much of their heart and energy went into the product she'd just enjoyed.

She shut down the Internet and stood to stretch.

A tall man approached the checkout desk. The sun snaking past the front window caught in his silvery hair. Anne estimated him to be in his early fifties. He wore a pair of slacks with the crease ironed and a tweed sports jacket, looking every bit the role of a college English professor. "Hello I'm looking for the librarian, Anne Gibson," he said. His voice was as distinguished as his stature.

"I'm Anne Gibson." She smiled at him. "How may I help you?"

"My name is Rodney Kelley," he said. He pulled a copy of Grace's article from his jacket pocket. "I believe this book might belong to my family."

Anne nodded at Remi as she moved from behind the counter. She waved toward the little sitting area. "Please, let's sit to talk."

Mr. Kelley sat, stretching his long legs in front of him and crossing them at the ankles. "Thank you for talking with me."

His calm, easy demeanor put Anne right at ease. "Of course," she said. "Please explain why you think the book might belong to your family."

"My grandfather, Gus, was a huge Edgar Allan Poe fan. He was also an avid book collector with an extensive collection of various authors' early- and first-edition copies. He passed just a few months ago."

"I'm so sorry," Anne said. She remembered the first year after losing Eric. Those days had been very hard.

"Thank you." Mr. Kelley took a deep breath before continuing. "Several boxes of my grandfather's books have been in my garage following his passing, and despite my wife's multiple requests to go through them and determine what to keep and what to give away, I didn't sort through them."

Anne held her breath, almost sure of what Mr. Kelley would tell her next.

"My wife didn't realize my grandfather had some rare and valuable books mixed in his collection. When I didn't take the time to go through the boxes in the garage, my wife assumed they weren't valuable. She saw the call the library put out for the used-books sale and decided to get rid of the boxes cluttering our garage."

Oh my... Anne could only imagine the conversations between this husband and wife after Mr. Kelley found out.

"Obviously, I'm not positive that the book was one of my grandfather's, but if there's even a chance that it is, I must, understandably, follow up."

Anne nodded. "Of course, I understand," she said. "Do you have any type of documentation that would be proof of ownership?"

Mr. Kelley straightened in his seat, pulling his legs up and leaning toward Anne. "My father is out of town at the moment, but when I called him to inform him of the boxes of books being lost, he gave me some description of the interior of the Poe books his father owned. In very explicit detail. If I could just see the book, I could determine pretty quickly if the book was one that belonged to my grandfather."

"I'm sorry, Mr. Kelley, I can't show you the book."

He sat up even straighter. "Someone has already claimed it?"

She smiled. "I've received some interest from parties who believe the book belongs to them, but no one has produced documentation to prove ownership."

"I see."

"But I can't show it to you because the book is in a safety deposit box at the bank." Anne was very relieved she'd already taken the book.

"Oh," he said. "Well." His brows furrowed. His face went slack. "Well, let me give you my number. If the others' claims of ownership turn out unfounded, call me and I'll come take a look at the book to see if my grandfather's marking is inside. I can bring you other papers of his with the same marking. Would that suffice as proof of ownership?"

"I believe it would," Anne replied with a nod.

"Very well." He pulled out a business card and handed it to Anne. "Here is my number. If you could call me one way or another by week's end, I'd greatly appreciate it." He stood and extended his hand. "Thank you for your time, Mrs. Gibson. It was lovely to have met you."

"And you as well," Anne said as she shook his hand. "I'll call you by Friday."

Mr. Kelley made long strides out of the library.

Anne straightened several books at the end of the display counter and watched him leave with such grace in his movements. She compared his attitude to that of Jenna Coleman's. Of the two, she was more inclined to think the book belonged to the Kelley family. His story just resonated with her.

Anne recalled how many times she'd nagged Eric about something she wanted him to do: fix the slow drain in the bathroom sink, tighten the faucet in the kitchen, change out the filter in the water softener. There were a couple of times when she got tired of waiting for him to get around to the chores, so she'd either done it herself, such as changing the water filter, or she'd hired someone to fix the issue. Eric had been upset she'd wasted money to hire someone, but she'd been tired of waiting. She could only imagine how Mrs. Kelley felt about boxes of books in her garage that she'd nagged her husband to go through for a couple of months. Like Anne, she must have finally been fed up and took matters into her own hands.

Yes, Anne could easily see how a valuable book would have been donated to the sale. It made clear sense.

A lot more than Jenna's. Who didn't have the appraisal and police report of such a valuable theft?

Anne's hands paused on the glass case. If Jenna's book had been owned by her business, wouldn't she have carried insurance on such a valuable piece of property? The police report would be adequate documentation to file an insurance claim for the loss of the book. If the insurance company paid a claim on the book, and it was the one lying in Anne's safety deposit box, did that mean Jenna had to return the money to the insurance company?

If the book was the one listed on Jenna's police report, could she want it back so she could secretly destroy it in order to avoid paying back the insurance money? Especially considering how expensive some of the Edgar Allen Poe titles were. That might explain her rude and confrontational behavior. It didn't excuse it, but it would explain it a bit.

Chapter Six

"Mommy, I hafta go see Cindy and Becca this weekend. We're gonna do some trading," Liddie said as she danced around the kitchen.

"You don't *have* to visit your friends, Liddie," Anne said, sidestepping her daughter as she tried to finish cooking dinner.

"But we wanna trade."

"It's *have to* and *want to*, sweetie, and I understand you want to go. I said we'd see." Anne stirred the spaghetti sauce while keeping an eye on the boiling pasta. It would probably be a good idea to have Liddie safely under someone else's care while she gave attention to the book sale on Saturday afternoon. "Where's your brother?" she asked.

"I dunno. I think he went to his room," Liddie answered.

"It's *don't know*, Liddie. Please find Ben and tell him dinner is almost ready. Both of you need to wash up."

"Okay," Liddie said as she turned and skipped from the kitchen.

Anne normally would have had dinner ready by now, but she'd gotten busy in the library. So many people had dropped by just to ask about the Poe book, but no one other than Jenna and Rodney Kelley had laid claims to it. Many of the visitors promised to come to the book sale on Saturday afternoon.

The timer on the pasta started buzzing. Anne turned off the burner on the stove and grabbed the pretty bird-design colander that had been Aunt Edie's.

Birds! She'd totally forgotten to call Coraline. Anne checked the oven's timer. She still had four minutes left on the bread. She quickly grabbed the phone and dialed Coraline's number.

Brrring!

She pulled down three bowls and three glasses from the cabinet.

Second ring.

She grabbed the strainer spoon from the drawer and set it beside the sink.

Third ring.

Anne set the bread knife by the cutting board on the counter.

"Hello, this is Coraline. I can't answer your call, but please leave me a message. Have a great day." *Beep!*

"Hi, Coraline. It's Anne Gibson. If you could give me a call at the library when you have a moment, I'd appreciate it. Thank you," Anne said before hanging up and replacing the phone to its base.

"Ben! Liddie!" She used the hot pads to pour the pasta and hot water into the colander in the sink, then turned the hot water on to rinse the pasta. "Kids!" Where were those two?

The oven's timer blasted.

She held on to the hot pads and opened the oven door. The bread bubbled, with edges slightly brown and crispy. The distinct aroma of garlic filled the kitchen. Anne's stomach growled in response.

Had she even had lunch today? She honestly couldn't remember. It'd been one of *those* days.

Anne slipped the open-faced loaf onto the cutting board and turned off the buzzing timer. "Ben! Liddie!" What could be keeping the kids? They loved spaghetti.

She used the pasta utensil to stir the pasta under the hot water, then turned off the tap. She tossed the hot pads onto the counter and stepped into the living room.

Liddie hop-skipped from down the hall. "My hands are all cleaned good, Mommy."

"Good girl. Where's your brother?" Anne asked.

"Dunno—I mean, I *don't know*, Mommy. He was in his room and I told him to wash up and that dinner was almost ready, just like you said, and he said he would in a minute, but he was reading. I went and washed my hands like you told me to."

She planted a kiss on the top of Liddie's head. The scent of sunshine and shampoo filled her senses. "Get up to the table. I'll get Ben and be back in a minute."

So he's reading again. Anne smiled and shook her head as she made her way to Ben's bedroom. Ever since last year, Ben had been catching up on a twenty-book series titled "Coastal Club" by R. W. Winger. All the middle graders, especially boys, seemed to devour the books. She sure couldn't keep them in the library. The hold list on almost every volume of the series was at least three or four people deep. That was saying a lot here in Blue Hill.

She pushed open Ben's bedroom door. "Ben?"

He looked up from the book and his face turned red. He slipped a bookmark between the pages before shutting the book and setting it on his bedside table. "I'm sorry, Mom. It was just a really good part," he said, ducking his head as he stood.

Anne grinned, despite herself. She, too, could easily get lost in a story and forget place and time. Aunt Edie used to call it *adventuring*. "Hurry and get washed up. We don't want the garlic bread to get cold."

"Hey, Mom?"

"Yes?" Anne answered, turning back to him.

"The newest book in the Coastal Club series is coming out on preorder soon, and I really want to order the book," Ben pleaded.

"I'll think about it. What is it that makes the series so interesting?" Anne asked, her hand resting on his bedroom doorknob.

"The plots are all really cool. The main characters solve mysteries on Lagoon Beach. Each book is a new mystery with new suspects and all."

"That could be appealing. What are the main characters like?" Anne asked, wondering how they related to children nowadays. She'd grown up reading Trixie Belden and Nancy Drew books, so she had a special place in her heart for children's mysteries.

"Nick is the leader of the group, and he is really brave and daring even though his parents are divorced. I think that makes him strong." Ben ran a finger over the spine of the book. "Macy is the bookworm. She knows all about plants and animals. The last main character is Gino—but everyone calls him G—and he is very technologically advanced."

"That's great detail, Ben." She had to admit she was impressed with her son's insight into the characterization of the main characters. She might have to read this series. "How did the three of them meet?"

"Well, Nick and Macy were childhood friends and they are neighbors. They met G when they needed to find information on the computer about a mystery, and they bonded. Then all three of them formed the Coastal Club."

"That sounds interesting. We'll see about preordering the latest release, okay?" She pushed his bedroom door open all the way.

"Okay, Mom." He flashed her a smile and rushed toward the bathroom.

Anne returned to the kitchen to find Liddie in tears, sopping up a large puddle of milk dripping down the counter and onto the floor.

"I'm sorry, Mommy. I was tryin' to help," Liddie cried.

"*Trying to*, sweetie." Anne grabbed paper towels from the counter. "Honey, I've told you over and over not to try and pour the milk yourself. Especially when it's a new gallon."

"I'm sorry, Mommy," Liddie said through her tears.

"Here," Anne said as she handed Liddie more paper towels. "Keep working at it. You need to clean up your mess." She refrained from just doing it herself as Liddie made smears on the floor. Liddie had to learn to obey, and when she didn't, she needed to deal with the resulting mess herself.

How many times had Anne had to deal with a life mess when she hadn't obeyed God? The lessons Anne learned that way were the ones she remembered the most.

"What happened?" Ben asked.

"Your sister tried to help. Will you please pour the milk while I make our spaghetti?" Anne answered.

Ben opened the refrigerator and stepped around Liddie, who was still sopping up the spill. Anne filled all their bowls with food and set them on the table before slicing the bread. "Hurry up, Liddie," she said over her shoulder.

"Almost done," Liddie answered as she put the wet paper towels into the trash.

"Ben, please get the Parmesan cheese and set it on the table," Anne said. She finished slicing the bread, then wet two paper towels and handed them to Liddie. "Now follow up with these wet ones so the floor isn't sticky."

Once Liddie had finished, they sat down at the table.

"Who would like to say grace?" Anne asked.

"Me!" Liddie bounced in her seat.

"Okay, go ahead," Anne said.

"God is great. God is good. And we thank Him for our food. By His hands we all are fed. Give us, Lord, our daily bread. Amen," Liddie prayed with her sweet, pure voice.

"Thank you, sweetie," Anne said. She twirled the sauce-coated spaghetti around her fork. "Liddie told me about her day, Ben. Tell me about yours."

His face lit up like it did on Christmas morning. "I have the permission slip for you to sign so I can try out for football."

Anne had to force her mouthful down with two swallows before she could speak. "Football? But you're such a great baseball player."

"Different season, Mom."

She mentally raced through everything she could remember having read about different sports. "Umm, but aren't you building different muscles, and building up too many designed for football player isn't good for baseball players, right?" Anne asked. She *thought* she'd read that somewhere. Once.

Ben laughed. "Mom, you're so funny. You don't bulk up for flag football."

"Have you thought about what might happen if you get tackled and hurt? It could put your arm in a cast for many weeks," Anne said.

"It's *flag* football. No tackling," Ben said as he shoved another forkful into his mouth.

"I want to play football," Liddie said.

"Girls can't play football." Ben rolled his eyes.

"Can too."

"No, they can't," Ben said.

Liddie's bottom lip protruded. "Can too. We can do anything boys can do."

Ben shook his head. "Tell her, Mom. Girls can't play football. They'd get hurt." He poked his chest out a little.

Anne raised a single eyebrow. "Are you saying boys can't get hurt playing football?"

* * *

"No. We're just tougher and less likely to get hurt than girls."

"I want to play football, Mommy," Liddie said.

"No, sweetie," Anne told Liddie but kept her gaze on her son. "But boys can and do get hurt, Ben."

"Yeah, in tackle football. Not so much in flag." Ben gulped his milk.

"You could still trip and fall while running down the field," Anne said, even though she knew she was grasping at straws.

"I could do that playing baseball, Mom," Ben said.

"I want to play baseball too," Liddie said.

Ben shook his head. "Girls play softball, Lids, not baseball." He looked back at Anne. "I'll bring you the permission slip after dinner. It's due back to the coach by Friday. That's when tryouts are."

"Tryouts?" Anne asked. "You have to try out for the team?"

He scowled. "Well, yeah, Mom. You don't want a bunch of guys on the team who can't play. You have to try out. That's why Alex has been helping me and Ryan. We've asked Mr. Pyle to help us too, and he said he would for a little while on Wednesday evening."

Anne took a sip of her milk. Alex hadn't mentioned he'd been helping the boys get better in football. That was an activity she wished he'd talked with her about before engaging in it. She'd have to discuss it with Alex. Soon.

Ben scooped his last forkful into his mouth. "May I be excused?" he asked.

"Don't talk with your mouth full. You know better," Anne answered.

He swallowed loudly, then drank the last of his milk before standing. "Now may I be excused?"

"Rinse your bowl and glass and put them in the dishwasher," Anne said as she took another sip. "What's your hurry? A lot of homework?"

"I did my homework in class. I need to finish this book tonight. Ryan said the next one in the series is even better." Ben put his dishes in the dishwasher, then gave Anne a quick kiss on the cheek. "Thanks for dinner, Mom. It was good."

"Can I be excused too?" Liddie asked.

"It's *may I*, and set your dishes in the sink." Anne absentmindedly wiped her mouth with the paper napkin, thinking.

On one hand, she was terrified to let Ben try out for the football team. He loved playing on a team and clearly wanted to try out. But, flag or not, he could get hurt. On the other hand, she didn't want him becoming too much of a loner, burying his nose in a book all the time. Oh, she loved to read and was thrilled her children loved books as much as she did, but she knew how important being outdoors and getting exercise and playing with friends was too.

She'd have to think really hard about what the right thing to do was. She and Eric had never really discussed this. It was times like this that Anne felt the weight of being a single parent.

Sometimes, being both Mom and Dad had its downside.

Chapter Seven

"Coffee?"

Anne smiled into the phone on Tuesday morning. "Grace, you are singing my tune."

"Can you meet me at Coffee Joe's in ten minutes?" Grace asked.

"Perfect. I'll see you there." Anne hung up the phone and told Bella that she'd be out for about an hour or so. She jumped into her car and steered toward the coffee shop.

Coffee Joe's small building was nestled between the health food shop and the sporting goods store. Along with the wide variety of teas and coffees, Joe's also offered bakery goods and sandwiches. It was the mouthwatering aroma of some type of cinnamon pastry that welcomed Anne as she entered.

Grace, already in line at the counter that ran the length of the room, waved her over.

"You beat me," Anne said as she stepped beside the newspaper editor.

"Just got here." Grace gave her order to the barista behind the counter.

Anne did the same, then moved along to the end of the counter. "I was so happy you called. For some reason, it seems I'm in desperate need of caffeine this morning." She yawned. "See?"

Grace chuckled as the barista handed her a cup of steaming coffee. "I'll grab us that table over there," she said with a nod toward the corner table.

"Here you go, Mrs. Gibson," the barista said. "I'm looking forward to the book sale this weekend."

"Thank you. I'll be looking forward to seeing you at the sale." Anne picked up her own mug of piping hot java and followed Grace. She sank into the chair and took a moment to just inhale the rich scent of her coffee.

"I have to confess, I wanted to meet you not just to see you and have a cup of coffee," Grace said.

"Oh?" Anne asked, then took a sip from her mug.

"I had a gentleman call the paper yesterday, asking about the Poe book."

Anne set her cup on the table. "I guess that's to be expected since you wrote the article."

Grace shook her head. "Actually, no. He's the only call I've received." She took a sip of coffee. "He asked a very unusual question."

"What's that?" Anne asked, her curiosity simmering as hot as the coffee.

"He asked if there were any papers inside the found book," Grace said.

"Papers? Like, loose pieces of paper?" Anne asked.

Grace nodded. "That's what he asked. I wondered why he'd contacted the paper instead of you, since you have the book and would be able to check and see if there are any loose papers."

"That is odd. What did you tell him?" Anne took another sip of coffee, letting the heat sink down to her toes.

"The truth: that I didn't recall seeing any papers in the book, but it would probably be best for him to contact you at the library."

Anne nodded. "Did you get his name?"

"Rodney Kelley. The name sounds a little familiar, but I can't place from where or get a mental image of the man," Grace said.

"He came by the library yesterday about the book." Anne told Grace about their meeting. "But he never said anything about loose papers."

"Like I said, peculiar."

Anne thought about the book. She'd inspected it fairly well before she'd put it in the sleeve. "I guess I could have missed a single piece of paper tucked inside, but it's highly unlikely."

"Well, I just thought it extremely strange that he would call the paper rather than just ask you."

Unless he was fishing before he bothered with Anne. "What time did he call you?" Anne asked.

Grace shrugged. "I'd just gotten to work, so it was around eight thirty or nine. What time did he go by the library?"

"Afternoon." Interesting. Anne took a sip of coffee. "He calls you and asks about papers, then he comes to see me but doesn't even mention them." Something didn't make sense.

"Wonder what is up with that?" Grace asked. "You know, I said his name sounded familiar. I think I'll do a little digging and see what I can find out about him. At least figure out why his name rings a bell."

"He seems nice enough. He was sharply dressed and very well-mannered." Anne nodded. "But I'd appreciate your seeing what you can find out about him. I'm curious, that's for sure."

"Well, I've got to get back to the paper. I just wanted to share the info — and a cup of coffee — with you," Grace said as she stood. "I'll let you know what I find out on Mr. Rodney Kelley."

"Thanks, Grace," Anne said. "For the information and the coffee break."

Grace rushed out the door, leaving Anne sitting alone with only a few sips left. The cinnamon smell made her mouth water, enticing her to buy one of the yummy pastries. Anne resisted the temptation, drank the last sip of her coffee, and left.

Anne stepped outside the coffeehouse and slipped her purse strap over her shoulder. The front window of the sporting goods store caught her eye with its blue-and-white display, the colors of the Blue Hill Panthers. Footballs and pompoms decorated the base of the display, reminding Anne of the permission slip Ben had left on the kitchen table for her.

She pushed open the door and stepped inside the store for the first time since moving back to Blue Hill. Unlike the shop next door, the smell here wasn't warm, enticing, or comforting but was instead filled with the odor of plastic and rubber and... well, Anne thought she might be imagining the hint of sweat in the air.

"Hello. My name is Ron. How can I help you?" a young man approached her. He couldn't be more than twenty.

She bit her tongue, trying not to correct his grammar. "I'm just looking, thank you."

"Certainly. If you need any help, just holler for me."

The sales team must work solely on commission. Anne moved from the front of the store, following the football sticker on the floor that directed shoppers to the football section — as if the large, inflated football hanging over the rack of football cleats wasn't enough of an indication.

A couple of men roamed the aisles, looking at different items. Mouth guards. Chinstraps. Shoulder pads. Helmets. Hip pad sets and rib protectors? Anne stared at the contraptions. Seriously? And her son wanted to play a sport that required such equipment?

"Hey, Anne," Alex said as he approached. "What are you doing here?"

"Hey there. Frankly, I'm wondering if you've lost your mind."

Alex frowned. "What are you talking about?"

"Ben said you were helping him and Ryan prepare for the football tryouts on Friday." She waved toward all the protective gear on the racks. "It's obviously very dangerous, even more than I remember, so why would you encourage the boys?"

"Oh, Anne," Alex chuckled. "This equipment is for full-contact football. You know, where the guys get tackled? The boys are trying out for the community flag football league. No tackling. They pull flags off the belt. That's it."

"So they don't wear any of this stuff?" Anne asked.

"Our league requires them to wear helmets and mouth guards, but that's it. They don't even have to wear shoulder pads."

"I don't know, Alex," she said.

"What are you worried about? He already plays baseball. They have protective gear too."

Anne took slow steps down the aisle, back toward the front of the store. "He doesn't get tackled in baseball, Alex."

Alex fell into step beside her. "No, and he won't in flag football either. Besides, in baseball, he can get hit with the ball, which is hard as all get-out. He can hurt himself sliding into base. There is danger in every sport, Anne, but it's important to boys. It's important to Ben."

She paused and pushed her glasses back up the bridge of her nose. She needed to get them tightened the next time she was by the optometrist's office. "I know, but…"

"Anne, Anne, Anne—"

"Don't you *Anne* me. I have to protect him." An unexpected, unexplained, near panic attack hit her. If something happened to Ben or Liddie…

"Anne, I'm just saying flag football is even less dangerous than the sport you already let him play."

He was being logical, but still. She let out a slow breath, releasing the panic that had nearly choked her. "I'm thinking about it."

"He'll be very disappointed if you don't let him," Alex said.

"I know. I know." She laid a hand on his forearm. "Thanks for the information, Alex. I have to get back to the library to let Bella go to lunch."

"You know, you could bring Ben over to the house this afternoon. I told the boys I'd work with them, and even Chad's going to drop by. You could stay and watch. See for yourself how it is."

She smiled. "Thanks, Alex. I just might do that."

* * *

Here comes trouble.

Anne stared at Jenna Coleman as she marched toward the checkout desk, her high heels tapping on the floor in an oddly rhythmic beat. She stopped in front of Anne and set her clutch-style purse on the desk. "Hello, Mrs. Gibson," she said.

"Hello, Jenna. Did you bring those papers?" Anne asked as she stood.

Jenna's brow creased. "I'm afraid I must insist that you give me the book now because it might take some time for me to locate the police report and appraisals. I just realized that they might be in my poor, deceased husband's papers."

"I can't do that," Anne said. "I explained I can't, *won't*, hand over the book to anyone who doesn't have adequate proof of ownership."

"Then let me see the book. Perhaps my store's stamp is within."

Hardly likely. Any book collector and rare-book store owner knew that the value of any book is depreciated with markings. "I'm sorry," Anne said, although she didn't really feel very sorry, "but the book isn't here to show you."

"Not here? What?" Jenna's eyes widened as she spoke.

"It's in a safety deposit box for security purposes, obviously," Anne said.

"I don't understand why you won't let me have my book," Jenna said with the stomp of one of her little pointy-toed shoes.

"Because it's not proven that it's your book," Anne replied.

Jenna let out a huff, snatched her purse and tucked it under her arm, then turned on her heel. "I'll be back with proof. You'll see I'm not making this up."

Not bothering to respond, Anne just watched Jenna storm off. The woman was delusional and probably never owned a book by Edgar Allen Poe in her life.

Anne bit her lip. That was an ugly thought. And unfair. She didn't know Jenna Coleman, didn't know her personality. Even though Anne hadn't said a single rude thing out loud, she was wracked with guilt. Maybe she could help Jenna find the police report.

She looked up the number for the Blue Hill Police Department, then dialed the number.

"Blue Hill Police Department, how may I direct your call?" the female operator asked.

"Michael Banks, please," Anne said.

"One moment." The phone clicked. For a minute, Anne didn't know if she'd been put on hold or hung up on.

"Michael Banks."

"Hi, Michael, it's Anne Gibson."

"Hello, Anne. How are you?"

"Good. How about you? And Jennifer?"

"We're doing great. What can I do for you?"

"I'm trying to find a copy of a police report. It would have been several years ago."

"What kind of report?" Michael asked.

"Theft," she said, then realized it might have been classified another way. "Well, someone broke into a bookstore and stole items from a display case."

"Ah, okay. Probably a B and E. Breaking and entering."

Even *she* knew that. "Yes."

"Do you have a month or year?" he asked.

"No. I'm sorry I don't have that."

"That's okay. What's the name of the shop?"

"Um, I think the owner may have mentioned the name but I really don't recall it now." Anne realized she really didn't have much information to help him find the report. "The owner is Jenna Coleman."

"That will help. Hang on."

Anne could hear taps on a computer keyboard over the phone.

"It's not in our system, so it must be over two years ago," Michael said.

"Probably." That sounded about right.

"I'll have to go to the records room to locate a copy."

"I'm sorry, Michael. I don't want to put you out. I'm trying to help someone," Anne said.

"I'm working on something right now, but when I get a free minute, I'll go check it out, okay?"

"That would be great. Thank you so much."

"I'll call you if I find anything."

"Thanks, Michael. Tell Jennifer I said hello," Anne said.

"I will. Bye."

Chapter Eight

Anne hung up the phone and turned back to the computer sitting on the counter. She opened the Internet browser and ran a search on "flag football injuries." Her heart caught sideways in her throat as she looked at the first headline: "Flag Football Injury Leads to Fifteen-Year-Old's Death."

She clicked the link and read, slowly letting out her breath. The boy and another kid both went to catch the football and collided, smashing bare heads. A freak accident.

Alex had said the Blue Hill league required the boys to wear helmets. Surely a helmet would prevent serious injuries. But would it prevent death?

She returned to the search results page and clicked on the next link, this one listing flag football injuries as documented by a particular hospital over a three-year tracking of injuries. Anne scanned the information. The most common injury was a sprained ankle, something that Ben had already incurred in baseball.

Maybe Alex was right and flag football was no more dangerous than baseball.

Could she take the chance? Anne imagined Ben's face if she refused to let him try out. He'd be beyond disappointed.

Anne closed the Internet window on the computer, her decision made. She'd sign the permission slip. If this was what Ben wanted to do and it was relatively safe, she'd support him any way she could.

She wanted her children to be happy, and for the most part, Ben was. She knew he missed his dad, but he'd dealt with losing Eric pretty well for a ten-year-old. He showed responsibility with Hershey and in helping with Liddie. He was a great baseball player and would probably be just as good on the football team.

Then the thought occurred to her—what if Ben didn't make the team?

* * *

"Touchdown!" Alex threw his hands up over his head, still clutching the football. Ben and Ryan were a good three or four feet behind him. He spiked the ball in the makeshift end zone, then proceeded to do what Anne could only guess was a victory dance.

Anne giggled. She'd forgotten what a lousy dancer Alex had always been. Like having two left feet.

Ryan and Ben giggled.

"Come on, Uncle Alex, you weren't *that* far ahead of us," Ryan said.

"Puh-leeze!" Alex rubbed his nephew's head, then gave him a playful shove. "I was at least six feet ahead of you."

"Nuh-uh, no way," Ben said.

"Does this mean Ben and Ryan lost?" Liddie asked, looking up from her doll-accessory catalog.

"Yes, honey, I believe it does," Anne answered.

Alex ran in front of Anne and Liddie's lawn chairs, plopping down beside Anne's feet. "I might be an old man, but I still got it."

"You've got something, all right," Anne answered, but she couldn't help laughing. Especially when Ryan and Ben walked over.

"Come on, Uncle Alex, let's run another play," Ryan said.

"Nope, boys, I'm beat."

"Oh well, we wouldn't want your heart to give out or anything," Ryan said, laughing with Ben.

Alex reached out and grabbed Ryan, pulling him to the ground. He put the boy in a loose headlock and with his knuckles, rubbed Ryan's head. "Are you saying I'm out of shape, young man?"

Ben erupted in laughter—until Alex let Ryan go and then grabbed Ben and did the same to him. In seconds, both boys were reduced to squeals of laughter.

"You two are the ones who have tryouts coming up," Alex said. "Get in shape. Run up and down our field three times each. Race. Winner gets bragging rights!"

Ryan and Ben grinned at each other, then took off.

Liddie set down her catalog. "I wanna race too," she announced, propping her little hands on her hips.

"It's *want to*, sweetheart, and I don't think the boys want you to play with them. Are you finished looking at your catalog?" Anne said.

"Nonsense," Alex interrupted. "Go ahead and give them a run for their money, Liddie. I heard you're pretty fast."

Liddie smiled. "I am." She took off, pumping her legs as fast as she could.

Anne watched the kids run back and forth. It was a beautiful afternoon. Not too hot and not too chilly. Cool and crisp enough for a sweater. The air smelled clean and fresh. Anne loved Blue Hill during this time of year. She always had.

"So you see how harmless flag football is?" Alex asked, nudging her leg.

He'd played with the boys, working with them on cutting directions for when someone reached to grab one of the three colored straps of fabric worn on a belt around their waist. Time and time again, Alex had thrown the football or caught it, chased or was chased...and not once did anyone come even close to being hurt.

Of course, it was Alex and not another team. And Alex was an adult and the other team would all be boys who were Ryan and Ben's age. And rowdy.

"Do you think he has a chance of making the team?" Anne asked.

Alex watched the boys running, Liddie on their heels. "I think Liddie has a good chance. That girl can run." He flashed Anne his easy smile.

She smiled back. "Liddie sure loves to run. She enjoys chasing her brother — and loves to beat him even more."

Alex chuckled. "I bet she does."

"You didn't answer my question," Anne said, turning serious. "Do you think Ben has a chance of making the team?"

"I don't know. I haven't seen any of the other kids trying out, except for Christian, and he's good. Then again, what should we expect from Coach Pyle's son?"

"I don't want Ben to be disappointed if he doesn't make it." Anne knew all too well how such disappointment stung. It really hurt.

"If he doesn't make it, yeah, he'll be disappointed, but he'll be okay," Alex said as he moved from the ground to the lawn chair Liddie had been sitting in. "He's a lot more mature than you give him credit for, Anne."

Her spine automatically stiffened, and she had to take a moment to breathe slowly. "I give him plenty of credit, Alex. I think I know my son pretty well." She stopped herself. Alex didn't mean to offend her. He had given her son a compliment. It just felt like a backhanded insult to her.

She forced her tone to come out even. "I know he's mature for his age. He had to grow up quickly and face reality when Eric died."

"I'm sorry, Anne. I didn't mean to imply you—"

She laid a hand over his arm. No, he didn't. She was just too sensitive. "I'm sorry. I didn't mean to snap at you. I just don't want him to be hurt."

He nodded. "I understand," he said. "But you can't protect him from the world all the time."

"I know," she said softly. How well she knew.

Ben and Ryan approached, out of breath, and dropped onto the ground, rolling onto their backs and panting.

Liddie ran up. Her face was flushed, but her eyes shone with excitement. "I almost beat them, Mommy," she said as she crawled into Anne's lap.

"You sure did, sweetheart." Anne hugged Liddie, inhaling the distinct smell that was all outdoors. Sunshine and fall.

"Are you coming to the tryouts?" Ben asked Alex.

"Nah. I think I'm gonna stay home and wash my hair." Alex laughed, leaning over and tweaking Ben's ear.

"You should say *going to*, Mr. Alex," Liddie said as she crossed her arms over her chest, "*Gonna* is mmm-proper grammar, huh, Mommy?"

Alex hid his smile behind his hand.

"It's *improper*, sweetie, not *mmm-proper*, but you are correct that *gonna* is supposed to be *going to*." She leaned forward and whispered in Liddie's ear, "But we don't correct adults, remember? That's rude."

Liddie clamped a hand over her mouth. "I'm sorry, Mr. Alex."

"It's okay, sweetheart. I should use proper grammar so I'm not a bad influence," Alex said, winking at Liddie.

Anne shifted Liddie off her lap and stood. "We'd better get home, kids. Dinner is ready and waiting."

"Aw! I was going to ask Uncle Alex if we could go out for pizza and see if all of you wanted to come," Ryan said.

"That's sweet, but I put a roast in the slow cooker this morning, and after dinner, I have to finish up everything for the book sale on Saturday," Anne said. "Maybe next time."

"How's this? If you guys make the team, I'll treat you to pizza." Alex glanced at Anne. "Okay?"

She shrugged. "Sure. Why not? I'll get everybody ice cream after the pizza."

"Yes!" Ryan fist-pumped the air.

"What if we don't make the team?" Ben asked in his quiet, serious voice. "Or if only one of us makes it?"

Alex grinned and pulled Ben into a manly bear hug. "Then we'll still go to eat away our sorrows. Especially the ice cream."

Ben and Ryan laughed while Liddie grabbed her catalog.

Anne smiled at Alex, hoping he knew how thankful she was for the smooth way he'd handled the question—letting Ben know that even if he didn't make the team, it was all still okay.

* * *

Friday snuck up on Anne. She'd been working every night to get things finished and ready for the book sale on Saturday afternoon. Liddie was the first to remind her.

"Mommy, I hafta—I mean, *have to*, carry my suitcase to school. I can't wait to sleep over with Cindy and Becca," Liddie practically sang as she finished her breakfast.

Anne gripped the handle of her coffee cup so hard, it was a miracle it didn't snap off and crash to the floor. "Um, sweetie, why don't I pack your suitcase later and I can take it to you when I pick you up from school?"

"No, Mommy. I'm riding home from school with Cindy and Becca."

Oh, Anne had forgotten about that. "Tell you what: I've got to go to the school to pick up Ben anyway, so why don't I just take your suitcase then? That way, you don't have to carry it around with you during school."

"Okay, Mommy." Liddie jumped up from her kitchen chair and started to skip down the hall.

"Dishes, Liddie," Anne said, pointing at the plate and cup her daughter had left on the kitchen table.

"Sorry," Liddie said as she skipped back, grabbed the dishes, and put them in the sink. "I forgot."

"Don't forget to brush your teeth before you get dressed," Anne said. "And please find out what's keeping your brother."

"I'm right here," Ben said. He dumped his backpack on the counter before reaching for a plate.

"You pour your milk, honey. I'll fix your plate," Anne told him. She slipped the rest of the scrambled eggs from the skillet onto his plate and added two slices of bacon before setting it on the table.

Ben finished pouring his milk and sat down. He bowed his head, was still for a moment, then lifted the fork and shoveled eggs into his mouth.

If Anne hadn't already eaten with Liddie, she would have certainly lost her appetite watching her son eat. It wasn't that he didn't use good table manners, because he did. It was just that he ate so fast. Today even faster than normal.

Usually the three of them ate breakfast together, but today, Ben had said he needed to take a shower before school. Anne had started to argue but realized he needed to make such choices for himself. It didn't matter that he'd showered last night before bed.

There was nothing wrong with being clean.

"Are you nervous about this afternoon?" she asked Ben.

He lowered his fork and swallowed, his Adam's apple becoming more visible. She swallowed the lump in her own throat.

Anne took a sip of coffee. Her baby was growing up too fast. At least she still had time. A few more years before he'd be more interested in real cars than the toy versions.

"I'm a little nervous." He pushed eggs around the plate. "I mean, I think I'm ready because of Alex and Ryan, but you never know what the coach is looking for. At least that's what Coach Pyle says."

"Just do your best and let God handle the details, right?" Anne smiled.

"I know." Ben stopped playing with his breakfast. "I just really want to be on the team. You know?"

She nodded. "I do. I've seen how hard you've practiced." Anne worked to sound bright and cheerful. "You've practiced almost as hard as you did for baseball."

"It's different than baseball. Everybody made the baseball team. We didn't have to try out. The tryout means you only get on the team if you're good enough." He lifted his face and stared at Anne. "I want to be good enough."

Anne's heart nearly broke in two. She crossed the room and gathered him into a hug. Holding him tight, she inhaled the scent of shampoo. "Oh, sweetheart, you *are* good enough. You're perfect just the way God made you."

This was a prime example of another reason she'd hesitated to sign the permission form.

Ben hugged her back and stood, pushing away from her a little. "I know that, Mom. I meant I want to be a good enough football player to make the team," he said with the quiet seriousness that reminded Anne so much of Eric.

"Well, you've done all the practicing and learning possible. You're as ready as you can be."

"Yeah, I guess." He took his plate to the kitchen and scraped the rest of the eggs into the garbage disposal before rinsing both his and Liddie's dishes and placing them into the dishwasher. "I just really, really want to be on the team."

"I understand." She glanced at the clock. "But you'd better hurry and feed Hershey before school."

Anne returned to her coffee, topped off the cup, then savored the strong, hot brew. She loved her children with all her heart, but sometimes, well, there was only one of her and there were many days when she longed to have someone to help her with the kids on a full-time basis.

Today was just one of those days.

Fifteen minutes later, Anne led both kids down the back stairs to the car. As she pulled around to the front, where the library patrons parked, Anne noticed something grayish lying in the middle of the driveway. She put the car in park. "Stay in the car. I'll just be a minute." She undid her seat belt and stepped out of the car.

Anne approached the object carefully. It was very possible she'd encounter a dead animal...like a raccoon or squirrel.

"What is it, Mom?" Ben had lowered his window and stuck his head out to holler at her.

She waved him back into the car. If it was a dead animal lying there, she certainly didn't want her children to see it. She'd have to get rid of it before the kids were out of school. She waited until Ben was totally back inside the car before continuing her approach.

Bigger than a squirrel. Maybe a raccoon. The same gray color as a raccoon.

Only when she stood directly over the object did she realize it wasn't a dead animal. It was a piece of clothing.

She carefully picked it up. It was a good quality ladies' cardigan. One of the popular over-sized ones. It was vaguely familiar... Anne just couldn't place where from. Maybe Wendy had one similar. She checked the pockets, hoping to find something that would identify the owner, but all she came up with was an old Spider-Man figurine. Ben had one like it, while Ryan doted on Iron Man.

Anne glanced toward the parking lot to make sure no cars were there. She hadn't noticed the cardigan in the drive when they'd come home from Alex and Ryan's last evening, and the library had already been closed.

So since no one was at the library this early, where had the garment come from? When had it been left?

"Mom?" Ben yelled through the open window again.

"Coming." Anne draped the cardigan over her arm and carried it with her. She would put it in the library's lost-and-found box. Maybe she'd just been too tired to see it in the drive last night. It *had* been a long day.

She slipped behind the wheel and tossed the cardigan into the backseat, then put the car in drive. She glanced at Ben beside her. "Put your seat belt back on."

He did, but he shot her a funny look.

"What?" she asked as she turned on to the road.

"Why was Ms. Winn's sweater out there?" Ben asked with wide eyes.

She glanced at the cardigan, then back to her son. No wonder it had looked familiar. It *was* Rachel Winn's.

Now Anne really had questions. When and how did the cardigan get left in her driveway? And, most strangely, what was the reclusive Rachel Winn doing with a boy's superhero figurine?

Chapter Nine

Mercy. Anne sucked in air.

Ben held out his hands to catch the football.

Anne wanted to shut her eyes, but she knew she couldn't. Or rather, shouldn't. Parents sitting in the stands at the tryouts yelled to the kids on the field. Not Anne. She just prayed Ben would do his best.

The boy with the ball threw it through the air, straight toward Ben. Higher. Higher.

Heading straight for Ben's outstretched arms.

Another boy, wearing the opposing team's colored "flags" shot out toward Ben. He was so much bigger than Ben. Taller. Wider. More than likely a whole lot stronger. He picked up speed as the ball lost height, heading directly into Ben's outstretched hands.

Anne gasped and clenched her hands.

Ben caught the ball, then spun and started running. Fast. The other boy was behind him by at least two feet.

Three feet.

Alex, sitting beside her on the metal seats, chuckled and patted her shoulder. "He's doing great," he whispered.

But she paid Alex no mind. She used her hand to shield her eyes from the sun. Her entire focus was on her son, now a good four feet in front of the other kid. Everyone ran after Ben, but he had the lead.

Another yard.

He ran hard, cutting fast to the right to dodge an opponent who flew across the field, then he shifted back left to step out of reach of another boy grabbing for his flag.

Another yard. And another.

Ben spun out of reach of a boy blocking his path, hands out to snatch Ben's flag. He grabbed nothing but air.

One more yard. Two.

Touchdown!

Anne was on her feet, jumping and hollering before she realized it. Beside her, Alex stood and yelled too.

"Oh my goodness! He made a touchdown!" she said. "I can't believe it. He made a touchdown."

"I told you he was good." Alex gave her a teasing smirk.

Anne sat back down, but her eyes were glued to Ben, who accepted congratulations from his teammates on the field. He'd scored a touchdown! Her son scored a touchdown.

Pride swelled in Anne's chest, and for a very brief moment, she wished Eric were here to see their son in his moment of glory.

Chad Pyle clapped Ben's back as he came to the sidelines. Ben's smile spread fast as the high school football coach gave him a few words of praise. When Chad turned his attention back to the field, Ben's face lifted. His eyes scanned the stands until...

Anne locked stares with her son. Unshed tears filled her eyes as she gave him a thumbs-up. He grinned, the special smile that always melted her heart, and flashed her sign language for "I love you" before going back to talking with his teammates on the sideline.

"I'm so proud of him," Anne said a little breathlessly.

"You should be. He's done amazing," Alex said. "Look, Ryan's going in now."

Anne didn't know a lot about football, but she understood that Ben played offense and Ryan played defense, so they weren't on the field at the same time.

The other team hiked the football into action. Ryan took off at a dead run toward the guy about to throw the football. The boy took two steps back and to the right. Ryan kept charging. Faster...spinning...cutting.

Ryan ducked low, reached out, and yanked the boy's colored flag.

The referee blew the whistle. Alex was on his feet, whooping and hollering along with several other parents. The boys on Ryan's team rushed him, giving out high fives and clapping him on the back.

"Did you see that?" Alex hugged Anne, then quickly released her. "Ryan sacked the quarterback!"

Anne wasn't quite sure what all that meant, but she knew enough to know that Ryan had done an outstanding job.

Out on the field, the junior-league coach blew his whistle. He motioned for all the kids to sit on the sideline benches. "All of you boys did really well out there today. I'm proud of each one of you," he said. "My assistant coaches and I need to go over our notes together to decide on those who've made the team, so grab a bottled water from the cooler and give us about fifteen minutes or so."

"Now what?" Anne asked Alex.

"The coaches will check to make sure they decide on every position's players. Then they'll announce who made the team."

"In front of everybody?" Anne asked. How horrible. It was bad enough if you didn't make the team, but for everybody you tried out against to know too, well, that was humiliating. She gripped her hands together in her lap.

Alex chuckled. "Yeah. Didn't you girls do this for anything back in school?"

"Not that I recall," she said. It seemed almost cruel to rub it in someone's face that they didn't measure up. Her heart ached, not just for Ben and Ryan and Christian but for all the boys out there who'd had the guts to try out.

"The waiting can be the hardest part," Alex said, standing to stretch.

The man sitting on the other side of Alex asked a question about the Pittsburgh Steeler's upcoming season.

Anne took off her glasses and wiped them on the bottom of her shirt. She didn't agree with Alex. The hardest part would be hearing your friends' names called and not yours.

She stared at Ben and Ryan on the sideline. Both boys guzzled from water bottles and laughed with several other boys. They looked so carefree, so happy.

Maybe Alex was right—this was just the way it was done, and to boys, it didn't matter as much. But she couldn't forget Ben's face from this morning...wanting to be considered good enough.

It could be that it was a rite of passage from little boy to young man. While that was something to celebrate, it was also something for mothers to mourn. He'd stopped calling her Mommy. He didn't want her to kiss him in public, but hugs were still okay. For now. Lately, he'd become more interested in sports and book series to talk about with his friends than hanging around the library and staying near her.

Yes, her son was growing up.

"When do you have to pick up Liddie?" Alex asked.

"Yvette, Cindy and Becca's mom, is going to keep her until after the book sale."

The whistle blew, and Anne's stomach contorted into a tight knot. The coach and his assistants lined up in front of the boys sitting on the bench.

"First off, we want to thank each and every one of you for coming to tryouts. You made our decisions pretty tough. We'd also like to thank you parents for being so encouraging to your sons and bringing them out this afternoon," the coach said. "Unfortunately, the league only allows us to have thirty-five players on the team."

Anne wiped her palms on her jeans. She hadn't realized they'd become sweaty until she reached to clean off her glasses.

The coach held his clipboard and read from it. "This year, our defensive-line players will be: Donald, Randall, Noah, and Jeff as cornerbacks; Marvin, Chuck, Brian, Thomas, and Warren at safety; Alexander, Brody, and Ryan as linebackers; Paul, Kyle, and Sam as defensive ends; and Gene and Kenny as nose tackles."

Applause erupted among the boys, right along with Alex and Anne. Ryan had made the team!

"Now, our offensive line players will be Christian and Felix as quarterbacks; Darren and Ty as running backs; Robert and Peter as centers; Gary, Tim, and Sean as guards; Mark, Luke, and Scott as tackles; Roger, Ron, and Fred as tight ends; and Boyd, Ben, and Sam as wide receivers."

Anne jumped to her feet and clapped just as hard as she could, as did many other parents in the stands. Ben had made the team too! The boys down on the sidelines were just as excited.

Except for the dozen or so whose heads were bent. Anne silently prayed for God to bless each of them abundantly in some other way to fill their hearts with joy and ease the sting of rejection.

"That's our team, folks. Parents, I need you to grab one of these practice and game schedules on your way out. Our first practice is tomorrow," the coach said. "Congratulations, boys. I think we're going to have an amazing season this year."

Alex led the way from the stands to the boys. Ryan, Christian, and Ben were quick to high-five Alex as he approached. Anne and Alex took the schedule from the coach, then focused on the boys.

"Did you see me sack him, Uncle Alex?" Ryan asked, his face beaming.

"We did see it. Great job, champ." Alex ruffled Ryan's short hair.

Ben rushed Anne. "I made a touchdown, Mom. A real touchdown." His eyes were brighter than Anne had seen in a long, long time.

"I'm so proud of you, honey." She gathered him into a quick hug. "Congratulations." She included Ryan and Christian with her smile. "You all did wonderful."

"Yeah. And you know what that means?" Alex asked.

Ryan and Ben grinned and answered in unison. "Pizza and ice cream!"

Alex nodded. "That's right." He turned to include Chad and Christian. "We promised the boys pizza and ice cream after tryouts. Would you like to join us?"

"Can we, Dad?" Christian asked.

Chad shook his head. "Son, I've got to get you home and then hurry to the high school away game. Besides, your mother would have my head if I took you out for pizza and ice cream and didn't take your brothers and sisters."

"But I made the team," Christian said, his displeasure lined in every curve of his young face. "I worked hard practicing."

"And making the team was your reward for your hard work. You set a goal and put in the work to achieve it," Chad answered.

Christian didn't say anything, but his expression conveyed his disappointment quite clearly. Anne could only imagine how he felt. Being one of the middle children in a crew of seven, he might get lost in the shuffle sometimes. Not that Chad and Wendy weren't amazing parents, they were, but Anne really wanted to include Christian in their celebration.

Anne touched Chad's arm. "Would it be okay if Christian went with us? I'd take him home afterward," she whispered.

Chad glanced at his son, now horsing around with Ben and Ryan, then nodded. "But if Wendy hits the roof, I'm blaming you." He grinned, so Anne knew he was only teasing. Well, half teasing.

"I'll take the heat." Anne assured him, then raised her voice toward the boys. "How about we send your dad on his way, Christian, and you come with us?"

"Yes!" Christian yelled, then sobered and looked at Chad. "Can I, Dad? Please?"

"Yeah, buddy. On one condition."

"Anything."

Chad grinned at his son. "You can't tell your brothers or sisters. They'd eat me alive for not bringing them anything."

"Done. Thanks, Dad," Christian said, then turned back to Ryan and Ben—the three of them talking over one another about plays and downs and other football terms that were lost on Anne.

Alex and Anne followed the boys heading to the parking lot.

"I doubt the boys will want to be split up, so how about we menfolk ride together and you meet us there?" Alex asked, using a deep, caveman-like voice.

"Of course. I can do without the close confinement of sweaty, postgame bodies." Anne pulled her keys from her purse. "I'll meet you at Stella's Pizza." She slipped behind the wheel of her Impala.

It didn't take long to reach the restaurant. She pulled into the parking lot right behind Alex and the boys. They spilled out of vehicles and into Stella's Pizza. Stella's was a small joint a couple of blocks from the high school. Its rather cheap and worn decor and low prices were offset by fantastic pizza. The wonderfully unique recipe is what had kept Stella's in business all these years. The tangy aroma of tomato and spices filled the air, as if welcoming them in a comforting, familiar hug.

They quickly found a table large enough for the five of them and sat down. Anne excused herself to go visit the ladies' room and wash her hands. When she returned, the boys were still talking nonstop about the practice tomorrow. The waitress came over directly, took their drink orders, and left menus.

"How about we get three large cheeses and three large pepperonis?" Alex asked.

"Yes," the boys answered in unison.

"Six large pizzas for five of us?" Anne asked, incredulous. She usually ordered a medium for herself and the kids when they had pizza delivered. "That's more than a pizza a person. I won't eat but a piece or two, at most."

"These boys worked up a serious appetite," Alex answered, waggling his eyebrows at the boys.

"I'm so hungry I could eat a horse, huh, Uncle Alex?" Ryan asked with a big grin.

"You betcha. One of those big ole' Clydesdales too." Alex's smile was contagious.

"A horse, huh?" Anne asked.

"Me too," Ben chimed in, followed immediately by Christian's agreement.

"That's what we'll order," Alex said.

"Okay, boys. Go wash those grubby, sweaty hands," Anne said.

The boys scooted back their chairs and headed to the men's room.

"I need to wash up as well." Alex pushed to his feet. "Oh, and Christian can take home whatever is left to his brothers and sisters. I don't want Wendy after our heads." He grinned, then followed the boys.

Anne laughed as he headed to the men's room, but she was very touched by Alex's generous gesture. Sure, he could joke that he did it just because he didn't want to rile up Wendy, but truthfully, he did it because he wanted to be kind to the rest of the Pyle kids. Sometimes, his thoughtfulness reminded her of the sweetness he possessed even as a child that drew her to be friends with him.

The waitress delivered their drinks, took their order, then whisked away. As the sun set over the beautiful Pennsylvania Friday night, more townsfolk filed into the pizza joint. The noise level became a hum with all the different conversations, along with the added background of music spilling out from the old-time jukebox. The enticing smells mingled over the dining room. Anne closed her eyes and inhaled deeply, savoring the moment.

"Mrs. Gibson, may I speak with you for a moment, please?" A woman's voice disrupted Anne's chaotic, yet peaceful moment.

"Excuse me?" Anne startled.

"I'm sorry for disturbing you, but I simply must speak with you." The middle-aged woman with gray roots had angst weighing down every crease around her eyes.

"Do I know you?" Anne asked. Shouldn't Alex and the boys be back by now?

The woman pressed her lips together, looking as if she might cry at any second. "I'm doing this all wrong. I'm sorry." She wrung her hands in front of her. "My name is Evelyn Kelley. You met my husband earlier this week. Rodney Kelley."

Ah yes. The mysterious Rodney Kelley. Now his wife was here, of all places.

Wasn't this just curious?

Chapter Ten

Alex and the boys noisily returned to the table. Alex stared at Evelyn Kelley, as if trying to place her.

Anne stood. "Alex, will you watch the boys for a few minutes, please? I need to speak privately with Mrs. Kelley."

"Sure," Alex said, but he watched her with a worried stare.

Anne led the way to a quieter part of the restaurant and sat in a small booth.

Evelyn sat opposite her. She took a deep breath, then let it out in a rush. "Thank you for listening to me. I'll get right to the point. The Poe book."

As if there was anything else they'd have to discuss? "I already told your husband that I would need some sort of documentation," Anne said, "proof of ownership before I could turn the book over to him."

"I understand that, but this is all my fault." Tears welled in her big hazel eyes. "You see, after his grandfather passed and we received so many of his belongings to go through, Rodney and his father were so wrapped up in settling the estate that everything just seemed to pile up in my garage...to the point where I had to park my car on the street."

Anne just nodded.

"I'd asked Rodney to go through the boxes and put what he wanted to keep in storage. I can't tell you how many times I asked," Evelyn said, shaking her head. "It got to the point where even I felt like a nag, but I wanted my garage back. I know that sounds petty, but winter's coming and I don't relish the thought of having to go out in the cold to get into the car in bad weather."

Anne understood. When she and Eric had lived in their apartment in New York, sometimes the weather was downright brutal with snow and ice. It'd made even going to the grocery store a huge challenge, especially using public transportation. "Not having a garage is certainly inconvenient."

"That was the point. I have a garage. I just can't use it," Evelyn said. "I finally got so frustrated because Rodney started tuning me out whenever I brought up the subject." She wiped a tear that had escaped down her cheek.

Anne found herself choking up.

"Anyway, I saw the flyer about the used-book sale to benefit the library, and I thought I'd kill two birds with one stone—make enough room in my garage so I could park my car, which would hopefully motivate Rodney to clean out the rest of the boxes, and help the library."

Flashing an understanding smile, Anne waited for what she was sure she already knew what was coming.

"As soon as Rodney's father saw the article in the paper about the Poe book, he immediately called us to check on the boxes we had. I had to tell them both what I'd done." More tears shimmered in Evelyn's eyes. "Needless to say, they're both furious with me."

"I'm sorry," Anne said, not sure what else she could say.

"Not only are Rodney and his father mad at me, but my father-in-law is just as angry at Rodney. It's caused a big uproar in the family like you wouldn't believe." Evelyn let out a heavy sigh.

"Rodney told me about your conversation with him at the library, and I understand your position. I do. I'm just asking you to reconsider."

Anne shook her head, but before she could say a word—

"I'm just hoping that you'll at least let him see the physical book. It's possible there's an identifying mark inside that would prove it belongs to the Kelley family."

"I'm sorry, Mrs. Kelley. I can appreciate the situation you are in, but you must realize mine as well," Anne said as softly and gently as she could. "Someone else has also come forward with claims of ownership. They are working to find documentation to prove their ownership. Because the book doesn't belong to me or the library, I have to secure it, so I put it in a safety deposit box. That's why I can't just show it to him."

"I'm begging you, Mrs. Gibson. I don't know if my marriage can survive this mistake I made," Evelyn said. She didn't bother to wipe away the tears flowing freely now.

"I'm sorry. Even if I wanted to show it to him today, I couldn't. The bank won't open until Monday morning."

"But can you give it to him on Monday? Please?"

While Evelyn's pleas were certainly heartfelt, there was just something...off about it. Anne couldn't forget what Grace had told her. "Is there perhaps something else in the book that could prove ownership?" she asked Evelyn. Like a paper?

Evelyn stopped crying and her eyes widened. "Not that I know of. Why? Was there a slip of paper in the book or something?"

"Not that I recall," Anne said.

Alex rounded the corner. "I hate to interrupt, but the pizza's on the table. Ben wanted to wait for you to say grace."

"I'm coming," Anne said as she stood. She looked at Evelyn. "I'm sorry I can't be of more help right now."

"Maybe we'll call you Monday and see about going to the bank?" Evelyn's voice held layers of hope.

"Call me first. I might not be able to get away. Or I might receive documentation from the other person." Anne secretly doubted that Jenna Coleman would produce anything, but Michael just might.

"Okay," Evelyn said, standing as well. "I'm sorry again for disrupting your evening."

Anne turned and followed Alex to their table.

"What was that all about?" he asked as he pulled out her chair for her.

"Long story. Will have to tell you later," she replied, then smiled at Ben. "This looks and smells delicious. Who wants to bless the food?"

Ben jumped at the chance. Everyone bowed their heads and Ben said grace, then began the feeding frenzy of three athletic boys who thought they were starving. Their moans of appreciation for the crust-and-sauce sensations echoed around the table. Even Alex and Anne sighed as their taste buds were satisfied.

Anne had barely finished a single piece when the three boys declared themselves full, each having devoured three pieces. "Did you even chew the pizza, or did you just inhale it?" Anne asked Ben.

He ducked his head. "I was hungry, Mom."

"Uncle Alex, can we have some quarters to play the video games?" Ryan asked.

Anne glanced at the two video games in the corner by the jukebox. Those things had to be almost as ancient as the jukebox. They were probably a novelty for the boys.

"Sure." Alex pulled out a five-dollar bill from his wallet and handed it to his nephew. "Get change and then each of you can have a dollar's worth of quarters. I want the other two dollars back."

Ryan grabbed the money. "Thanks, Uncle Alex."

Christian and Ben shoved to their feet. "Thank you," they both chimed out before rushing behind Ryan to the counter for change.

"You're a softie," Anne admonished softly.

"I remember what it's like." Alex glanced to the games in the corner. "Mom and Dad couldn't take us out for pizza very often, so it was a real treat. I like that Ryan enjoys it almost as much as I do. He deserves to have as much of what's left of a carefree childhood as he can."

Alex's parents were missionaries who were out of the country much of the time, which is why he, instead of his mother and father, was raising Ryan after his sister and brother-in-law died in a car wreck.

Anne nodded as the boys grouped around the video games. "Hey, I need a favor," she said to Alex.

"What?"

"I can drop Ben off at football practice tomorrow, but I need to get back to the library to finish setting up for the book sale. Could you take Ben home?"

"Sure," Alex said. "Happy to take him to practice as well, if you need me to."

"I appreciate that, but I want to watch a bit of his first practice. The sale doesn't start until one, and the sheet said practice would be over at the same time. I just need to leave a little early to make sure everything's set right. Both Remi and Bella are working, so it should be okay."

"That's fine." Alex glanced at the boys, then back to Anne. "So what did Mrs. Kelley want to talk with you about that was so urgent?"

Anne quickly told him what was going on with the Kelley family's claim to the Poe book, as well as Jenna Coleman's. "I need to remember to ask Grace tomorrow if she learned anything about Rodney Kelley."

"She volunteered to help at the sale?" Alex asked.

"No. She's covering it for the paper."

The waitress appeared with the check, and Alex requested several takeout boxes for the leftover pizzas. All four and a half of them. When she returned with Alex's credit card receipt, Alex boxed up the four whole pizzas to drop off at the Pyle home. "Want to split the rest of this half?" he asked.

Anne put her hand on her stomach. "Oh no. I'm full, and Ben ate well more than he usually does, and Liddie's spending the night over at Becca and Cindy's, so it would go to waste. You take it all."

Alex grinned. "Okay. Breakfast of champions in the morning."

"Please tell me you're kidding," she said.

"What? You've never had cold pizza for breakfast?"

"In college, yeah, but not since becoming a real adult." Anne chuckled.

Alex laughed. "You don't know what you're missing."

"Um, empty calories?"

"Ha. It's got dairy and vegetables and meat and bread...that's four of the six major food groups. Throw in a banana and it's a complete, well-rounded meal."

"Ugh." She rolled her eyes but couldn't stop the grin from spreading. "You're incorrigible. Please tell me you don't let Ryan have that for breakfast."

Alex widened his eyes in exaggerated surprise. "What? That's not a good parenting habit? We only have it about four mornings a week."

She gave him a gentle shove. "You're bad."

He laughed, then motioned the boys over. Ryan handed him two dollars.

"Who won?" Alex asked.

"I did," Ben said, the grin he'd been wearing all afternoon and evening carved permanently on his face.

"I came in a close second," Christian said.

Anne stood along with Alex. "Can anybody eat some ice cream?"

"Me!" the three boys chimed together.

Anne chuckled. "Then let's walk over to Thrifty's before it closes."

The boys raced to the door. Anne and Alex followed at a much more reasonable pace. Alex stopped at his vehicle and put the leftovers inside before leading Anne across the street.

"I don't know where they're going to put ice cream. I don't think I can squeeze in anything after the pizza I ate," Anne said.

"Aw, c'mon. Surely you can eat a cone," Alex said.

Anne shook her head. "I don't think so."

"How about we split something?" Alex asked. "Just one scoop of Rocky Road in a bowl? You know you want at least a spoonful."

She grinned. He'd remembered her favorite flavor. "Okay. Just a little bit, though. You have to eat most of it."

"Deal."

The young girl behind the counter smiled as the boys decided what flavors they wanted, then changed their minds a few times before finally placing their order.

Alex ordered the bowl for himself and Anne, but she demanded to pay. "I told the boys I'd get the ice cream. I insist."

"Mom, aren't you having any?" Ben asked, licking his cone.

"She's gonna share with me," Alex said.

Anne grinned. "I only want a spoonful or two."

Ben frowned. "You still like ice cream, don't you?" he asked Anne.

"Of course. I'm just full from all the pizza. Why?" she asked.

"Just making sure because I hope we're going to have some for your birthday," Ben answered.

Anne reached for a spoon. She'd hoped to let her birthday go by without mention, but leave it to Ben to remember. "We will, honey."

Alex snapped his fingers. "That's right. You have a birthday coming up soon, don't you?"

"It's just another day on the calendar." Heat filled her cheeks. She never wanted a big deal made out of her birthday.

"Don't be silly. Birthdays are special days. A cause for celebration," Alex said.

"Not when you reach my age."

Alex gave her a nudge. "Hey. I'm older than you."

She kept the spoon in her mouth. "*Umm-mhh.*"

He made a face at her.

She laughed, then wiped her mouth with a napkin. "You said it, not me."

"Age is only a number," Alex said.

Anne hid a yawn behind her hand. She glanced at the table beside them where the boys had finished off their cones and were talking over one another again, but they were a little quieter now than before — and had a little less energy.

The anxiety and physical exertion of the tryouts, as well as full stomachs, had apparently caught up with them.

"Time for us to head home," she said, stretching. "I have a busy afternoon tomorrow with the used-book sale at the library."

"But I have practice tomorrow," Ben said, a horrified expression replacing the smile.

She ruffled his hair. "I know that, honey. I'm taking you. I'll leave a little early, but Alex has agreed to take you home after practice. How's that?"

Ben nodded. "Oh, okay."

"Who am I riding home with?" Christian asked as the group poured out of the drugstore and headed toward their vehicles.

Anne smiled. "Ben and me. I have to drive right by your house on my way home."

"Then you'd better take these." Alex opened his car door and handed the four large pizza boxes to Christian.

"What's this?" Christian asked.

"The leftovers. So your dad doesn't get in hot water with your mom," Alex said.

Christian grinned. "Thanks so much! See you tomorrow, Ryan."

The boys said their good-byes.

"Drive carefully," Alex told Anne.

"Always." She slipped behind the steering wheel and started the car.

Within ten minutes, Anne had dropped Christian off at home. Wendy was thrilled to see the leftover pizza.

As Anne drove home she asked Ben, "You don't mind that I'm going to miss the last few minutes of your first practice, do you?"

"I understand, Mom. You'll be there for most of it."

It seemed like he had matured by the hour the last week or so. Anne didn't quite know if she liked that or not.

Chapter Eleven

At least the sun shone brightly over the football field, even if the temperature had dipped down into the low forties.

Ben rushed from the car as soon as Anne parked. Good thing she'd already wished him luck today. She climbed into the stands and sat beside Wendy and Alex.

"Hey, thanks for the pizza last night, guys," Wendy said. "I had a piece this morning for breakfast."

Alex grinned and pointed at Anne. "See? I told you."

"You're both hopeless." Anne rolled her eyes but smiled at her two friends.

"Are you ready for the sale today?" Wendy asked.

"I hope so. Remi and Bella were both getting things set up when I left. I told them I'd be there around twelve thirty since Alex is taking Ben home from practice," Anne answered.

Wendy nodded. "I'll be there as soon as practice is over. Chad and I brought separate cars so he could stay around after and take Christian home. Hannah will be more than ready to see her dad get home."

Hannah, the oldest of the Pyle children, was fourteen and earned extra money by babysitting her younger siblings when both Wendy and Chad couldn't be home.

"Although," Wendy continued, "Christian has given me orders to look for any copies of the last two books in the Coastal Club series. He already read a friend's copy, but he wants his own."

Alex stretched his long legs out across the bleacher in front of him. "Ryan too. What is it about that series? Whenever a new one comes out, Ryan has his nose stuck in it and I can't get him to do a thing until he finishes it."

"That's Christian exactly," Wendy said. "Anne, do you have any information on the author, that R. W. Winger? I've tried to find some information on him online and in the library catalogs, but he's very elusive."

Anne shook her head. "I did the same thing and couldn't find anything. From what I understand, he's a recluse. Just writes those books the kids absorb."

"Don't get me wrong, I'm as avid of a reader as anyone, but for days at a time, it's like Christian disappears. I have to go hunt him down. It's insane," Wendy said.

Anne chuckled. "Ben's reading the last one now, so I completely understand."

"It's like every kid between the ages of eight and fourteen is totally hooked by the series," Alex said.

"That's true," Anne volunteered, "but at least the main characters aren't vampires or wizards. I love that Ben reads and can get lost in a series, and I like that these characters are at least based on humans."

"True," Wendy said with a nod. "But there's something to be said about some specific vampires and werewolves."

Alex laughed and shook his head. "Check it out. The coach is running them."

Anne focused on the field. The coach blew the whistle, and the four boys on the line took off running across the field. The coach would blow the whistle again when they reached a certain point, and the next four boys on the line would take off.

"Checking their speed," Wendy said.

"Is that what they're doing?" Anne asked. It looked to her like they were just running.

Wendy nodded. "Chad does that to the new players on the high school team. He says it helps him figure out what position to play some of them."

"But the coach already said what positions they'd play," Anne argued.

"He's determining what string each kid will play," Alex said.

"String?" Anne was totally confused. What did string have to do with football? Maybe it was part of the flag uniform part?

"The players who are selected to start the game are called the first string," Wendy explained.

"The other boys who play the same position but don't actually start the game are called second string," Alex said.

"And if there are extra players in that same position, they're called third string," Wendy said.

"Oh. I see." Anne stared at the field. Ben stood on the line beside two other boys. She recognized them from the library — Boyd and Sam. The coach had also called their names as wide receivers.

The whistle blew, and the boys took off running. Ben and Eric were neck-and-neck until they'd run about thirty yards. After that, Ben picked up speed, leaving Eric behind.

"So the coach will pick the fastest out of Ben, Sam, and Boyd to see who will start?" Anne asked.

"Not necessarily," Wendy answered.

"I don't understand." Anne watched as the coach blew the whistle and Ben—still at least ten yards ahead of Sam, and Boyd even further behind than that—slowed and moved off the field.

"Ben is playing wide receiver," Alex said.

"The coach said Sam and Boyd were wide receivers too," Anne pointed out. "So one will be first string, one second string, and the third one will be third string, right?"

Alex shook his head. "There are usually two wide receivers on the field at a time."

Oh, this was really confusing. "How does that work?" she asked.

Wendy laughed. "It can be quite complicated. The way Chad explained it to me is that there are usually two wide receivers to start each game. They are the ones the quarterback primarily throws the ball to way down field. They have to be very fast, and able to zigzag well."

"Okay." Anne nodded. "That I can understand."

"If Coach decides to have two wide receivers on this team, then both boys will be considered *first string*. Understand?" Alex said.

"Yep. Got it." Anne smiled as the coach blew the whistle again. It all looked really tiring to her.

Anne's cell phone rang. She dug it out of her purse quickly, checked the caller ID, then answered, "Hello, Grace."

"Hey, are you busy?" Grace asked.

"Just at Ben's first football practice."

"He made the team? That's great."

"Yeah." Anne nodded, even though Grace couldn't see her. "What's up?"

"I found out why the name Rodney Kelley sounded familiar."

Anne sat up straighter. "Yes?"

"His grandfather, Gus Kelley, died not too long ago. I remember the obituary. It was hard to write because not many had anything nice to say about him. Most everyone said he was, and I quote, 'meaner than a snake to everybody who knew him.' End quote."

"Interesting," Anne said, but it didn't help her figure out anything about Rodney and his father and the book.

"There was something really odd about his estate, though. Seems old Gus had argued so many times with Rodney's dad, Jeff, that Gus had told everyone in town over and over again that he was going to cut his son out of his will and leave everything to the Blue Hill Garden Club."

"Really?" Anne asked.

"Yeah. According to my interview notes, several people mentioned they were surprised that Jeff and Rodney were left Gus's entire estate."

"Gus Kelley had a large estate?" Anne asked, more out of curiosity than thinking it would help uncover the Poe book's owner.

"Not really. Don't get me wrong, he was comfortable, but he wasn't rich or anything. He had some good investments, and he did have quite a book collection, so I'd noted."

Well now. *That* was useful. "Did you learn anything else?"

"That's it," Grace said.

On the field, the coach motioned for all the boys to huddle around him.

"I appreciate your looking for me, Grace," Anne said.

"Of course," Grace replied. "Hey, I made our hair appointments for Monday morning at nine, then figured we'd have lunch in town if that's good for you?"

"That's perfect," Anne said. "The kids are out of school for an in-service date, so Wendy already invited Ben and Liddie to spend Sunday night with them. She'll take the kids home after lunch."

"Okay. I'll see you later at the sale."

"Thanks, Grace." Anne hung up the phone and watched the boys begin doing exercises that looked almost like Anne's calisthenics.

"Everything okay?" Wendy asked.

"Yeah." Anne told them what Grace had said about Rodney Kelley. "So I guess that means the book is probably theirs."

"But how can you prove it?" Alex asked.

Anne shrugged. "If it was Gus Kelley's, then it should be listed in his estate value since it's worth a lot of money."

"That makes sense," Wendy said. "I would imagine Rodney would have that information or his father would before he comes back to try and claim the book again."

"I guess," Anne said. She would have checked that out first, had it been her, before ever going to the library to show an interest. It didn't seem to make sense.

* * *

The sale had been, in Anne's estimation, a success. She hadn't tallied the profits yet, but from the steady stream of people buying books for the last four hours, she guessed she would have a tidy sum to spend on the audio/video equipment.

She felt confident they'd taken in enough money to buy the system she had been eyeing in the catalog. The number of books remaining on the tables indicated that over half had been sold today. She would put the leftover books in storage and perhaps hold another sale in the spring.

Wendy came by and handed her a cup of coffee.

"Thank you," Anne breathed as she took a sip. Caffeine. Blissful caffeine. Just what she needed to break the early evening sleepiness.

"I'll start clearing the rooms and turning off the lights. Maybe that'll motivate the last of the shoppers to hurry up and make their choices," Wendy said as she turned back toward the library's main rooms.

Anne was almost dead on her feet. She hadn't slept very well last night, what with worrying about the sale and fretting over Ben's first practice. And, to be honest, she never slept really soundly when either of the kids weren't home.

The front door opened and she swallowed a groan, reminding herself that every sale meant money for the new equipment. She plastered on a smile and lifted her face—then let the smile slip off as Rodney Kelley approached.

"Hello, Mrs. Gibson."

She forced herself to be cordial. "Mr. Kelley. Did you come to look over the books for sale? We were just about to pack up and call it a day. Is there something specific I could help you with?"

He shook his head, not a hair out of place. "I wanted to let you know that my father and I have gone through all of my grandfather's books and the rarest of his, an Edgar Allan Poe title, is definitely missing."

Anne sighed. While she believed his story, and certainly his wife's, there was still something a bit off about the whole situation. Time to call his bluff. "I'm sure, considering the title's worth that I found, that the executor of your grandfather's estate will have some sort of documentation—an appraisal, insurance papers, something—that lists the book's title. If you'll just bring me a copy of that, I'd be more than happy to hand over the book."

"If you could just let me see the book, I'd be able to tell if it's my grandfather's." The irritation was as clear in his voice as it was in his expression.

"I've already explained, Mr. Kelley, the book is in a safety deposit box." She'd explained it to him. And his wife. And now him *again*. Did he think she was lying?

"Just one look at it and I'll be able to tell."

Enough! Anne fisted her hands on her hips. "Mr. Kelley, I've told you more than once that the book isn't here. I can appreciate your thinking you'll know if it's your grandfather's by looking at it, but if it's not here for you to inspect, it's not here. Period. End of discussion."

He ground his teeth.

"Hey, Anne, do you need help packing…" Wendy rounded the corner with Donald Bell on her heels. "Oh. I'm sorry. I didn't realize you were helping someone."

Anne kept her stare locked on Rodney, whose face had turned red like he'd been in the sun all afternoon. "It's okay, Wendy. Mr. Kelley was just leaving."

Rodney looked at Wendy and Donald, then back to Anne. "I'll be in touch," he said.

Anne nodded. "Of course. I would, however, strongly suggest you get in contact with the executor of your grandfather's estate and bring me a copy with that title listed."

He didn't answer, just turned on his heel and stormed out of the library.

"So that's Rodney Kelley," Wendy said. "What did he want?"

"To see the book, of course," Anne answered. "Just like before."

"I thought you explained the book isn't here."

Anne nodded at her friend. "I did. More than once."

"Maybe you should call the police, just in case," Donald Bell said.

Anne smiled and shook her head. "No. It's okay." She let out a quick breath. "Now, did I hear an offer to help me pack up books?"

"I did," Donald said, his cheeks turning a little pink. "If you need help, I mean."

"Of course we need the help," Wendy interrupted. "I'll go hurry these last two customers along and lock the door." She pointed to the table with a scattering of books no one was looking at. "Go ahead and start boxing those up, Donald. Empty boxes are hidden under the tables."

Anne smiled as Wendy took charge. She was grateful, as she was flat worn out. Maybe age was more than just a number. She sure felt every bit of her thirty-four years right now.

The last customer approached Anne and handed her the money for the four books she held. Anne gave the lady her change, thanked her for her support, then slipped the books into a bag. Exhaustion pushed her into a chair after the lady had left. She glanced over the tables...they'd sold a lot, yes, but she still had plenty to box up.

Every muscle in Anne's body threatened to revolt if she dared try to lift a single book, but she couldn't just leave the library in such a state.

"Okay, we're officially closed," Wendy said. "You count the money, Anne. I have Alex with Ben, Ryan, and Christian ready to help Donald pack up the books and store them."

Anne smiled at her friend, whose words were pure music to her ears. "Thank you, Wendy. I don't think I can lift another book today."

Wendy grinned and gave her a big hug. "I figured, so I recruited help. And since Christian and Ryan want the two copies of the latest Coastal Club books, they are more than happy to pitch in and help."

"You found some copies of them?"

"I did. Actually four copies. One for Ryan and one for Christian, and I held another one in case you want to give it to

Ben. He said he didn't have it yet." Wendy grinned and waggled her eyebrows. "Bribery is a staple in my house."

"You, my friend, are a genius." And Anne meant it.

"Yes, I know." Wendy laughed. "Oh, and Yvette called. She has to run to the grocery store so she'll drop Liddie off here when she's done." She checked her watch. "In about fifteen more minutes, give or take a few."

Anne hugged her back. "I adore you."

"I know." Wendy nodded as Alex and the boys slipped in from the back. "You guys start packing books. The empty boxes are under the tables." She pointed at Anne. "You start counting the money. I want to know how much we made today."

"Yes, ma'am," Anne said. She opened the drawer and pulled out the cash bag.

Anne counted the money. That couldn't be right. She recounted.

Alex, Donald, and the boys packed up all the books and put the boxes in storage. Wendy placed all the tablecloths in her tote bag to take them home and wash them, then instructed the guys to break down the tables.

She had to have miscounted. Anne started with the one-dollar bills again.

"Anne?" Donald said softly.

Looking up from the money, she smiled. "Yes?"

"I have to head home. I need to let my dog out," he said.

Anne widened her smile. "Thank you so much for all your help today. I really do appreciate it."

"Yes, ma'am." He ducked his head, but not before she noticed the pink coloring his cheeks. "I'll see you later."

"Good night, Donald."

He shuffled away, asking Wendy to unlock the front door so he could leave. Anne returned to counting the money. Again.

She concentrated as she counted every bill and every cent. The total was the same. For the third time. It couldn't be a mistake, but...

"So how'd we do?" Wendy asked.

"More than I thought we would raise," Anne answered.

"Really? That's awesome," Alex said.

"I know. I counted it three times because I couldn't believe it." Anne's excitement rushed through her veins, her earlier exhaustion gone. "I can get the complete system I wanted but never thought we could afford."

Wendy grinned. "Told you this was a great idea."

"You were right," Anne said.

Car headlights flickered through the window. Everyone turned.

"Wonder who that could be," Alex said.

"Probably Yvette dropping off Liddie," Anne said. "Let me go see." She headed to the library's front entrance, unlocked the door, and stepped on the sidewalk.

The temperature had dipped with the setting sun, sending a chill down Anne's spine. Sure enough, Yvette headed up the walkway with Liddie in tow, arms carrying her overnight case and another tote.

"Mommy!" Liddie rushed into Anne's arms. "I missed you."

"I missed you too, sweetheart. Did you have fun?"

"I did. I got lots of trade stuff," Liddie said, opening the other tote. Feathers from a boa drifted in the cool breeze.

"We'll look at everything inside, honey," Anne told Liddie. She smiled at Yvette. "Would you like to come in?"

Yvette shook her head, her short curly hair grazing against her cheek. "Another time. I left the girls in the car with the ice cream."

Anne laughed. "Thank you so much for having her. I hope she behaved."

"She was as good as gold." Yvette smiled at Liddie. "Bye. We'll see you at church tomorrow."

Anne waited until Yvette had gotten back in her car and shut her door before following Liddie into the library.

Alex, Ryan, Wendy, and Christian met her at the door.

"We're heading home too," Wendy said. She gave Anne a quick hug. "See you tomorrow at church."

"Bye. Thank you all for everything."

Anne locked the door behind them, put the cash bag in the bottom drawer and locked it up, and then put her arm around Liddie and Ben. "Let's head upstairs, kids. I'm about ready for a hot shower and my bed."

"But I've got lots to show you, Mommy," Liddie said.

"And I want to see it all." Anne kissed the top of her daughter's head. She did want to see everything, if she could stay awake.

When Anne finally made it up to Liddie's room later, she sat on the foot of the bed. Liddie's comforter was laid neatly across her bed. Anne studied the décor and furniture in Liddie's bedroom. The décor Anne had let Liddie pick out included light pink walls, a pink ceiling fan, white carpet, a full-length mirror, a dollhouse, and more. The chair rail that wove around the room was covered in zebra print wallpaper. It was a rather loud room.

Liddie had finally unpacked her clothes and sat on the floor to show Anne. All her new things were neatly laid out in the space on the floor in front of her.

"Look at this necklace, Mommy!" Liddie said as she held up a costume diamond necklace.

"Pretty, honey." Anne nodded, trying to keep her eyes open.

Liddie showed Anne about twenty-five new things including a pink boa, a Hello Kitty charm bracelet, and a dazzling tiara. Anne tried to pay as much attention to her daughter's new items as possible, she really did, but her mind kept wandering to how comfortable the bed looked.

Anne nodded at each thing Liddie held up and made the appropriate *ooh*s and *ahh*s.

But despite Liddie's excited talk, Anne eventually dozed off, only to be awoken by Liddie shaking her wrist.

"Did you fall asleep, Mommy?" Liddie asked, blinking her big brown eyes.

"No, honey, my eyes just needed a rest." Anne smiled and hugged her daughter.

"Okay. Will you help me put it in my chest?" Liddie asked.

"Of course. Bring your trunk we got for you at the flea market over here," Anne said.

Liddie obediently went over and retrieved the old wooden domed trunk.

"Be right back, Mommy," Liddie said, heading toward the door.

"Where are you going?" Anne asked.

"To the bathroom." Liddie walked out of the room, leaving Anne with all the costume jewelry and accessories.

Anne began to admire the smooth surface of the trunk's dark wood. She also looked at the yellow shiny metal around the edge. Copper maybe?

Anne sighed as she sorted through other items Liddie had obtained from her game of trading treasures. She especially liked a very pretty necklace with a metal chain and a green four-leaf clover charm hanging from it. It was simple but looked very chic.

Another treasure was a pair of pink clip-on earrings. Anne chuckled. Liddie would have a ball playing dress up with those.

"I'm back!" Liddie said as she walked into her room.

"Ready to put your treasures away?" Anne asked.

Liddie carefully placed each item in the trunk in the order she felt best. Then she hugged Anne. "Thank you for letting me go, Mommy," Liddie said, smiling. "I had a good time."

"Oh, you're welcome, sweetie." Anne smiled and then yawned. She was ready for bed.

Chapter Twelve

The sun had already climbed high into the noonday sky when Anne walked out of church. Too bad the temperatures hadn't risen with the sun. Anne wrapped her sweater more tightly around herself as she moved to say hello to Reverend Tom.

"Lovely service today," she said.

"Thank you," he answered before bending to say hello to Liddie.

"I'm going to spend the night with Miss Wendy and Justin and Ethan and Jacob and Christian and Emily and Sarah and Hannah," Liddie told him. "Ben is coming to spend the night too. Not 'cause I'm a baby, but 'cause he wants to play football with Christian."

"Really? What will your mom do all by herself?"

Liddie looked up at Anne. "Mommy, are you gonna be okay while we're gone?"

Anne and Reverend Tom both chuckled. "It's *going to*, Liddie, and yes, I'll be just fine. Miss Grace and I have appointments to get our hair done in the morning and reservations to have lunch together." Anne hugged Liddie closer as she led her daughter into the parking lot, Ben trailing behind them. "I will, however, miss you two like crazy." She turned to include Ben.

"M-o-m. It's just for one night," Ben said.

Anne laughed and pulled him into a hug. "I know. But I still miss you guys when you're gone." Yet she knew it was good for them to spend time away from her and with their friends. She didn't want to smother them. Well, she did...but she knew she shouldn't. Besides, she was looking forward to a girls' pampering morning and lunch alone with Grace.

"I thought you were going to bring their suitcases to church," Wendy said as she joined them in the parking lot. "We're heading home to a cookout."

"Their duffle bags are in the backseat," Anne answered. The kids would have a great time cooking burgers and hot dogs with Wendy's crew. She unlocked the door and handed Liddie's duffle bag to Wendy while Ben grabbed his own.

"Bye, Mommy." Liddie gave Anne a tight hug.

Anne squeezed her in return, then showered kisses all over Liddie's face. "You be good for Miss Wendy and Mr. Chad, baby girl, okay?"

"I will, Mommy. I love you." Liddie's sweet voice tapped against Anne's heart.

Anne blinked away the emotion and grabbed Ben before he could escape without a hug. "I love you, Ben. Be good," she whispered.

"Bye, Mom. See you tomorrow."

"I'll make sure they call you tonight before bed," Wendy said with a smile.

"Thanks." Anne waved as her kids and the Pyle crew climbed into Wendy's van. With a quick honk, they were gone.

Not sure what to do with herself as she drove out of the church parking lot, Anne decided she'd treat herself to a drink at Coffee Joe's, and maybe one of the delectable pastries that always smelled so good.

A few minutes later, she stepped into Coffee Joe's and grabbed a coffee and a blueberry scone. She'd just sat down at a table by the window when Coraline Watson came in. Anne waved her over. "It's getting chilly a bit early this year, isn't it?" Anne asked as Coraline sat down with her large cup of coffee.

"It is, but I love it," Coraline said. "Of course, I miss being able to see all my birds in the winter, but I do enjoy the change of seasons."

Anne hid her smile behind her cup of coffee as she took another sip. Coraline claimed to be an avid bird-watcher, and she was, to a certain degree, but she also watched the people of Blue Hill just as intensely as the birds in the trees around the park.

"So have you found the owner of that Edgar Allan Poe book yet, dear?" Coraline asked.

Anne shook her head. "Not yet. I have a couple of people whom it could belong to, but no definite proof yet." She took a bite of the blueberry scone. Yummy sweetness danced over her tongue.

"Mildred should be home late next week. Maybe she'll remember something about the book being donated," Coraline said.

Mildred had been Aunt Edie's best friend, and ever since Anne had moved back to Blue Hill, she'd graciously stepped into the role of older confidante to Anne. Her wisdom and insight were nearly as much of a blessing as Aunt Edie's had been.

"I hope she remembers something," Anne said. "Do you know Rodney Kelley, Coraline?"

"Well, now, dear. I know who he is, but I don't really know him. I know his father, Jeff, a bit better." Coraline took a sip of her coffee. "Poor dear."

Anne swallowed the bite of scone she'd been chewing. "Why poor Jeff?"

Coraline shook her head. "His father, Gus, was so hateful. For years, he told everyone in the Blue Hill Garden Club that he was going to leave his estate to them and cut Jeff out of his will entirely."

Anne couldn't imagine being so upset with Ben or Liddie that she'd even threaten to cut them out of her will. "Why would he do that?" she asked Coraline.

"I don't know for sure, you understand, but the way I heard it, Gus wanted Jeff to go to medical school and become a plastic surgeon, then he could support Gus for the rest of Gus's life. But Jeff didn't have the stomach for the medical field, which disappointed Gus to no end."

"That's sad," Anne said, taking another sip of coffee.

Coraline chuckled. "Maybe so, but the final laugh was Jeff's. I understand Gus had been quite wealthy back when Jeff was a boy, but the toll of living a longer life took most of Gus's investments. He was financially comfortable until the day he died, so Jeff and Rodney got some money but mainly property."

"Well, that shows that amends must have been made somewhat since Jeff wasn't cut out of Gus's will," Anne said, finishing off the scone.

"Apparently so." Coraline took another sip of coffee. "How is everything else going with you, Anne dear?"

"Everything's great," Anne said, then proceeded to bring Coraline up to speed with the kids and happenings at the library. She sipped the last of her coffee.

Coraline drank her last sip as well. "I've got to run, dear." She gave Anne a wave. "I'll see you later."

"Bye," Anne said. She threw away their trash, nodded at the barista behind the counter of Coffee Joe's, then headed out into the street.

The afternoon wind had picked up a bit, rustling the late autumn leaves that still clung to the trees and littering the sidewalks with the dried leaves that had already fallen. Anne pulled her sweater more tightly around herself and headed to the car.

One of the things she enjoyed about being back in Blue Hill was the lovely slower pace. Even the speed limits in town were slower than the average thirty-five miles per hour. Going only fifteen miles an hour allowed people to wave at the Main Street storekeepers who were out sweeping the sidewalks in front of their stores. Or the young people out walking their dogs.

Anne turned off the town's main thoroughfare and steered toward Bluebell Lane. She passed Rosehill Park, which was Blue Hill's park; it boasted a small pond and a rose garden. Years ago, Aunt Edie had belonged to the park's garden club. As a matter of fact, the garden club had placed a commemorative brass plaque honoring Aunt Edie in the planter of Japanese rosebushes.

As Anne slowed even more, she noticed a young couple pushing a stroller with a giggling little blonde-headed girl. Anne used to play here as a young girl. She smiled to herself and then glanced toward the big old swings. She remembered coming to the park as a child, swinging on those old swings with the creaks and squeaks, higher and higher, until she thought she was flying. Those were the days.

She tapped her brake as she caught movement on the swings, but it wasn't a child soaring through the air. Instead, an older woman pointed her toes skyward, slicing through the last rays of the late afternoon sun. The older woman was Rachel Winn, without her cardigan.

Anne pulled the car into the park's lot and turned off the engine. She grabbed the gray cardigan from the backseat, where she'd left it after finding it in the library's driveway, and she headed toward the swings.

Rachel slowed, then dragged her feet on the dusty ground to stop as Anne approached.

"I think this belongs to you," Anne said, holding out the garment.

Stepping from the swing, Rachel took the item of clothing and slipped her arms into the sleeves. "Thank you. I thought I'd lost it. Did I leave it at the library?"

Anne nodded. "I found it in the driveway the other day." She waited to see if Rachel would explain.

"*Hmm*," Rachel said. "Well, thank you. See you tomorrow."

Before Anne could say another word, Rachel turned and hurried in the opposite direction. Anne watched her go. The woman was a little eccentric, but not in a concerning way. As Anne watched her walk away, she couldn't help but wonder about the superhero figurine in the pocket. That was just a little odd.

Rachel gave off signals of wanting to be left alone, and those signals came across loud and clear. Yet her aloofness and oddity also made people want to get to know her and find out her secrets. She was quite the enigma.

Anne got in her car and drove home. The whole building was quiet. A bit lonely. Anne finished the laundry and carried the kids' clothes to their rooms. In Liddie's room, Anne smiled at the open trunk sitting on top of her dresser. Some of Liddie's *treasures* had spilled onto the floor. Feathers from a bright pink boa. A string of blue glass beads. A lady's cocktail ring.

Anne held the ring, which featured a large pearl, in the palm of her hand. It must be one of the cool things Yvette gave Cindy and Becca to trade that Liddie was so enamored with. Anne would go through her costume jewelry soon and pass on to Liddie anything she didn't want to keep. Here in Blue Hill, she really didn't have any need for costume jewelry, even the good quality stuff she'd collected over the years.

After putting away the clothes and folding the quilt at the bottom of Ben's bed, she ate a simple supper and enjoyed reading for a while in total peace and quiet. Growing tired, she laid out her clothes and set her alarm. It was still early, but she could use the extra sleep, and tomorrow would be a busy day.

Her last thought after crawling into bed was that she needed to remember to call Coraline and see what she knew about Rachel Winn. Something about the woman was definitely strange, and it involved more than just some caped superhero figurine.

* * *

"This has been wonderful," Anne told Grace over lunch at the quaint little restaurant in the mall in Deshler, a neighboring town to Blue Hill.

"I love the new highlights in your hair," Grace said. "They're very becoming."

Anne's hands went automatically to her head. She hadn't been able to get more than just a trim off her shoulder-length tresses, but she'd let the stylist and Grace talk her into having layers cut around her face to frame it and to add just a few highlights to fancy up her common brown color.

She wasn't sure yet if she liked the result.

"Thanks," she told Grace, then took the last sip of her tea. "I guess we should start heading back to Blue Hill. I bet Wendy's ready to drop my kids off."

"I bet she didn't even notice she had two extra ones," Grace said, laughing as she reached for the check.

Anne handed Grace some cash. "Does that cover mine?"

"Of course." Grace added her own cash to the top of the plastic tray. "Should cover the tip nicely as well."

Anne stood and waited for Grace to join her. "I've really enjoyed this."

"Me too. We should make this a monthly habit at least," Grace answered, then turned and led the way out of the restaurant and into the mall.

"Definitely. And maybe next time we can get Chad to watch the kids so we can drag Wendy out with us."

They walked toward the mall's exit. A huge banner going up outside the bookstore drew Anne's attention. "Oh my goodness," she whispered.

"What?" Grace asked and she turned to read the banner as well. "A new Coastal Club installment will be releasing just in time for Christmas," she read out loud. "Is that the kids' series everyone's raving about?"

Anne nodded. "Ben's reading the latest one now. I'll definitely have to get him this one for Christmas. I wish I could get in touch with the author to get Ben an autographed copy. Ben would be over the moon."

"Can't you just contact the author and buy an autographed copy? Or send him the book you buy and have this"—Grace squinted as the workers moved the banner—"this R. W. Winger sign it and mail it back?"

"I've tried to locate the author, but it seems he's quite hard to pin down. No interviews. No pictures of him. No signings. No tours. Nothing."

"Can't you use your husband's contacts to track him?" Grace asked as they headed out of the mall.

"I hadn't thought about that." She didn't really know many in the publishing business, despite Eric having been an editor for one of the major New York publishers. She did, however, know of a couple other editors who had worked with Eric. "Maybe I'll call someone and see what I can find out."

"There's an idea. If this R. W. Winger is as mysterious as he seems, then getting anything from him would make Ben flip," Grace said, leading the way across the parking lot to where their cars were parked side by side.

She would be the best mom ever if she got Ben an autographed copy of the latest Coastal Club book. That alone was plenty of motivation to try and hunt down R. W. Winger.

Chapter Thirteen

"I hope the kids weren't a handful for Wendy," Anne said as she stepped out of her car at the library and nodded at Wendy's van. "Or that there isn't something wrong."

Grace put her arm through Anne's. "Maybe Wendy was just being nice and thoughtful to bring them home so you wouldn't have to wait. She knows how much you miss the kids when they aren't with you."

True. Anne smiled but still walked a little faster in through the door.

"Surprise!"

Anne froze as many people jumped out at her. Liddie and Ben ran to her, hugging her.

"It's a surprise party for you, Mommy. For your birthday," Liddie said.

"Happy birthday, Mom," Ben said.

Anne pointed at Grace. "So that's why you ate so slowly at lunch. I thought maybe you had a sore tooth or something."

Grace laughed and gave Anne a hug. "Nope. I was under orders not to let you get back here before one thirty."

"I threatened her, of course," Wendy said as she gave Anne a hug too. "Now, come on and check out your cake before my motley crew messes it up. They've been hammering for a piece ever since I took it out of the oven this morning."

"It shouldn't have smelled so good," Chad said. "Happy birthday, Anne."

"Thank you," she answered, smiling at people as Wendy led her to the library's refreshment area.

"Happy birthday," Reverend Tom and his wife, Maggie, said in unison.

"Thank you."

"Well, what do you think?" Wendy asked as she waved toward the cake, which was the centerpiece of the table.

It was a beautiful cake in the shape of a book, decorated to look like the cover of Anne's favorite title, *Moby Dick*.

"Oh, Wendy, I love it," Anne said.

Coraline stuck a candle at the top and struck a match to light it. In her clear, soulful voice, she led the well-wishers in a loud round of the Happy Birthday song.

"Make a wish and blow out the candle, Mommy," Liddie said as soon as they'd finished singing.

Anne smiled, closed her eyes, then opened them and blew out the candle in a quick puff.

Everyone clapped.

Wendy handed Anne a bright orange gift bag. "Here, this is from me, Chad, and the kids. You open your presents while I cut the cake." Wendy turned to Grace. "Take her over to the presents while we make a mess."

"I don't need presents," Anne said, heat fanning her face. A surprise party was more than enough. She felt uncomfortable with gifts.

"Just open the present and love it," Chad playfully demanded. "There's no point in arguing with her over anything. You should know that by now."

Anne laughed. He was right. She pulled away the tissue paper to find a beautiful stained-glass bookmark. "Oh, it's exquisite. I love it. Thank you," she told both Chad and Wendy.

Wendy paused in her task of cutting the cake and handing plates to her kids to pass around and returned Anne's smile and said, "I saw that and knew it was you."

"Here, open mine next," Ben said, putting a messily wrapped box in her hands. "I made it and wrapped it myself."

She set the bookmark down on the table and slowly peeled back the paper and opened the box. Inside was a wooden frame painted red, with *ANNE* burnt into the wood at the top. "You made this, Ben?"

He nodded. "Alex helped me so I wouldn't burn myself, but I wrote it out and traced it all by myself. Painted it too," he said, pride filling his voice.

"It's beautiful, honey. I love it. Thank you." She pulled him close and gave him a hug and a kiss. He didn't even pull away.

"Mine next, Mommy," Liddie said, shoving a small gift bag at her.

"Okay. Okay," Anne said, setting the frame beside the bookmark. She reached into the bag and pulled out a costume tennis bracelet. "Oh, Liddie. It's beautiful."

"It's a bracelet, Mommy."

"I love it. Thank you, honey." She hugged and kissed her daughter. Liddie accepted the affection, then rushed off to get a piece of cake.

Remi and Bella moved through the crowd and handed Anne a bag. "This is from us."

Anne let out a little sigh as she slipped her opened presents into the orange gift bag. "You didn't have to get me anything." She hated being such the center of attention.

"We made it together," Bella said.

Anne reached into the bag and pulled out a long, red scarf. She wrapped it around her neck. "I didn't know you girls knitted."

Remi nodded. "It's one hobby we both love."

Bella grinned. "And we're pretty good at it too."

Anne snuggled the soft yarn. "I'll say. Thank you, girls. I love it."

"Here," Alex said, putting another gift into her hands. "This is from Ryan and me."

"You didn't have to, Alex." Her discomfort rose again.

Alex ignored her admonition. "Ryan actually picked it out." Alex's nephew stood beside him, chewing on his bottom lip.

Anne opened the present to find a beautiful set of wooden, world-shaped bookends. "They are perfect. Thank you," she said.

"You're welcome," Ryan said before rushing off to join the other kids in choking down big pieces of cake.

"Now you can say that I gave you the world," Alex said softly.

Heat flushed across her face. "You shouldn't have." She set the bookends on the table by the rest of her gifts.

"Here. This is from me," Grace said, handing her yet another present.

"You all are spoiling me," Anne said.

"Everybody needs a little spoiling on their birthday," Grace said.

Anne opened the gift to reveal a Visa gift card.

"So you can get whatever you really want," Grace said.

"Thank you. It's perfect," Anne said, slipping the gift card into the orange gift bag.

"Now, taste your cake." Wendy handed her a paper plate with a big chunk of cake in the middle. "It's wonderful, if I do say so myself."

Anne took a forkful into her mouth. The cake was perfectly moist, perfectly chocolate, with just the right amount of icing that didn't leave a greasy aftertaste. "It is wonderful."

Wendy grinned. "I know. It's my grandmother's recipe."

"I want it," Grace said, reaching for another piece. "I just ate until I was stuffed and I inhaled the first piece."

"Happy birthday, Anne," a deep voice behind her said.

Anne turned to see Donald Bell standing, looking quite sheepish.

"Hello, Donald. Thank you. It's been quite a surprising day, that's for sure," Anne said with a smile. "Would you like a piece of cake? Wendy is a fabulous baker, and she's outdone herself this time."

"No, thank you." He glanced over her shoulder at Alex and Grace. "Um, could I speak to you for a moment?"

"Oh. Sure." Anne set her plate on the edge of the table and followed Donald to a quiet corner of the checkout area. "Is anything wrong?" she asked.

"No. Nothing's wrong. I—uh—" he glanced around, then let his gaze settle on the floor in front of him. "I was, uh, just wondering if you'd like to go out to dinner one night. With me." He lifted his stare for just a split second, then dropped it right back to the floor. "On a date."

"Oh." She wasn't sure how to respond. What was she supposed to say?

Donald lifted his head and made eye contact. His cheeks were bright red.

She'd better figure out something to say. Something that wouldn't hurt his feelings. "I'm flattered, Donald, I am," she started, then realized how lame it sounded. "And if I was ready to date again, I'd be thrilled to go out with you," she said. "But I'm not ready yet."

"Oh. I understand," he said.

Did he? "I've just really gotten settled back into Blue Hill. And then there are the kids, and I don't know how to explain to them if I decided to start dating now."

He shook his head. "No, I understand. I just thought I'd ask," Donald said, then ducked his head again.

"I'm glad you did. I'm flattered." She reached out and squeezed his forearm. "Really, Donald. I am. Truly."

He met her eyes, then nodded.

"Mommy, you need to put on your bracelet," Liddie said, running to Anne with the tennis bracelet in her hand.

"I will, sweetheart. I just need a little help with the clasp," Anne told her daughter, but she held Donald's gaze.

After another moment, he smiled. "Happy birthday, Anne."

"Thank you, Donald," she said, before letting Liddie lead her back to the refreshment area, where Wendy waited to secure the bracelet on Anne's wrist.

"Everything okay?" Alex appeared at her side and asked quietly.

"It's all fine," Anne answered. And it was. If Donald was interested in her, that explained his hanging around the library all the time without checking out books. It explained his volunteering when he didn't seem interested in reading.

Actually, it was almost funny. Her imagination had worked overtime, dreaming up crazy, ominous, and sinister scenarios for Donald's constant appearance at the library when it was just a man interested in a woman.

Anne gave a little chuckle at her own silliness.

"Good," Alex said, his eyes questioning but not saying anything.

It was nice to be close enough friends that the unspoken was comfortable between them.

* * *

"See, Mommy, I'm 'sponsible enough for a kitten. I gave Hershey fresh water without you or Ben asking," Liddie said on Tuesday afternoon.

Ben had gone over to Wendy's after school to practice football with Ryan and Christian. Chad had been working with his son on some high school moves, and Christian had been chomping at the bit to teach Ryan and Ben.

Because Ben had gone directly to the Pyle's house after school, Liddie had taken it upon herself to make sure the chocolate Labrador had fresh water.

Anne was actually impressed. "Thank you, Liddie. That is showing great responsibility. I'm sure Hershey appreciates the fresh water too."

Liddie grinned. "So can I have a kitten? Please?"

Anne shook her head as she sliced the apple and placed the pieces on a plate beside the spoonful of peanut butter. "I explained that we'd discuss it when you got to be as old as Ben was when he got Hershey," she said, then placed a kiss on the top of Liddie's head. "Now, go wash your hands before you have your snack."

"Okay, Mommy, but I still want a kitten," Liddie said before she skipped down the hallway to the bathroom.

"And I want a million dollars," Anne whispered under her breath.

Speaking of money, Anne was a little shocked she hadn't heard from Jenna Coleman or Rodney Kelley yesterday or today. She'd been prepared to go to the bank and get the book out of the safety deposit box if they had proof, or at least to check it for loose papers, but there was no contact from either of them. It was almost as if they'd given up on claiming the Edgar Allan Poe title, which made Anne consider that neither of them were the owners. If that were the case, she was back to square one:

Who did the book belong to?

Anne rinsed the knife and put it in the draining rack as Liddie skipped back into the kitchen. "Hands all clean?" Anne asked her daughter.

Liddie's head bobbed up and down.

"Okay. You eat your apple, then come down to the library to do your homework while I finish some work I need to do." Like ordering the new audio/video equipment.

"Okay, Mommy."

Anne headed downstairs to the library. Remi glanced up and smiled as she approached. "Hey, Mrs. Gibson. I set up a nice homework station for Liddie over there," Remi said, gesturing to the corner of the checkout area where she'd pulled a small desk and chair and set a little battery-operated lamp on the corner.

"Thank you, Remi. That's so thoughtful."

"I remember what a big deal homework was to me back at that age."

"It's very nice of you." Anne reached for the equipment catalog under the counter, but movement registered from the corner of her eye. She turned to catch just the edge of Rachel Winn's gray cardigan flashing past the doorway.

Anne couldn't get the image of Rachel on the swings at the park out of her mind. No more than she could forget about the figurine she'd found in Rachel's sweater. She needed to get some sort of handle on Rachel Winn.

She headed toward the Nonfiction Room, marching straight for Rachel Winn's setup at her usual table. Rachel glanced up and must have caught the determination on Anne's face. She stood and rushed toward the ladies' room.

Frustration rose in Anne's chest and she was almost tempted to wait directly outside the restroom door. Almost, but not quite.

Anne walked back to the checkout counter just as Coraline walked in, her arms loaded down with library books.

Remi rushed to help her. "Let me take some of these for you."

"Oh, thank you, dear," Coraline said as she transferred about five books into Remi's open arms. She laid the other half dozen or so on the counter. "I know, I know, I should carry them in one of those many totes I have. I just forget every single time."

Anne smiled as she began to check the books back in. The bathroom door opened with a *whoosh*. Anne glanced over her shoulder to spy Rachel Winn slipping back into the Nonfiction Room.

"Coraline," Anne started, carefully considering her words so as to not offend the lady, "do you know Rachel Winn?"

"Know her?" Coraline asked.

Anne nodded. "Yes."

"Rachel Winn?"

"Yes," Anne answered. Never before had she got the feeling that Coraline was hemming and hawing on purpose. It just wasn't like Coraline. She enjoyed—no, she relished, being in the center of discussions. She loved knowing things. So why the hesitation now, over Rachel Winn?

The library's phone rang. Remi reached for the receiver. "Blue Hill Library, Remi speaking, how may I help you?"

"I believe she's staying over at the Blue Hill Inn, isn't she?" Coraline asked. "I guess you could ask Charlotte for more details." Charlotte and her husband, Henry, owned and operated the Blue Hill Inn.

Anne set the book she'd been checking back in on the counter and met Coraline's wide-eyed stare from behind her thick glasses.

"Coraline Watson, you know she's been staying at the Blue Hill Inn for weeks. What's going on with you?"

"Mrs. Gibson, excuse me," Remi interrupted. "It's Wendy on the phone for you. She says it's an emergency about Ben."

Ben?

Anne felt lightheaded as she grabbed the phone. "Wendy? What's wrong?"

She was sure Wendy spoke in complete sentences, but all she heard was, "Ben...hurt...Chad took him...clinic."

"I'm on my way there now," Anne said, then handed the phone back to Remi. "Ben's hurt. He's at the clinic. I have to go."

"Ben's hurt, Mommy?" Liddie asked, coming up behind Anne.

"Oh, honey," Anne said, giving Liddie a hug. Not knowing how bad it was, Anne needed to protect her daughter. She wanted Liddie close. But she didn't want to upset Liddie if Ben was seriously hurt. Yet the warmth of Liddie's hug comforted Anne. Liddie was only—

"Liddie, your mom's going to go check on your brother. I need you to stay here and help me run the library while she's gone, okay?" Remi said, gently prying Liddie away from Anne and moving her toward the checkout counter.

"Yes. You stay and help Remi. I'll be back," Anne said. She kissed Liddie, thanked Remi, then grabbed her purse and headed toward the door.

"We'll all be praying," Coraline called out after her.

But Anne kept on moving as fast as she could without running. She had one focus, and one focus only: get to her son.

Chapter Fourteen

"Lord, please watch over Ben. Let him be okay. Please." Anne repeated her simple prayer over and over and over. On the entire ten-minute drive to the Blue Hill Medical Clinic, she recited her prayer. Even during the four minutes it took her to park and jog across the lot, she prayed. And once she got inside and located which room Ben was in, she prayed.

She pushed past the curtain in the examining room to find Ben lying on his back, his leg elevated with an ice pack on the ankle area. Chad sat beside him, but he jumped to his feet as soon as Anne barged in.

"Ben! What happened?" Anne moved to his side and smoothed the hair off his forehead before kissing him.

"I'm fine, Mom. I just tripped up and fell." Ben's cheeks turned red. "It was a stupid mistake."

"Hey, buddy," Chad said, "errors happen all the time. Everybody makes them. No need to be so hard on yourself."

"Yeah, but this stupid mistake could cost me my starting place on the team," Ben said, closing his eyes as he propped his head back on the flat pillow on the small bed. "Stupid," he muttered under his breath.

Anne smoothed the long sleeve of Ben's shirt and stared at Chad over Ben and the bed. "What happened?"

"He was practicing some cutting moves I'd been helping him and Christian with and somehow or another, his ankle got twisted and he fell." Chad nodded at the ice-pack-covered foot of Ben's. "He couldn't bear his weight, so I had him hold ice on it and drove him right over."

If Ben was going to get hurt playing football, at least he was at the high school coach's house.

Anne pressed her lips together and nodded. She knew it! Knew Ben would get hurt. She'd ignored her gut feeling, letting Alex and Ben talk her into letting him try out. And now look what had happened.

"Mom," Ben said, opening his eyes and staring at her. "This was my fault, not football's. I wasn't paying attention to where I was running."

Anne pinched her mouth shut. Could her son now read minds?

"Actually, if it's anybody's fault, it's mine," Chad said. "I shouldn't have let the boys work on moves in the backyard. I should've taken them to the school's field and let them practice there where I know the ground's level and without roots or holes."

"Well, what have we here?" Dr. Anthony Shields drew back the curtain and stepped into the room. Tony had been a year behind Anne in high school. He'd been short, a little nerdy, and had run the Tech Club. But now, all these years later, he was a doctor, married, and expecting their first child next year.

"I just misstepped is all," Ben said, sitting up.

"Why don't you let me check it out though, just to be sure?" Tony set down Ben's medical file that he'd carried into the room, washed his hands at the little sink in the corner of the room, then dried them. He pulled the ice pack off of Ben's foot and pressed. "Does this hurt?" he asked, keeping a close eye on Ben's face.

Ben shook his head.

"What about here?" Tony moved his fingers and pressed again.

Ben shook his head.

"Here?"

Again, Ben shook his head, but his face twisted into a little grimace.

Tony sighed. "Ben, if you don't tell me if it really hurts, I can't help you."

"It's just a little sore there. Where you touched it last," Ben said.

Tony nodded, then moved to wash his hands again. "I don't think there are any broken bones, but I'd like to take an X-ray, just to be sure."

"Broken?" Ben asked, the hysteria rising in his voice.

"I said I don't think anything's broken. I just want to check to make sure."

Ben threw himself back on the pillow and put his arm over his eyes. "I'll be cut from the team," he whined.

"You won't be cut from the team, Ben," Chad said.

Tony shot Chad, then Anne a quizzical look.

"League flag-football team," Chad explained.

"Ah," Tony said with a nod. "Well, Ben, I'm trying to rule out serious injury so I can get you up and back playing as soon as we can. How's that?"

Ben sat upright again. "Yeah!" He did a fist pump through the air.

Tony laughed. "The nurse will be here in a minute to take you to X-ray. I'll see you soon." He left, his Croc-style shoes squeaking against the tiled floor.

Anne didn't know how to react. She didn't want her son to have any broken bones, but she didn't want him to play football and get more seriously hurt either.

Before Anne could decide what to say, a nurse in pretty pink scrubs came in, pushing a wheelchair. She was about middle-age, Anne would guess, with a kind, weathered face. "You must be Mr. Ben Gibson," she said with a smile. "I'm your nurse, Kathy, and I'll be taking you to get those fancy pictures of your foot and ankle."

Ben sat up and worked with the nurse to get transferred from bed to wheelchair.

"It will take us about half an hour. Why don't you two go get some fresh air?" Kathy said to Anne and Chad. "I'll be taking him back to room number four across the hall just there." She pointed at the little hallway with eight doors, each with a big number painted on the outside.

Anne nodded. "Thank you."

Chad and Anne stepped outside into the cool air. The sun had disappeared behind the tree line, leaving only streaks of orange against the early evening darkness. The temperature seemed to have dropped with the setting of the sun.

"I'm going to grab my sweater from the car," Anne said. She always kept a sweater for herself and the kids in the trunk of her car, just in case of an emergency. Like this.

"I need to call Wendy," Chad answered, pulling his cell phone from his pocket. "I promised her I'd let her know something as soon as we saw the doctor."

"You don't have to stay, Chad. We're fine," Anne told him as she pulled her car keys from her purse.

"Don't be silly. I'm just going to call Wendy right quick."

Anne smiled and headed to the Impala. She popped open the trunk and pulled out her soft, cashmere sweater. It was a green one that the kids had gotten her last Christmas because Liddie said it matched her eyes. She put it on, then debated whether or not to take Ben's in. He'd probably think she was smothering him if she did, so she left it in the trunk and locked her car.

She stared at the Blue Hill Medical Clinic as she strolled across the parking lot. The aged building had been a bank when Anne lived in Blue Hill before. Now, ivy spread across the faded brick walls like fingers stretching over the building until finally winding around to grip the corner pillars in a tight embrace. The front white steps were cracked, but that gave them character, at least Anne thought so.

Chad joined her at the front of the clinic and pulled open one of the double black doors to allow Anne to enter first. The outside of the building might be in need of a little attention, but the inside was modern with blinding white walls and tile flooring. The harsh odor of disinfectant filled the air. Anne had been so worried about Ben earlier, she hadn't even noticed. She did now, and sneezed. Again. And a third time.

"You okay?" Chad asked.

Anne snatched a tissue from the check-in counter and blew her nose. "Just the smell, I guess," she said while shoving the tissue into her purse. "Room four, right?"

Chad nodded.

Anne opened the door to an empty room. "Guess we beat them back," she said. Nothing like stating the obvious.

A younger lady wearing blue scrubs ducked into the room. "Hi, I'm Emma. Just need to make sure your information and Ben's insurance information are still the same." She handed a clipboard to Anne.

Anne scanned the information and nodded, handing the clipboard back to Emma. "It's all the same."

"Great." Emma flipped the page. "I just need you to sign here so we can file this on your insurance."

Anne signed her name, then handed the pen back to Emma, who thanked Anne before she left. Staring after her, Anne couldn't help but think about Jenna Coleman and her possible insurance claim on the Poe title. Maybe the book really *did* belong to her, but what if she'd gotten paid from the insurance company when it was stolen and Jenna had learned that, if the book was returned, she might have to pay back the money?

Anne didn't know for sure if that was the way Jenna's policy worked. Anne knew that the library's insurance policy stated that in the event the insurance company paid a claim on a stolen insured item, the insurance company would own the item if the item was ever recovered. However, there was documentation in the policy that, given such a circumstance, the insurance company could give the library the option to buy back the recovered item if the value of the item had not increased considerably since the item was stolen.

Maybe Jenna's policy wasn't like that.

Either way, no one had asked about the book in the last couple of days. Anne wondered what she would do if no one came forward to claim it with proof.

The door creaked open and Kathy wheeled Ben inside the small room. "Hope you don't mind, but we took the scenic route back," the nurse said, grinning.

"She let me pop a wheelie in the hall," Ben said.

"A wheelie? That's impressive, champ," Chad said, helping the nurse move Ben to the bed.

Kathy plumped the pillow behind Ben's head and adjusted the bed for his comfort. "You weren't supposed to tell anybody," she said. But she winked at Anne before setting the ice pack back on Ben's ankle.

"How'd he do?" Anne asked.

"He was a perfect patient. As soon as Dr. Shields reviews the X-rays, he'll be in to give you the diagnosis and treatment plan." She ruffled Ben's hair. "You behave, young man. No racing down the hallways, you hear?"

"Yes, ma'am," Ben said, grinning and giving the nurse a salute.

Anne moved to his side. "Are you cold, honey?"

He shook his head. "I'm fine, Mom."

"Okay. Sometimes X-ray rooms can be rather chilly," Anne said. She smoothed the edge of his shirt. She felt so utterly helpless.

"Has anybody seen a wheelie-popping rider in here?" Tony stepped into the room and went automatically to the sink to wash his hands.

Ben giggled at the doctor.

"Aha! It was you." Tony pointed at Ben as he moved to stand by Ben's feet. He removed the ice pack. "X-rays look great. Except for this little guy," he said as he handed a little Spider-Man figurine to Ben.

Anne's son blushed as he took Spidey and shoved him into his front jeans pocket. "I had to take him out for the X-ray machine."

"Hey, I'm a big fan of Spider-Man, but I personally loved Captain America. He's my hero," Tony leaned in and stage-whispered to Ben.

Anne pressed her lips together to hide the smile. Tony's wife was a lucky woman. Tony would be an amazing father.

The doctor straightened and met Anne's anxious stare. He smiled. "No broken bones, no small fractures." Tony removed the ice pack and palpated Ben's foot. "I don't even think it's a sprained ankle. It's more just like a hard external bump. It'll probably bruise really well, but there's not much swelling, thanks to Coach putting the ice pack immediately on the injury."

Chad ducked his head.

"Just to be safe, no running for a week, and I'm going to wrap it up in a bandage to wear for the next day or so. I'd like you to stay home from school tomorrow. Just tomorrow, to make sure you don't have excessive swelling. If you don't, then you're okay to go to school and you don't need crutches. Keep the foot elevated as much as you can over the next few days but after that, I think it'll be fine." He pulled open a drawer and pulled out a tray filled with colorful Coban Wrap. "What color would you like, sir?" he asked Ben.

"Can I play football this weekend? It's our first game," Ben said.

Tony shook his head and set the tray on the bed beside Ben. He pulled the stool on rollers beside the bed and plopped down. "I'm sorry, but no. Not this weekend. We want you to get back to one hundred percent before you take the field again, right?"

Ben's whole face fell. "But I'm supposed to start." His voice wobbled like it did just before he cried.

Anne wanted to speak up, but Tony cut her off. "What position? I never could play football when I was young. I was such a nerd." He grabbed a roll of the green Coban and held it up for Ben, twisting it.

Ben's eyes widened. "You're a doctor, though. That's cool."

Tony chuckled as he began opening the roll of green Coban. "It's cool now, but I was a bookworm back in school." He carefully made the first loop around Ben's foot, right by the arch. "Ask your mom. She knows what a geek I was."

"Mom?" Ben asked, his eyes still wide but without tears now.

Yes indeed, Dr. Tony Shields would be an amazing father.

"He was a little short for his age...," she began.

Tony shook his head as he continued wrapping the length of Ben's foot. "Come on, Anne. Tell the truth."

"Well, he was short. And he led Tech Club." She caught her bottom lip between her teeth. "Back when we were in school, that was kinda nerdy."

"I bet it's still nerdy," Tony said, wrapping up the ankle. "So what position do you play, Ben?"

"Wide receiver."

"That must mean you're really fast." Tony secured the wrap and closed the simple fastener on the top of Ben's foot.

"Oh, he's fast all right. And he has good hands," Chad said.

Ben smiled.

"Well, just sit out this one game, champ, and you should be good to go for the next one, okay?" Tony patted Ben's leg, then stood and put the tray back in the drawer. "Keep him home from school tomorrow and his foot elevated. If you notice any swelling or if he complains of pain that ibuprofen won't knock out, bring him back in," he told Anne.

"I hope I don't get kicked off the team or lose my starting position," Ben mumbled.

"You won't," Chad said. "I know Coach Walden and he's a good guy. He won't want to lose such an awesome player, Ben. Don't sweat it."

But Ben look worried.

Tony signed Ben's chart and held the clipboard to his chest. "Mike Walden?"

Chad nodded.

The doctor grinned at Ben. "I just treated his baby for colic. Would it make you feel better if I called Mike and told him that you'll be ready for next week's game, fast as ever?"

Ben nodded, his eyes widening. "Would you?"

Tony laughed. "Sure thing. I wanted to check on the baby anyway. I'll call tonight." He patted Ben's shoulder. "Now stop worrying." He nodded at Chad and Anne. "Kathy will be in with the discharge papers in just a second."

"Thanks, Tony. I really appreciate everything," Anne said. Not many doctors would take the time to reassure a kid about his football *career* during a treatment.

"You're welcome," Tony said, then grinned at Ben. "I'll have to try and make it to a game this season just to watch you run. So follow my orders!"

"Yes, sir!" Ben gave a salute as Tony left the room.

"Hey, I'll call Mike too, and explain what happened," Chad told Ben.

"Thanks, Mr. Pyle."

Anne stood and hiked her purse strap up her shoulder. It sounded as though if she wanted to pull Ben from football she'd have an uphill battle with her son. While she wanted to protect him, she realized that keeping him from doing what he wanted would really hurt him. She couldn't allow that. She'd just have to deal with her nerves every time he took the field.

Or practiced.

The door swung open and Kathy handed Anne a stack of papers. "Discharge orders. Home care instructions are printed, along with the clinic's number in case you need us." She put her hands on her hips and grinned at Ben. "Okay, Mr. Wheelie. Ready for another ride in my shiny wheelchair?"

Chapter Fifteen

"There. How's that?" Anne asked Ben. Chad had helped get Ben upstairs and settled in the living room before heading home to Wendy. Ben sat back on the couch with his foot resting on a pillow on the coffee table. He was pretty excited about getting to use the elevator for the rest of the week, since she usually preferred the children take the stairs.

Remi, ever thoughtful, had made sure Liddie completed her homework, and she had closed up the library for Anne. "I've got a chair and ottoman with a side table all set up in the Nonfiction Room for Ben tomorrow," Remi said.

Those twins sure had been a lifesaver to Anne on more than one occasion. Remi handed the library's master set of keys to Anne. "Can I get you anything else? Make all of you a sandwich or something?"

"I'll figure something out for dinner," Anne said. "I can't thank you enough for everything as it is."

"It's what we do here in Blue Hill, right?" Remi grinned.

Anne turned back to Ben. "Liddie's taking care of Hershey. Is there anything else I can get you right now?"

Ben straightened the small fleece throw blanket in his lap. "I'm fine, Mom." He leaned back against the throw pillow Anne had fluffed behind his back. "I'm just bummed and bored."

"Bummed and bored?" Remi asked. "Now that's a depressing combination if I ever heard one."

"He's not happy about having to miss the football game this weekend," Anne explained.

"It's our first game," Ben told Remi. "I was supposed to start."

Remi shrugged. "So you'll start the next game. It's no big deal." She leaned forward to get on his eye level. "Trust me, it's not who starts the first game that matters, but who finishes the last game."

He grinned up at her. "I guess so. Dr. Shields said I should be able to play next weekend."

"See," Remi said, winking at him. "There you go."

Anne shook her head. Ben had whined about missing the game the whole ride home from the clinic and she'd said basically the same thing as Remi, to no avail. Then again, Remi was young and pretty, and Ben probably had a healthy schoolboy crush on her.

Liddie marched up the stairs. "There. I fed and gave Hershey water just like you do, Ben." She skipped over and stood by the arm of the chair. "I told him about your foot and 'splained why you couldn't play with him right now."

Warmth spread throughout Anne's stomach. Liddie was so sweet and adorable to her brother that Anne didn't even correct Liddie's pronunciation.

"Thanks, Liddie," Ben said.

"Well, if I can't get you anything else, I'd better run. Bella has texted me twice already," Remi said. "She's working tomorrow, but I'll stop by in the afternoon to check on you, Ben. See you then."

"Thank you again, Remi," Anne said as she let her out the back door.

"Are you hungry?" Anne asked Ben.

"A little," he said with a shrug.

Lately, when hadn't he been hungry?

"I'm hungry too," Liddie chimed in.

Anne could always order a pizza, but they'd just had that. There surely wasn't a lot of nutritional value in having pizza twice in a week, but as much as she hated to admit it, she just didn't feel up to cooking tonight. Her nerves had been through the wringer, leaving her emotionally and physically exhausted.

"What would you like for dinner?" Anne asked the kids.

"Cereal!" Liddie said.

"A kid's frozen dinner," Ben said.

"You aren't having a frozen dinner." Anne headed into the kitchen and opened the refrigerator door. No leftovers. Not even enough lunchmeat to make sandwiches for everyone. She really needed to go to the grocery store. She glanced at the counter and saw the waffle iron. Anne took inventory in the fridge. Milk, check. Eggs, check. Butter, check. And some strawberries to go on top, check.

"How about waffles?" she asked the kids.

"Yea!" they said in unison.

"Great. Liddie, come help."

She pulled a chair up to the sink and gave Liddie the task of washing strawberries while Anne mixed the batter. Ben flipped through television channels with the remote. Just when the volume would level off, he'd change the station. It was really annoying, or perhaps Anne just needed a good amount of sleep.

"I'm done, Mommy," Liddie said.

"Good job. Why don't you pat them dry?" Anne handed her daughter a couple of paper towels. "Just gently pat them. We don't want to squish them."

Liddie giggled. "Squished strawberries. That's how they make jam."

Anne shook her head but smiled. "Kind of." She sprayed the waffle iron and poured in batter. "Why don't you get the butter out, sweetheart?"

As Liddie moved to do her bidding, Anne put away the chair and pulled out three plates and three cups.

"Want the milk too, Mommy?"

"Sure, honey. Thank you."

Twenty minutes later, they were finishing their waffle and chocolate milk picnic in the living room.

"Does it hurt?" Liddie asked Ben, pointing at his foot.

"Nah," Ben brushed off the concern.

Anne inspected his wrapped foot and ankle. "It doesn't look like it's swollen any more than before. That's good. Would you like an ibuprofen before bed?"

"Well…" Ben glanced at the ceiling. "Maybe I should take one, just to be sure it doesn't swell overnight or I don't kick it in my sleep."

So it probably was hurting a little, he just didn't want to admit it. "That sounds like a smart plan. I'll get you one," Anne said as she gathered their plates and cups and took them into the kitchen.

After giving Ben his medication, Anne worked to get Liddie into the bath, then directly into bed. Dinner had been late, so their entire routine had been off. Liddie had begged for a third bedtime story, but Anne just couldn't read anymore. Every muscle in her body threatened to revolt in sheer exhaustion.

"It's way past your bedtime, sweetie. Snuggle down," Anne said.

"Mommy, are you excited about this weekend?" Liddie bounced in her bed, looking not at all tired.

"This weekend?" Anne put the storybook back in its place on the shelf.

"Tea Time, silly." Liddie plopped back onto her pillow.

Anne's hands froze on the comforter she'd been tucking around Liddie. She'd completely forgotten about the library's first tea time. Months ago, Liddie and Wendy had come up with the idea for a high tea, as described in one of the books the library had featured as part of the children's summer reading program. It was to be a big event—ladies in dresses, hats, and even gloves, all bringing their special teacups and saucers to the formal event.

Most of the girls in Liddie's class were excited. Even some of the older ladies in church had mentioned they were digging out their old hats to wear to it.

Anne hadn't even thought about the tea. She couldn't believe she'd let it slip her mind! She'd have to check the supplies. And cookies. They'd definitely need cookies.

"You didn't forget, did you, Mommy?" Liddie asked, blinking those big, chocolate-colored eyes of hers.

Anne bent and kissed Liddie's forehead. "Don't you worry, sweetheart. The tea will be a wonderful event. We'll have a grand time." Mercy! She needed to get to the mall and pick out hats and gloves at the formal shop for herself and Liddie. When was she going to be able to do that? And make sure they had plenty of tea and cookies? She let out a quiet sigh hidden behind her smile. "Say your prayers, sweetie."

"Now I lay me down to sleep, I pray the Lord, my soul to keep. Watch over me through the night, and wake me with the morning light. God bless Mommy, and Daddy up in heaven, and Ben, and Hershey, and" — Liddie yawned — "and everybody else. Amen."

Anne felt like condensing everything she could herself, so she kissed Liddie one more time, told her good night, turned off the light, and pulled the bedroom door almost closed behind her as she left.

It was a blessing in disguise for Ben's injury. Not that he was hurt, not at all, but that he couldn't play in the game on Saturday. How she would have managed tea time in the morning and a football game that afternoon, well, she would've managed, but now she didn't have to.

God sure worked in mysterious ways. Indeed.

* * *

"You did not have to do this," Anne told Wendy, even as her stomach growled at the enticing smell of hash brown casserole that wafted up from the dish on the counter.

"I know I didn't have to, but I wanted to." Wendy adjusted the potholders and lifted the casserole pan. "I'm going to run this upstairs and stick it in your fridge right quick, okay?" She didn't wait for Anne to answer before she marched up the stairs.

Anne didn't bother saying anything. She'd learned long ago that arguing with Wendy when she had her mind made up was like spinning her tires on an icy patch in the middle of a snowstorm.

She headed into the Nonfiction Room, where Bella had helped her pull the chair and ottoman closer to the fireplace. There wasn't a need for a fire just yet, but the fireplace itself just made the room feel cozier, more welcoming.

Ben sat in the chair with his foot propped up, a bottled water on the table beside him, and the first Coastal Club book open in his lap. Anne hadn't wanted to leave him upstairs alone. She wanted to be able to be nearby in case he needed something. He'd decided if he had to be bored, he'd start rereading the series from the first.

Anne sure hoped that Jayden James's mother returned the second book sometime today. At the rate Ben was reading the first book, he'd be done and chomping for the next one after lunch. Bella would be back from lunch soon and Anne could sit down and eat with her son.

"Mrs. Gibson," a woman's voice sounded from the front checkout area.

Anne hurried out of the Nonfiction Room. The voice sounded almost like— "Oh, hello, Ms. Coleman." Yep, she'd been right: It was Jenna Coleman. And Anne so wasn't in the mood for any of her shenanigans today. Not with Ben in the library. "What can I do for you?"

She could only hope Jenna was here to check out a book, but Anne knew better.

Jenna pulled a paper out of her purse. "I brought you this," she said with a smug look.

Anne took the paper that was folded. She carefully opened the single sheet that was almost torn in the crease marks and gently smoothed it. The entire print on the paper was faded as if it had been left out in the sun for a long time. Or it had originally been on thermal paper and dimmed in months instead of years.

The top of the paper had a printed letterhead that was a little difficult to make out. Anne squinted behind her glasses to read the business name—*Andy's Appraisals of Antiques and Rare Items*. In even smaller print underneath the name was the address. Anne couldn't make out the street number, but the city was legible enough to read: Deshler.

"I think that should suffice as proof that I own the book," Jenna said, her shrill voice bouncing off the walls of the library's entry area.

Anne inspected the paper again. It was dated almost three years ago and was clearly an appraisal for an Edgar Allan Poe first edition valued at twenty-two thousand dollars, but the title of the book was entirely illegible.

And the actual appraiser's signature? Nothing but a scrawl. Anne didn't want to accuse anyone of being dishonest, but this was ridiculous.

"Shall we go to the bank and retrieve my book now?" Jenna asked.

Anne gestured to the paper. "I can't accept this as proof of ownership."

"Why not? You can clearly make out that it's an appraisal of an Edgar Allan Poe first edition," Jenna said, plopping her designer purse onto the counter.

"You can't even read the title of the book," Anne argued. "How can you claim it's the one I have?"

"How many first editions of a Poe book do you think are running around in Blue Hill?" Jenna asked.

True. "But you can't even tell me the title."

"That doesn't matter!" Jenna's voice rose again. "That proves I own a first edition of an Edgar Allan Poe book. You found a first edition Poe book. There isn't more than one floating around this little town. I don't understand why you won't give me my book." Jenna stomped her heeled foot against the floor of the library.

What, was the woman a sullen teenager? She certainly acted like it.

"Because this doesn't prove you own the particular book I found," Anne said. She handed the paper back across the counter. "And I can't even read the name of the appraiser on this paper."

"Are you saying I forged it?" Jenna asked, snatching the delicate paper from Anne. "I assure you, I didn't forge his signature."

"No. I'm saying that where the appraiser usually signs an appraisal, there's usually their name typed underneath. There's nothing like that on this paper."

"So? I don't see how that matters."

Anne glanced over her shoulder toward the Nonfiction Room, praying Ben couldn't hear the woman's harsh tone. "I don't know what else to tell you, Ms. Coleman." She snapped her fingers. "You know what? Appraisers keep copies of all the appraisals they issue. Why don't you just go back to this appraiser and get a new, clear copy? Maybe on his copy, you can read the actual title of the book."

Jenna's face contorted into one of the most hateful expressions Anne had ever seen. Venom swam in the pools of her eyes.

"While I was up there, I went ahead and made some grilled cheese sandwiches and tomato soup," Wendy said from the refreshment area. "I brought that down and set it in the—" she rounded the corner where Jenna stood at the counter, glaring at Anne. "Oh. I'm sorry." Wendy smiled at Jenna.

"Wendy Pyle, this is Jenna Coleman," Anne introduced the two.

Jenna didn't even acknowledge Wendy. She continued to glare at Anne. "I'll be back," she said to Anne before turning and storming out.

"Something I said?" Wendy asked, staring after Jenna.

"Oh no. She's upset with me." Anne explained what had happened. "So it's not you at all."

"Anne, I know you can take care of yourself and all, but I think you should call the police about her," Wendy said, shaking her head. "There was something about the way that woman stared at you. Something sinister."

Anne laughed. "You've read too many suspense novels." She needed to change the subject, so she looped her arm through her friend's. "That grilled cheese sandwich and soup smells wonderful. You didn't have to make me lunch too."

Wendy shook her head. "Well, I still feel awful that Ben got hurt at my house."

"Kids are kids. It's not your fault," Anne said with a smile, taking note that she'd successfully changed the subject without Wendy really realizing what she'd done. "But I do love grilled cheese sandwiches and tomato soup."

"Then you go eat with Ben and I'll watch the front," Wendy said, giving her a little shove.

"Bella will be back in just a few minutes. I can wait," Anne said.

"Nonsense. You two eat. I'll head out as soon as Bella gets back." Wendy nudged her again. "Go. Eat while it's hot."

"Thanks, Wendy. I appreciate you." Anne gave Wendy a quick hug, then headed off toward the refreshment area in the back of the library.

She might have downplayed Jenna's attitude to Wendy, but Anne made a mental note to call Michael later. Jenna Coleman had made it very clear she was a time bomb just waiting to go off. The way she'd acted. Here. At the library. In such a public place.

Anne sure didn't want to be in the path when Jenna exploded.

Chapter Sixteen

"I'm sure she's cooled off," Anne said into the phone.

"I don't know, Anne. I think it still might be a smart idea for me to have a little chat with Jenna Coleman. From what you told me, it sounds like she verbally accosted you," Michael said. "That's illegal."

"I know, which is why I called you, because she reacted like that here at the library," Anne said, turning away from the front checkout counter, where Bella assisted Betty Bultman in checking out a mountain of books. "I really just wanted to know if you'd had time to look into Jenna's claim of that police report."

"I haven't but I will make it a priority tomorrow when I go into work," Michael said.

"Thanks. I really do appreciate it."

"It's my job. Are you sure you're comfortable with the way things are with her?"

"I'm sure. Thanks, Michael. Give my love to Jennifer," Anne said. "Talk to you tomorrow." She hung up the phone.

"Anne, dear," Mrs. Bultman called out. "I saw poor Ben. How long is he out of school with his injury?"

"Oh, he's fine to go back tomorrow. Thank you for asking," Anne said with a smile.

"Good. Good. With sports injuries, you never really know." Mrs. Bultman slipped books into her tote bag. "I would have inquired to him directly, but I noticed Ms. Winn talking with him. I think it's nice for library patrons to visit with the poor boy."

What could Rachel Winn be talking to Ben about? Anne turned toward the Nonfiction Room.

"Anne, dear, what time is the tea on Saturday?" Betty called again.

Rats! She'd forgotten about it again. What was wrong with her?

"It's at ten, Mrs. Bultman," Bella offered. "Are you coming?"

"Of course I'll be here." The wife of the mayor of Blue Hill would not allow an event such as Tea Time at the library to go by without making a grand appearance. "I pick up my dress tomorrow."

"Mom!" Ben called from the other room.

"I'm looking forward to a good time for us all," Anne said as she marched into the Nonfiction Room.

Rachel Winn was nowhere to be seen. Her laptop and cardigan weren't at the table she normally claimed.

"What is it, Ben?" Anne asked as she approached him.

"Can I use your laptop, please?" he asked.

"That's what you called me in here for?" She looked around the room, wondering where Rachel Winn had gone. Anne hadn't seen her leave.

He nodded. "I finished my book and you said the second one in the series hadn't been returned yet."

"So I did." She forced a smile and kissed the top of his head. "What do you want to do on the laptop?" Some people might say she was a little overprotective, but she wanted to know what her son was doing on the Internet. Especially at this very impressionable age.

"I want to visit the Coastal Club Web page. They have a fan forum and fan fiction site and everything." His face lit up like it did when he talked about football. "It's okay for me to visit that site, isn't it, Mom? It's run by the author and everything."

At least that was a safe site. "Sure, honey. I'll bring it to you. Do you need anything else?"

He shook his head. "I'm good. Still full from lunch."

"Okay." Anne ran upstairs and pulled her personal laptop from her bedroom. As she did, she noticed the time and rushed back downstairs. She handed Ben the laptop. "It has a full charge, so you should be good to go."

"Thanks, Mom," he said, already booting up the system.

"I'm going to run and pick up your sister. We'll be right back. You stay put and don't be a problem for Bella, okay?"

"Okay." His focus was already one hundred percent on the computer.

She told Bella she'd be back soon, then drove to the elementary school to pick up Liddie. She pulled into the school's lot just as kids spilled from the building. Many of them ran toward the big yellow school buses while others, like Liddie, raced to the lot where parents picked up their children.

The three-story-tall brick building was seventy years old. It previously housed the high school students but had recently been remodeled. Anne remembered they called the basement the dungeon. What Anne remembered was a huge, dark abyss that ran the entire length of the school, consisting of a myriad of rooms that interconnected in odd ways, like a macabre labyrinth.

Anne caught sight of Liddie waving at her. She pulled up in the car line and waved at Liddie's teacher, who opened the door and helped Liddie into her car seat in the backseat of the Impala.

"How was school today, honey?" Anne asked as soon as she was able to inch the car through the line.

"Good. Becca and Cindy said they got pink gloves to wear to tea on Saturday. Can I get pink gloves?"

Rats! She'd forgotten again. Maybe she should have Tony check her out because she sure seemed to forget details lately.

"Can I, Mommy?"

"It's *may I*, and I don't know about pink gloves. We'll see. You'll want gloves that match the dress you're wearing. We'll see what they have when we get to the store." Anne had looked at dressy hats and gloves over at the formal shop at the Deshler mall. But when was she supposed to find the time to stop by and pick out the ones they wanted?

She'd have to make time, that's all there was to it.

"Do we really drink hot tea?" Liddie asked.

"Yes. And we have petit fours and cookies," Anne said as she turned out of the school's lot on to Main Street.

"What are petty fours?"

Anne chuckled. "Petit fours are little individual cakes." She would not have time to make them. She'd have to order them. Soon. Maybe she could order them from Coffee Joe's.

"Yummy. How's Ben?" Liddie asked.

"His foot seems to be fine. No more swelling. He's just rather bored. I think he's ready to go back to school tomorrow." Anne smiled at her daughter's quick and constant subject change.

Anne's cell phone rang. She eased on to the shoulder and grabbed the phone from the console. She glanced at the caller ID before she answered. "Hi, Wendy."

"Hey. I have a quick question about Saturday's Tea Time. Hannah wanted to know if she would be needed to help watch the younger girls. She's volunteered to do that if you need her," Wendy said.

"I don't think so," Anne said. "I would think mothers will be watching their own daughters."

"Well, you just never know," Wendy chuckled. "Just keep her offer in mind in case it comes up."

"I will. Thanks."

"Is there anything you need me to do to help you? I know it's crazy when you have a hurt kid underfoot."

"Wendy, you're a lifesaver. Would you please order the petit fours for Saturday? If Coffee Joe's will make them, I can just have them bill the library, but if you need to get them from a bakery in Deshler, I can just call in the credit card to them." If Wendy could take care of this detail, Anne could breathe so much easier.

"Anne Gibson, we are not serving store-bought petit fours," Wendy exclaimed. "I'll make them, of course."

"I can't ask you to do that, Wendy."

"Well then, it's a good thing you aren't asking and I'm volunteering. No arguing."

Anne opened her mouth, then realized how futile disagreeing would be. She could say whatever she wanted, but Wendy would do as she pleased. Anne would be better off just to accept and move on. So that's what she did. "Okay. Thank you," Anne said.

Wendy laughed over the phone. "You're learning. Okay. I'll make the petit fours, and I've already got all the different teas. You just remind everyone to bring their own teacups and saucers as planned."

Anne grabbed her pen and notebook from the car's console and made a note. She'd have Bella send out a patron-wide e-mail this afternoon to remind everyone about the tea, and to bring their own teacups. "I'll get it done."

"Great. Okay, that's all I needed. Talk to you later. Bye."

Anne set her phone back in the console.

"Who was that, Mommy?" Liddie asked as Anne put the car back in gear and eased back on to the road.

"That was Miss Wendy, sweetheart. Talking about the tea." One major item off her to-do list. Now Anne just needed to figure out when to run over to the mall in Deshler to pick out hats and gloves.

Back at home, Anne asked Liddie to see to Hershey's food and water again. Then she talked with Bella about the e-mail blast to send out and went to the Nonfiction Room to check on Ben. His nose was almost *in* the laptop.

"What're you doing?" Anne asked as she gave his shoulder a pat.

"Playing on the Coastal Club Web site. Did you know you can post a question for the author and he'll answer you?" Ben's eyes were bright, holding excitement in every blink. "What do you think the R. W. stands for? I posted that question earlier. I hope he answers me."

"Does he post back often?" Anne asked, glancing over Ben's shoulder. The Web site's header was charming…a sea background with covers of the entire series tossed about.

Ben shrugged. "I've read some of the message boards and it looks like he posts every week or so."

"Well, that's interesting." She leaned over and planted a kiss on the top of his head. "Liddie's taking care of Hershey for you again. Don't forget to thank her when she comes inside." Anne headed upstairs and quickly cut up a banana and apple for Liddie's after-school snack.

While waiting on Liddie, Anne stepped out the back door, on the landing of the back steps. She stared out across the town. Autumn had fully arrived in Blue Hill, painting brilliant hues of yellow and orange on the trees lining the streets. Gone were the full, beautiful blooms of the bluebells that decorated the hill where the library and Anne's home sat, but the striking reds and yellows of the treetops were just as breathtakingly beautiful.

"Mommy?" Liddie called.

Anne stepped back inside. "Right here, sweetie." She pointed toward the bathroom. "Wash up. Your snack's ready."

Liddie did as she was told. Anne poured a small glass of milk and set it on the kitchen table beside the banana and apple.

"Mommy, I have homework. I have words on flashcards to study," Liddie returned and plopped down at the kitchen table.

"You do? Wow, you're getting so big. Homework and sight words." Anne kissed the top of Liddie's head. "I'm going back down to the library. Come down when you're finished with your snack, okay?"

"Yes, Mommy."

Anne made a point to check the back door and make sure it was locked before she left.

"Have we been busy this afternoon?" Anne asked Bella once she was back downstairs.

Bella nodded. "A little. Considering it's a weekday. I got the e-mail ready to send. I used the newsletter template. What do you think?" she asked, pointing to the computer.

Anne stared at the screen. Bella had taken pictures of Blue Hill at various times of year, then blended them all into one long picture that she used as the newsletter's header. The text on top of the header was a pretty handwriting-style font, with the library's name, address, Web site, and phone number.

Under the header, Bella had added in a border of sorts with images of little teacups and saucers. The information in the body of the e-mail gave all the pertinent details about the tea time.

"Oh, this is beautiful, Bella. You did a wonderful job," Anne said.

Bella smiled. "Good. I was just waiting for you to look it over before I sent it."

"Go ahead and send it. It's great. Thank you."

The library door opened and Ryan and Alex walked in.

"I heard about Ben. How's he doing?" Alex asked.

"Oh, he's fine. He'll be back at school tomorrow," Anne said.

"I got his homework for him," Ryan said.

"He's in the Nonfiction Room. Why don't you give it to him? I think he'll be very happy to see you," Anne said.

Ryan looked at Alex, who nodded. Ryan hurried off toward the Nonfiction Room. Anne and Alex followed at a much slower pace.

"Chad was pretty upset about Ben getting hurt at his house," Alex said.

"It happens. It wasn't his fault."

"I'm just glad he wasn't hurt seriously," Alex said.

"Me too," Anne agreed as they came up behind the boys.

"Ryan brought me my homework," Ben said with a groan. "Some friend, huh?" he teased.

"Hey, you don't want to get too far behind," Ryan said.

"Just teasing you." Ben shifted the laptop in his lap. "Check this out. They updated the Coastal Club Web site."

"Oh, wow. This *is* cool." Ryan leaned in next to Ben.

Anne shook her head. "Hey, why don't you shut the computer down and visit while Ryan's here?"

Ben sighed. So did Ryan.

"I'm bummed you have to miss our first game," Ryan said.

"Me too. I was supposed to start," Ben said.

"I heard Chad called Coach Walden, and you should be right back in starting position next week," Alex said. "There will be other games, and you'll be back soon."

"Does it hurt?" Ryan pointed toward the bandaged ankle.

"Not too bad," Ben said with a shake of his head. "I should be back at school tomorrow."

"That's great! School is so boring without you."

"Hey, I understand you have an errand to run," Alex said.

"Oh?" Anne stopped. What had she forgotten now?

"A run over to Deshler. You and Liddie. The mall," Alex teased.

Their hats and gloves! "Oh, right," said Anne. "But—now, with Ben hurt…"

Alex held up his hands. "I thought you could go now if I help Bella out here at the library and with Ben. You and Liddie could still run your errand and be back before it gets too late."

"I can't ask you to do that," Anne said. Alex was a great friend and the fact that he lived so close, just down the hill, was nice. But she needed to remember he did have a construction business he had to oversee.

He laughed. "Ryan's going through Ben withdrawal. Seriously, it's not a big problem at all. Let me help."

She only hesitated a moment more. "Okay. Let me grab Liddie and we'll get out of here." Anne grabbed her purse and slipped the shoulder strap over her shoulder. "Thanks, Alex. I appreciate it."

"Go on now," he said, his face turning red. He gave her a little nudge.

She really did love the feeling of community in the town of Blue Hill.

Chapter Seventeen

Deshler wasn't too far from Blue Hill, just one town over. Anne found herself appreciating the beautiful scenery of Pennsylvania as she drove. With all the tree leaves turning colors, the drive was lovely. So much so that Anne put the windows of her Chevy Impala down, and she and Liddie breathed in the fresh fall air.

Liddie bounced in her car seat in the back. "I'm so 'cited to get a hat and gloves. Will I look pretty, Mommy?"

Anne smiled at her as she parked in the Deshler mall's parking lot. "It's *excited*, sweetheart, and yes, you will be stunning."

After locking the car, Anne took Liddie's hand and led her into the mall.

They made their way toward the formal-wear store Anne had spied on her last visit. She'd seen some pretty hats in the back window. Aunt Edie had often worn hats to church. She had the perfect head for a hat, Aunt Edie had claimed, especially when her hair refused to behave.

"Mommy, look at the pretty jewelry," Liddie said, tugging on Anne's hand as they passed a jewelry store.

"It's all very lovely," Anne agreed, although the price tags on the items in the window could pay the library's bills for a month with no problem.

"Oh, look!" Liddie pulled Anne to the other side of the mall. "Look at that."

Anne smiled at Liddie's nose pressed against the glass display case, her eyes trained on the little ballerina doll pirouetting on the stand in the window. "She's beautiful," Liddie whispered.

"She's very beautiful," Anne agreed. It didn't matter how many dolls Liddie owned, she had never yet met a doll she didn't want. If Anne would let her, Liddie's entire room would be covered with every doll imaginable.

"Come on, we have to pick out our hats and gloves," Anne said as she gently turned Liddie from the doll store.

"I want a doll just like that for Christmas, Mommy," Liddie said.

"Christmas is still a couple of months away," Anne replied, but she made a mental note of the doll for Liddie's list.

They crossed from the center of the mall to one of the offshoot hallways. The smell of freshly roasted coffee wound down the hallway and teased Anne's senses. If Alex wasn't back at the library waiting on her to return, she would take the time to enjoy a coffee.

But she didn't want to infringe on his generosity, so she led Liddie into the dress shop she'd found.

"Hello. How may I help you ladies today?" an older saleswoman asked.

"We need hats and gloves for our tea time," Liddie announced.

"A tea?" The woman pressed a hand to her chest. "Oh my. Then we simply must find you ladies the perfect hat first." She waved toward the racks at the back of the store where hat upon hat hung. "Start looking there, why don't you?"

Anne smiled as Liddie ran to the back of the store. Her eyes were as wide as they'd been when looking at the ballerina doll.

The saleswoman gave a little laugh. "It's so delightful to see young ones excited about dressing up formally. Where are you attending this tea?" she asked.

"The library in Blue Hill is hosting it," Anne replied, grinning as another saleswoman in the back handed different hats to Liddie to try on.

Liddie checked all sides in the mirror with every hat she put on.

"Oh, I read in the paper about the librarian over there finding a rare Edgar Allan Poe book," the woman said.

That snagged Anne's attention from Liddie's enjoyment. She stared at the woman. "You did?"

"Yes, of course. Many of us over here in Deshler subscribe to the *Blue Hill Gazette*." She shook her head and made a clucking sound. "Have you heard if anyone's claimed the book yet?"

There was no sense in being coy with this woman. "I'm actually the librarian there, and no, we haven't yet found the book's rightful owner," Anne admitted.

The woman held out her hand. "LouAnn Patterson. Pleased to meet you," she shook Anne's hand.

"Anne Gibson. And that's my daughter, Liddie."

Liddie heard her name and lifted her head. "Do you like this hat, Mommy?"

"You look charming," Anne answered with a smile.

Liddie moved on to try a different hat.

"You know, my cousin's stepdaughter lives over in Blue Hill. She told us at church on Sunday that the Blue Hill Garden Club might have an interest in the book," LouAnn said.

"Really?" That was a new one to Anne.

"Yeah." LouAnn shrugged. "But what do I know, eh?" She gave Anne a little nudge. "You'd certainly know more about all that than I."

"No one's come forward with proof yet, that much I can tell you," Anne said.

"Well, you just be careful," LouAnn said as she pulled samples of different styles of gloves from the drawer behind the counter.

"What do you mean?" Anne asked.

"Well, several months ago, our local antiques dealer, Conrad Manson, was accused of falsifying legal documents to insurance companies, such as statements of how much something was worth."

"An appraisal?" Anne asked.

"Right. Like an appraisal. Anyway, everybody here was talking about how shocked we all were, because he went to church with us and lived right down the road from some of our neighbors and all. We couldn't believe the talk." LouAnn spread five different styles of gloves out on the counter.

"So what happened?"

"Well, before any charges could be officially filed, he just up and left in the middle of the night." LouAnn snapped her fingers. "Just like that. Disappeared into thin air."

That truly was odd. And Anne couldn't help but think about that fishy-looking appraisal Jenna Coleman had shown Anne. The address *had* been in Deshler. Maybe this scam artist had scammed Jenna too. Anne felt a little twinge...maybe she'd judged Jenna a little too harshly.

God, help me to stop jumping to conclusions. I need to just put everything in Your hands and stop trying to figure everything out on my own all the time.

"So which style of glove do you prefer?" LouAnn asked.

Anne ran her hand over the gloves before her. She preferred the short pair, but she already knew which ones Liddie would fall in love with. "Liddie, come look at the gloves," she called out.

Liddie, still wearing a hot pink hat, ran up the aisle.

"Which pair of gloves do you like best?" Anne asked.

Liddie touched them all, then stopped on the pink satin ones.

Anne hid her smile. She knew those would be the ones Liddie would pick.

"I like these, Mommy." Liddie pulled one of the long gloves on. It nearly reached her armpit.

LouAnn laughed. "Here, let me get you a pair of those in your size." She handed Liddie a glove.

Liddie put it on and waved her arm around like a queen addressing her subjects.

"Are those the ones you want?" Anne asked, although the answer was quite obvious.

"Yes, Mommy. Yes!"

Anne grinned. "Okay, sweetie. Take it off so we can get them in the box."

Liddie did and Anne handed it back to LouAnn. "Obviously we'll take this pair for Liddie."

"And for you?" LouAnn asked.

"I prefer the short cotton ones." Yes, those would be best. She might have to pour the tea, and the satin ones, while pretty, might be a little too slick.

"What color?" LouAnn asked.

"Um." Well. She didn't know.

"What color is your dress?" LouAnn asked.

Anne hadn't decided on what dress she'd wear yet either.

LouAnn gently shook her head. "I normally wouldn't recommend white after Labor Day, of course, but in your case...well, either the white or the candlelight, or if you think you might wear a darker dress, the black gloves are always elegant."

Choices, choices. Too many choices. Anne started to pick the white ones, but then she had a distinct memory of Aunt Edie.

Aunt Edie had been helping Anne get ready for the prom. Anne had been wearing a black strapless gown and didn't want to mess up the line of the dress with too much jewelry or frou-frou.

"I don't want to look all top heavy," Anne complained. "That would defeat the purpose of the clean and elegant lines of the dress."

Aunt Edie nodded, tapping her finger against her chin. "You're quite right, dear. Let me think. Classy. Elegant. Not overbearing, but just tasteful enough..."

"That's it!"

"What?"

Aunt Edie smiled. "I have just the thing. Hang on." She disappeared and returned a moment later with a small box, which she handed to Anne. "Here. See if these do the trick."

Anne opened the box and pulled out a pair of elbow-length black gloves. They were so delicate to the touch, like finely tatted lace.

She slipped them on. The material hugged her skin.

Anne looked at her reflection and smiled. So did Aunt Edie. "Perfect," she whispered.

Anne blinked as LouAnn pulled out a box in preparation for Anne's glove selection. How had she forgotten that dress memory with Aunt Edie?

"Have you decided?" LouAnn asked.

"I'll go with the black," Anne said. She smiled to herself. In honor of Aunt Edie and her impeccable and unique taste.

"Mommy, I want this hat." Liddie spun in front of Anne.

Anne bent over and lifted the brim of the big, white floppy hat. "I can't even see you, Liddie."

Liddie giggled. "I like it like that, Mommy."

Anne pressed her lips together. Speaking of unique tastes... sometimes Liddie reminded her of Aunt Edie, which could be a very good thing.

"If you just love it...," Anne began.

Liddie jumped up and down. "I do, Mommy."

"Then that shall be your hat." She caught the younger saleswoman's concerned look. She smiled. "I know it's a white hat and it's after Labor Day, but she's five. I think it'll be okay," she whispered.

LouAnn chuckled. "We're all north of the Mason-Dixon line, so I doubt the southern genteel fashion police will come out after us."

"True." Anne could appreciate LouAnn understanding that five-year-olds usually didn't play according to fashion guidelines.

"So what about you?" LouAnn asked. "What color hat?"

"You know, let's be bold." She pointed at the deep purple felt fedora-style hat. "Let me try on that one, please."

"Oh my. It's lovely," LouAnn said. She took it off the rack and handed it to Anne. "Here, try it on."

Anne did. She thought she'd feel awkward wearing a hat, but surprisingly, she didn't. It felt, well, it felt a little elegant.

"You look very striking," LouAnn said, holding up a mirror for Anne to see her reflection.

To be honest, she was pleased with how she looked. Maybe she'd been drawn to the purple because she had a lovely dress that would match.

"The hat will go along well with your gloves," LouAnn said.

Anne nodded and grinned at Liddie. "What do you think, sweetie?"

"I think you look beautiful, Mommy."

Anne smiled and handed the hat to LouAnn. "Then it's settled. I'll take it."

LouAnn and her assistant boxed up the hats and gloves, gave Anne her receipt after she paid, and wished Anne and Liddie a simply marvelous tea time, then told them good-bye.

"I love my hat, Mommy," Liddie said as they hurried along the mall's hallway toward the side of the building where Anne had parked.

"It's stunning on you too, sweetheart." Anne paused as they passed the bookstore.

The cardboard endcaps and displays were all dedicated to R. W. Winger and the Coastal Club series. Pictures of the characters. The setting. And, of course, a huge promo for the upcoming release, the one Ben wanted so desperately.

"Come on, Mommy," Liddie tugged Anne's hand. "I have to write my sight words."

Anne and Liddie sang as they drove back to Blue Hill. Despite everything that was going on with the Edgar Allan Poe book and her being so exhausted, Anne had truly enjoyed the shopping trip and the fun time with Liddie.

"...and Bingo was his name-oh!" she joined in the last stanza with Liddie just as they pulled into the detached garage next to the library.

"Come on, sweetheart. Hurry and finish your homework and I'll get started on dinner." Thank goodness she'd pulled a premade casserole out of the freezer this morning.

"Wow, did you buy out the store?" Alex asked as they went inside carrying their hatboxes and bags.

"Nope. Only got the hats and gloves we went for," Anne answered. "Liddie, go on upstairs and start your homework."

"Okay, Mommy," Liddie skipped toward the stairs.

Anne glanced at the clock. "I hope we didn't take too long."

"Not at all," Alex said. "We just locked the front door to the library."

"Would you like to stay for dinner? I took a casserole out of the freezer this morning."

Alex made a face. "I appreciate the offer, I do, but tonight's taco night at the Ochs/Slater *casa*."

She shook her head, smiling. "I really do appreciate your staying here and watching the library and Ben for me." She headed to the Nonfiction Room.

"I told you, no worries." He clapped his hands. "Hey, guys. Time for Ryan and me to hit the road."

"Aw, Uncle Alex. Ben's been showing me all the Coastal Club sneak peeks and stuff."

"You have homework to do, Ryan. And it's taco night," Alex said.

"Yeah. Okay." Ryan fist-bumped Ben. "See you tomorrow at school. Maybe I can help you carry your books to class and stuff."

"Yeah. That'll be fun," Ben said. "See you."

"Take care, Ben. We'll see you soon," Alex said as Ryan came out of the Nonfiction Room and across the library. "Let me know if you need anything," Alex told Anne. "Happy to help if you do."

"I appreciate it, but we're fine. Your staying here this afternoon was more than enough."

Ryan headed out the front door. Alex stopped and faced Anne. "I heard about Jenna Coleman's visit."

"Michael called you?" she asked.

"He's just a little worried about you and the situation. Promise me you'll call him, or me, if she comes back and tries to pull another stunt."

Anne grinned. "I'm quite capable of taking care of myself, you know."

"I do know," Alex grinned wider. "I'm more concerned about her well-being than yours."

"Well, in that case..." Anne shook her head. "I'll call Michael if she comes back and acts out like she did."

"Thank you." Alex started toward the door, then stopped and turned back to her. "I do worry, you know."

Heat spread out from her stomach. "I know. And I appreciate your concern for me and the kids. I really do."

He turned and left, leaving Anne standing there staring after him. It felt really good to have someone worry about her and the kids. Not that she wanted anyone to worry, of course.

It'd been a while since she felt like this. It made her... well, a bit giddy, almost. But it did feel nice.

Chapter Eighteen

"Sorry to drop by so late, but I just got finished with my shift," Michael said.

"No problem," Anne said, letting him into the library and locking the front door behind him. "I'm glad you stopped by."

Michael fell into step beside her as she led the way to the checkout area. "Why? Has Jenna Coleman been back to cause more trouble?"

"No, nothing like that." Anne took a quick inventory of her friend from high school.

Michael Banks was a broad-shouldered man, large and foreboding. He sported curly, dark hair that almost, but not quite, hid his growing bald spot. But it was his soft and kind blue eyes that made people trust him. Maybe that's why he was so good in law enforcement.

"Good."

"How about a cup of coffee? I just made a pot a few minutes ago," she said, leading the way to the refreshment area.

"None for me, thanks. I'm going to head home and sleep for at least twelve hours. Or however long Jennifer can keep the kids from waking me up."

Anne poured herself a cup, then took a slow sip. She leaned against the counter. "So what brings you by?"

"Oh," he said, shaking his head. "I'm so tired my brain isn't working. I found a copy of Jenna Coleman's police report." Michael pulled a paper from his pocket and passed it to Anne.

Anne quickly read the information on the first page. All basic information: name of person filing the report, address, personal information, date… "It's filed in the timeframe Jenna claimed," she said.

"Yes, that's true. Is it the book you found?" Michael asked, hiding a yawn by turning his head.

He'd probably worked close to fourteen or sixteen hours. Anne didn't want to keep him any longer than necessary.

She flipped the page to go through the itemization of what was stolen. She ran her finger down the page until she reached what she looked for:

> Novel-Tales: The Raven and Other Poems by
> Edgar Allan Poe
> Original brown cloth covering/published by
> New York: Wiley and Putnam, 1845

"That's not the same Edgar Allan Poe title of the book I found," Anne exclaimed. "It's not her book."

"So the book you have isn't the one that was stolen from Jenna Coleman's store three years ago?" Michael asked.

Anne shook her head. "Nope."

He took the copy of the police report and tapped the listed worth. "Do you think this book is really worth the twenty-two thousand dollars she claimed?"

Anne shrugged. "Possibly. I'm sure her insurance company wouldn't allow her to insure it for more than it's worth."

Yet something was stuck in the back of Anne's mind. What was it? Something about three years ago...

"Hey, can I see that again?" Anne asked.

"Sure. I made the copy for you." Michael handed the paper back to her. "What is it?"

"I'm not sure." She scanned the information again. Then it hit her.

"The date," she whispered.

"What?"

Anne pointed to the date of the police report. "This report is just two weeks after the date listed on the appraisal Jenna showed me." She stared into Michael's confused face. "Doesn't that seem a bit curious? To have an appraisal done and two weeks later, the item appraised is stolen?" she said.

"That is curious," Michael said. "I'll look into that."

"Well, at least now I can tell her the book I found isn't hers." She tucked the copy of the police report into her pocket. "Thanks for this, Michael. I really appreciate it."

"That's my job: to serve and protect," he said, grinning. "But now I'd better be getting home or I could fall asleep at the wheel. That wouldn't be so great."

Anne led the way to the front door. "Thanks again, Michael. Tell Jennifer I said hello and hug the kids for me."

"Will do. Night, Anne."

She locked the door behind him, yawning herself. Anne turned off lights as she made her way through the library. It had been a long Thursday.

Brrring!

Anne jumped, then laughed at herself. She'd forgotten to turn on the answering machine when she'd gone to lock the door before Michael arrived.

Brrring!

It was outdated to use an answering machine, she knew, but she preferred it over voice mail. She grabbed the library's receiver before it rang again. "Blue Hill Library, this is Anne. How may I help you?"

"This is Jenna Coleman. I'm calling about my book."

The woman's attitude of entitlement wore Anne out. She sank to the stool behind the counter. "Ms. Coleman, I obtained a copy of the police report you've referred to about the Poe title stolen from your store."

"Uh, good. So you know the book belongs to me," Jenna said, her arrogance seeping over the phone line like pine sap trickling down a tree.

The woman truly thought the book belonged to her. For some reason, that made Anne feel a little better. Jenna believing the book was hers made her attitude easier to take. Just a little. "Actually, it doesn't."

"Excuse me?" Jenna asked.

"According to the police report you filed, the book you owned that was stolen was written by Edgar Allen Poe, but it was titled *Novel-Tales: The Raven and Other Poems*."

"Okay?"

"But that isn't the title of the book I found," Anne explained.

"Are you sure?" Skepticism laced Jenna's voice. "There can't be two rare Edgar Allan Poe titles in Blue Hill."

As hard as it was to believe, there was no other explanation. "I'm positive. As unlikely as it seems, there apparently *are* two rare editions of Poe's work here in Blue Hill. Or there was before your copy was stolen three years ago," Anne said.

There was a heavy pause over the connection.

"Are you still there, Jenna?" Anne asked.

"I'm here. I just find it...oddly convenient that you have a copy of my police report," Jenna said.

"I got a copy from the Blue Hill Police Department because you were so insistent, yet you couldn't locate your copy."

"How do I know you're telling the truth?" Jenna asked.

Anne stiffened but told herself not to take the insult personally. She'd probably ask the same question if she were in Jenna's place. "If you'd like, you can meet me tomorrow and we'll go to the bank. I'll show you the book that I found, and you can compare the title against your police report yourself."

Another long silence.

"That's not necessary, I guess," Jenna said. "I doubt you'd volunteer to do that if you were lying."

Again, Anne refused to take offense. "I wouldn't lie."

"Well...sorry for having bothered you," Jenna said.

"It's o—"

The call disconnecting cut Anne off. She shook her head as she replaced the receiver onto the cradle.

She turned on the answering machine, shut off the computer on the desk, and grabbed her cell phone from under the counter. Anne made sure to check that she'd turned off the coffeepot in the refreshment area, then climbed the stairs to the third floor.

Anne could almost hear the hot shower calling her.

* * *

"Those look amazing," Anne told Wendy, staring at the boxes of petit fours Wendy slipped into the refrigerator in the refreshment area.

Wendy put the last tray on the shelf, shut the fridge door, and turned to Anne. "Don't you dare sneak one before tomorrow," she said. "I know exactly how many are in there, and there better be that many tomorrow at the tea." But Wendy wore the biggest smile ever.

Anne grinned back. "You shouldn't make them so tempting."

"Are you ready for tomorrow?" Wendy asked.

"I am now. I picked up my and Liddie's hats and gloves yesterday afternoon over at the mall in Deshler. What about you?"

Wendy nodded. "Yep. We found a bunch of old hats and dresses in our attic," she said. "I'm surprised you didn't find some up in yours, knowing how much Edie kept in the attic."

"To be honest, I didn't even look. I just didn't want to get distracted by all the goodies I'd find," Anne said.

"I understand. Well, I've got to get back. Hannah's got an eye on the kids while I ran these over since Chad's at the football game." She let out a heavy breath. "I'm kinda glad it's an away game so I didn't have to go. I have so much to do for us to be ready tomorrow."

"Thanks, Wendy. You're amazing," Anne said, following her friend through the library.

"Yes, I am. And don't you forget it," Wendy teased. She gave a little finger wave to Remi at the checkout counter, then left.

Anne turned to check on the order she needed to submit on Monday when she heard the door open again. She smiled. Leave it to Wendy to forget something. She set down the order and spun around. "What did you forget—"

It wasn't Wendy standing in the entryway, it was Evelyn Kelley.

"Oh. Mrs. Kelley. I'm sorry, I thought you were my friend coming back." She shook her head. "How are you?" Anne asked, trying to recover quickly.

"Not so good," Evelyn said. She glanced at Remi, then back to Anne. "May I speak with you? Privately?"

In reality, the Poe book probably belonged to the Kelley family.

Anne nodded, and led her to the little alcove in the History Room. She leaned against the display counter and waited.

Evelyn ripped at the tissue in her hands. "I hate to keep bothering you," she said, "but I'm afraid I don't have any other choice. You see, there is a very, very important document in the Poe book that is missing from Gus's collection. Rodney and his dad are positive the book was in one of the boxes I donated to the used-book sale." Big tears shimmered in Evelyn's eyes.

"I'm sorry, Evelyn, but there's not—" Anne started.

"No, please. I understand, I do, but this incident has caused such a rift between Rodney and Jeff, which has put a serious strain between me and Rodney...It's just a mess," Evelyn said, shredding the tissue and balling the pieces in her palms. "I'm afraid my marriage will be destroyed if I don't recover the document. It's all my fault it's missing. Jeff won't forgive Rodney for not going through the boxes sooner to get the paper, and Rodney won't forgive me for giving away the boxes. I just don't know what else to do but come here."

Evelyn lifted her face to Anne's. Tears ran freely down her rounded cheeks. "I'm begging you, please let me look at the book so I can find the document and save my marriage."

Anne couldn't stand to see her crying so. She hugged Evelyn. What kind of marriage couldn't withstand such a simple mistake? What kind of people were in the Kelley family? Anne glanced at her watch. "Evelyn, I'd love to help you, I truly would, but the book is in the safety deposit box at the bank, and the bank closed a good forty-five minutes ago."

Evelyn sobbed openly.

"Oh, please don't cry," Anne said, hugging her again. "I can't get into the bank to look inside the book for any document today, but I'll go first thing Monday morning."

Taking a step back, Evelyn stared at Anne. "You promise?"

Anne nodded. "I promise." She smiled. "Now, stop crying. It's all going to be okay."

She prayed that she hadn't lied to poor Evelyn.

Chapter Nineteen

"My, don't you look pretty?" Anne said, staring at Liddie's reflection in the mirror.

Liddie pirouetted in Anne's bedroom in front of the full-length mirror, so fancy in her ruffled turquoise dress and big white floppy hat. She wore the long pink gloves that reached just above her elbow. Anne smiled as she looked at her little girl all dressed up. She might not match perfectly, but that was okay. She was a lot like Aunt Edie in that way.

"Mommy, can I wear some makeup too?" Liddie asked, staring at Anne's makeup tray on the counter.

"Just a little bit." Anne smiled and put a little bit of translucent powder on her daughter's face. Even though it wasn't more than a brushstroke, it made Liddie happy.

Anne plopped the purple hat atop her head and smiled at Liddie. "How do I look, sweetheart?"

"Beautiful. Are you going to wear your bracelet I got you?" Liddie asked.

"Of course." Anne reached into her jewelry box and handed Liddie the Trading Treasures tennis bracelet Liddie had given her for her birthday. "Would you help me put it on, please?"

"Sure." Liddie struggled a little with the clasp. "I can't get it, Mommy."

"It's our gloves, probably. Let's ask Ben, shall we?" Anne walked across the hall to Ben's room and tapped on the door.

"Come in," Ben said.

They crossed into his room where he had the laptop sitting on his desk.

"What're you doing?" Anne asked.

"Reading." Ben frowned at her. "Why are you wearing that?" He nodded toward her hat.

Anne realized how ridiculous they must look to a nine-year-old boy. She decided to make it even more of a joke. She straightened her shoulders and pushed her nose into the air like a snob. "We're going to high tea," she said in a fake British accent.

Liddie and Ben both giggled. She joined in, then handed Ben the bracelet. "We can't get my bracelet on with our gloves. Will you fasten it for me, please?"

"Why would you wear a bracelet over those gloves anyway?" he asked, but he fastened the bracelet's clasp over her black gloves anyway.

"Because it's stylish," Anne answered in her accent. "And no one would see it if I wore it under the gloves. I want to show it off."

"Because I gave it to her," Liddie announced.

Anne nodded. "Because your sister gave it to me." She smiled at Ben.

"Okay, whatever." He smiled and plopped back down in front of the computer.

She ruffled his hair. "I'll save you a petit four," Anne said as she headed toward the hallway.

"A what?" he asked.

"It's a little bitty cake," Liddie answered in a know-it-all tone.

Anne smiled to herself and reached for the banister, when she heard voices drifting up the stairs from the library below. "We'd better hurry, Liddie. They'll start the tea without us."

"No, they can't," Liddie protested, but she hurried down the stairs before Anne.

Yvette and her daughters, Becca and Cindy, smiled at Anne as she joined the group of ladies. Young and old alike, everyone looked so formal in their gowns and hats.

Anne couldn't help but notice all the beautiful jewelry, divine dresses, super hats, and elegant gloves. Remi wore a green gown that flowed just under the bodice, gems shimmering around the top. Bella wore a gorgeous white hat to match her black-and-white polka-dot dress. Both girls looked as good as the petit fours.

Wendy had outdone herself with the table setting. A beautiful pink lace tablecloth, various patterns of antique china, a variety of tea cups and saucers, teapots, sugar cube dishes, petit fours, and spoons.

"Who would like to ask for blessings before we serve?" Anne asked the group of older ladies.

"I will," Nellie Brown volunteered. Betty Warring, Nellie's ever-present sister, thumped forward and leaned on her cane. She got around pretty well, or as she joked, she could make good progress if there wasn't any wind. The elderly sisters lived together and were an institution in Blue Hill. It seemed only right that Nellie would offer up grace.

Everyone nodded and joined hands with one another around the table, then bowed their heads.

"Heavenly Father, we thank You for this day. We thank You for gathering us here to enjoy a nice tea party. Thank You for the hands who prepared the food. Thank You for blessing us to get to enjoy the company of one another. Amen," Nellie prayed.

There was a chorus of "Amens" from the rest of the table. Everyone began to serve themselves tea and petit fours.

Wendy set napkins on the table with the petit fours and the teapot with the cold tea for the girls. The hot tea sat in the pot on the counter.

"Thank you, Wendy," Anne whispered. "You look amazing, as always."

"Thank you, kind gentlewoman." Wendy smiled.

"It's fancy to drink with your pinky up," Cindy said as she demonstrated.

All the girls giggled as they tried to drink with their little fingers pointing out. The girls were all sitting at one end of the table, giggling.

Anne laughed and poured herself a cup of hot tea.

"Mrs. Bultman, your dress is quite charming," Yvette stated, gesturing to the emerald green dress the mayor's wife wore.

"Thank you, it's been in my family for years." She smiled and took a sip of her tea.

Anne noticed she kept her little finger pointed out.

"Yvette, wherever did you find that dress of Becca's?" Wendy asked. "That red is absolutely beautiful on her."

"We actually found it in a thrift shop over in the Diamond District. We only had to do a few touch-ups and the dress was perfect." Yvette beamed.

The development of the Diamond District over on the west side of town had intended to provide a small, upscale shopping area that would attract shopkeepers and tenants. Despite an enormous investment into landscaping and cozy retail spaces, the development struggled to keep its tenants of various shops and offices, all fighting to compete with Blue Hill's thriving downtown. Anne had heard a couple of thrift shops had opened in that area, hoping to not have to compete with the flea market.

"Liddie's hat is stunning," Betty Bultman said. "They grow up so fast. All of the girls look so darling." She smiled as she looked at the pretty group of girls dressed up like dolls from another era.

"That they do," Anne said as she pushed her glasses back up the bridge of her nose. She should've worn her contacts, which she usually did on very special occasions.

"How do you manage the whole library?" Yvette questioned.

"I have lots of help," Anne answered, glancing at Wendy, Bella, Remi, and Betty.

"I was thinking maybe I could plant some different flowers in that planter by the front of the library. What do all of you think about that?" Bella asked.

"That sounds interesting. Maybe the garden club could help. What kind of flowers?" Wendy asked.

"I haven't quite decided yet. Something simple yet elegant. Like the library." Bella smiled.

"I think that would be nice," Betty Bultman said with a nod.

"So, Remi, do you enjoy what you do at the library?" Nellie asked.

Remi finished chewing her bite of petit four before she smiled and answered, "Of course. I love books, and I want to become a librarian, so naturally the library is like a second home to me."

"It's comfy to curl up with a good book in some of the big chairs," Bella added.

"The tables make laptop usage easy. I can e-mail my family here," Wendy said.

"Not to mention, if you sit by a window you can watch the wind blow through the trees. The leaves fly off, and it's lovely, really, a true part of nature's beauty," Anne stated. She'd spent more time than most doing that exact thing.

Everyone nodded in agreement, and then a couple of the ladies moved to refill their cups.

"Your dress looks wonderful, Mrs. Bultman," Bella complimented.

Bella reached to grab the sugar and accidentally hit the teapot. It spilled a little, but Anne caught it before too much damage was done. Bella covered her mouth with her hands, her cheeks blazing.

"I am so sorry, Mrs. Gibson. I should have been more careful," Bella apologized.

"It's okay. Accidents happen, dear. You didn't mean to. No harm done," Nellie said, patting Bella on the back.

"It's fine." Anne smiled at Bella.

Remi started to chuckle.

"What's so funny?" Wendy asked Remi.

"When we were children, Bella would always spill things, especially drinks in restaurants. We always called her bad luck. She thought it was over," Remi shook her head.

"Ha-ha, I remember that," Bella said, smiling.

"We better watch out for you," Betty teased.

Anne began to nibble on a petit four. She'd been so busy and stressed lately that the tea had seemed like it would just be a bother, but now she was thankful for the event—and for the fun and fellowship it provided.

"What a beautiful bracelet," Yvette said. "I have a Tiffany tennis bracelet almost identical to yours. Is it Tiffany?"

Anne laughed. "Hardly. Mine isn't a Tiffany. It isn't even real. Liddie gave it to me for my birthday last week."

Yvette reached out to her arm. "May I?" she asked.

Anne nodded.

Cindy and Becca's mother inspected Anne's bracelet. "Anne, perhaps you should check your real jewelry box because this bracelet most definitely is, in fact, a Tiffany."

"How can you tell?" Wendy asked.

"See the cut of the diamonds in the flower setting?" Yvette asked.

Wendy nodded. "Yes."

"Those are called rose-cut Tiffany diamonds, one of the earliest gemstone cuts, set in platinum," Yvette explained. She looked at Anne. "This is almost identical to my Tiffany garden flower bracelet from their collection."

Anne shook her head. "It can't be real because I don't own any Tiffany jewelry." Like she could ever have afforded such a piece!

"Oh, it's real. I'd bet my bottom dollar on that," Yvette said.

A sick feeling pitted in the middle of Anne's stomach. "Yvette, where is your Tiffany bracelet like this?"

"At home, in my jewelry box," Yvette answered.

"Where do you keep the jewelry you let Cindy and Becca use for their trading games?" Anne asked.

"In my room, on my dresser...Oh, I see where you're going with this," Yvette said. "Do you think it's possible?"

"Is the costume jewelry close enough to your real jewelry box that they might have gotten mixed up by mistake?" Wendy asked.

Yvette shrugged. "I don't think so." She gasped and covered her mouth. "Oh no. I wore my Tiffany bracelet to dinner with Greg a few nights ago. I know I set it on the dresser when I took it off, but I don't remember actually putting it back in my jewelry box." Her face flushed. "Becca helped me with the dusting the next day."

"I bet it accidently got mixed in with the costume jewelry," Anne said. She held out her arm. "Here, take it."

"Thank goodness it got to Anne and didn't get sucked up in a vacuum cleaner like it would've at my house," Wendy said.

Yvette took the bracelet off Anne's arm. "I'm so sorry, Anne. I feel bad because Liddie gave you this for your birthday."

Anne laughed. "At least I know she has good taste." She shook her head. "Seriously, we need to let the girls know what happened so they can be more careful." She motioned for Liddie "Liddie, could you and Cindy and Becca come here for a minute, please?"

The three girls rushed over.

"What, Mommy?" Liddie asked. Her eyes caught on the bracelet in Yvette's hand. "Did your bracelet fall off, Mommy? I bet Ben didn't latch it right."

Anne knelt down to be at Liddie's eye level. "Sweetheart, do you remember where you got the bracelet?"

Liddie nodded. "I traded Becca my diamond crown for it."

Anne smiled, then looked Becca in the eye. "Becca, sweetie, do you remember where you got the bracelet?"

Becca's bottom lip started to poke out. She shook her head.

"Think really hard, sweetheart," Anne gently pushed.

Becca stuck her thumb in her mouth and stared at the floor.

"She got it from Mommy's room," Cindy said.

"Shut up," Becca told her sister, sticking her tongue out at Cindy.

"Whoa, girls. That's not nice," Yvette admonished her daughters. She sat on a chair and turned both Cindy and Becca toward her. "Now, tell me how you got this bracelet," she said to Becca.

"I wanted the crown," Becca said, keeping her gaze on the floor. "Liddie wouldn't trade it for anything I had. She was gonna trade with mean ole' Mia Banks for a necklace to give Miss Anne for her birthday, but I don't like Mia and I wanted the crown," Becca said, shoving her thumb back into her mouth.

"Big girls don't suck their thumbs, Becca," Yvette said, gently pulling her thumb from her mouth. "Tell me how you got the bracelet."

Becca didn't say a word.

"Rebecca Renee, answer me," Yvette said, using a sterner voice.

Becca remained silent, gently swaying as she stared at the floor.

"She took it from your dresser, Mommy," Cindy said, the words tumbling out.

"Tattler," Becca said, sticking her tongue out at her sister again.

"Rebecca! Stop acting like that toward your sister," Yvette said. She frowned and touched Becca's chin and lifted her head until she looked in her mother's face. "Did you deliberately take my bracelet so you could trade with Liddie to get the crown?"

Big tears pooled in Becca's eyes. "I really wanted the crown, Mommy, and I didn't want Mia to have it."

Yvette let out a heavy sigh. "That was very wrong, Rebecca. You know better." She stood. "Come on, girls. We're going home."

"But Mommy, I didn't do nothing," Cindy cried. "I want another little piece of cake."

"You knew what your sister did and you didn't tell me," Yvette said. "Get your things. Now." She turned to Anne as Cindy and Becca scrambled to collect their teacups and saucers. "I'm so sorry, Anne."

"No. I completely understand."

Yvette bent over to Liddie. "I'm very sorry I have to take the bracelet back. It's very valuable, and Mr. Jacobs gave it to me on our ten-year wedding anniversary. How about I get your mom another bracelet you can give her?"

Liddie kept her mouth shut, just nodding. Her light brown curls with hints of blonde bobbed.

Yvette straightened and met Anne's gaze again. "I'm really very sorry."

"Don't worry about it," Anne said. "It's okay."

"No, it's not. Becca knows better," Yvette said. "Girls," she called out.

Becca didn't even look at anyone as she followed her mother from the library. Cindy gave Liddie a little wave as she left.

"Mommy, did I do anything wrong?" Liddie asked after they'd left.

"Oh no, sweetheart. You didn't." Anne squatted in front of her daughter. A thought occurred to her. "You didn't know the bracelet was really Mrs. Jacobs's and not one that Cindy and Becca could play with, did you?"

Liddie's eyes widened and she shook her head. "No, Mommy. I didn't know."

Relief washed over Anne. "Then you didn't do anything wrong, my sweet girl." She leaned over and gave Liddie a hug and a kiss. "But Becca knew the bracelet was her mommy's and not to be played with and she took it anyway. That was wrong. Mr. Jacobs gave Mrs. Jacobs the bracelet on a special occasion, so no matter what it's worth, it means a lot to her. Can you imagine how she would feel if she lost it?"

Liddie nodded.

"It could break her heart. It's a good thing she saw it today and recognized it so she was able to get it back," Anne said, then straightened. She gave Liddie another sideways hug. "Understand?"

"Yes, Mommy, but now you don't have a birthday present from me." Liddie's bottom lip started to tremble.

"You heard Mrs. Jacobs," Wendy interjected. "She'll get your mom a new bracelet so you can give it to her. It'll be even more special because your mom will always remember the time you gave her a Tiffany by mistake."

Anne chuckled. "That sure doesn't happen every day."

Wendy laughed.

Liddie laughed too. Then stopped. "Mommy, what's a Tiffany?"

* * *

"Ben, time for dinner!" Anne called from the kitchen.

There was no response. Where was he? It was unlike him not to come for dinner. Especially taco soup, one of his favorites.

Come to think of it, he hadn't seemed too upset to have missed the football game this afternoon. Either he'd decided to do a better job of hiding his disappointment, or something else had grabbed his interest.

Anne walked to his bedroom and knocked on the door before pushing it open. Ben sat at his desk, his eyes glued to the screen of the laptop.

"What are you doing?" Anne asked as she moved to stand behind him.

"Reading," he said, smiling but keeping his attention on the computer.

Anne crossed her arms over her chest. "Reading what?"

"A Coastal Club book," Ben said, eyes still focused on the screen.

Anne moved behind his chair and read over his shoulder. It looked like one of the Coastal Club books. Anne picked up the laptop and set it on his bed. "Ben, it's time for dinner, okay? The soup will get cold. Come on."

"Can I read just a few more pages? Just let me finish this chapter."

She chuckled. "No, honey. Come on. The book will be there when you finish." She headed back to the kitchen, wanting to laugh out loud. She could get just as lost in a book herself. Of course, the last book in the Coastal Club series had been released last year, so it wasn't like he didn't know what was going to happen.

Over dinner, Liddie talked on and on about the tea. Anne smiled as Liddie told Ben about Yvette's promise to get Liddie a new bracelet to give her.

Ben shoved the rest of his cornbread into his mouth—almost half a piece!

"Slow down, Ben. It's dinner, not a race," Anne said.

"Sorry, I just really want to read my book," Ben said.

"You can read it later, sweetie. Slow down eating. Your stomach will hurt if you eat too fast."

"Okay, Mom," Ben said, actually chewing his next bite.

As soon as the table was cleared, Ben rushed back to his bedroom.

Anne went in to check on him and found his nose in the laptop again. She moved behind him and read over his shoulder again. "Good book?" she asked, gesturing toward the laptop screen.

"*Mm-hmm.*" Ben nodded, then scrolled down to read more of the story.

Anne smiled, then kissed the top of his head. "Even though it's a weekend, don't stay up too late reading, honey. We have church in the morning."

"Okay. Night, Mom," Ben said, never taking his eyes off the computer monitor.

Anne pulled the door closed. At least Ben was reading, not playing online games or something.

Chapter Twenty

The Blue Hill Community Church's original bell rang out from the belfry as Reverend Tom led the congregation in the last notes of the closing hymn.

Anne grabbed Liddie's hand and led the way down the aisle. She shook Reverend Tom's hand before joining the rest of the townsfolk, spilling into the church's yard and parking lot.

The weather had turned out nice, warming up several degrees from yesterday. The early cold front had passed, and temperatures were now more in line with the norm for early October in Blue Hill.

"Anne, wait up," Michael hollered out.

She stopped, smiling as he and his lovely wife, Jennifer, whom Anne had also gone to school with, caught up with her. "Hi." Anne grinned at Tim, Jed, and Mia, Michael and Jennifer's children. "You three are getting so big."

Jed, at thirteen, seemed embarrassed by the attention. "Hi, Mrs. Gibson," he said quietly.

"Did you see my new shoes?" Mia asked Liddie.

"They sparkle!" Liddie exclaimed. "Mommy, I want some sparkly shoes."

Jennifer shook her head. "Come on, Mia. We have to get lunch started. Grammy's coming over today," she told her daughter.

"We need to get together soon, Anne. Maybe we can meet for lunch next week?"

"I'd like that," Anne said. "Nice to see you, Tim, Jed, and Mia."

"Bye, Mrs. Gibson," Tim said, following his mother, brother, and sister to the car.

"I wanted to let you know I followed up on that date of the police report," Michael said.

Anne turned around and saw Ben coming out of the Sunday school room. She motioned him over. "Ben, please take Liddie and get her in the car. I need to talk to Mr. Banks for a minute."

"Okay." Ben took Liddie's hand and led her to the silver Impala.

Anne nodded at Michael. "Jenna called me. I told her that the book I found wasn't the one stolen from her. I think I might've misjudged her because she really did think it was her book. She sounded pretty surprised when I told her the police report listed a different title."

"I bet she sounded surprised," Michael said.

"What do you mean?"

"Jenna Coleman *Franklin* has warrants out for her arrest for insurance fraud in Lumberton, New Jersey, and Warrick, New York, *and* Unity, Ohio," he told her.

"What?" Anne just couldn't picture the slight of a woman being so, well, devious. There had to be some mistake.

But Michael nodded and said, "Apparently she's been running scams in small towns where she would acquire appraisals on rare items, then a month or so later, file a police report claiming the item had been stolen and then file an insurance claim. The problem is, no one has ever actually physically seen any of the valuable items she claims."

That didn't make any sense. "The appraisers had to have inspected the items to have written appraisals on them to get insurance coverage," Anne said.

"She either forged the appraisals herself or had someone else forge them," Michael said. "Right now, the detectives I talked to are pretty sure she forged them herself."

Anne couldn't fathom such deceit.

She remembered her odd conversation with the talkative but nice saleswoman at the dress shop in the Deshler mall. "Michael, I wouldn't be so sure."

"Why is that?" he asked.

Anne told him what the saleswoman had told her. "It's possible that a local antiques dealer worked with Jenna on the fraud scam."

Michael pulled out his notebook and made notes. "What did you say his name was again?"

"Conrad Manson. And the saleswoman's name who told me all that is LouAnn Patterson. She works at the formal-wear shop at the mall in Deshler."

"Thanks, Anne. I'll run this through the system and see what we can find out."

The way people scammed... Anne shook her head. No wonder the insurance policy for the library was so expensive. With all the frivolous claims being made and all.

"I contacted all the detectives who were listed on the warrants and they want her arrested. They're on their way here as we speak.

I'm going to her house right now to take her into custody on their behalf," Michael said.

"Oh my," Anne said.

"I just wanted to let you know," Michael said. "I've got to run. I have to go by the station and pick up the warrants they faxed over. I'll talk to you later." He headed toward his car.

Anne slowly walked toward her car. She couldn't believe it. She would have never imagined that about Jenna Coleman. Never in a million years. Well, Eric had always said that her habit of looking for the best in people would often end up disappointing her.

She hadn't seen this coming about Jenna, that was for sure.

"Anne," a woman called out.

Anne stopped as Evelyn Kelley rushed up to her. "I haven't forgotten," Anne assured her. "I'm going to the bank first thing in the morning to get the book out of the safety deposit box to look for your document," Anne said. "And I guess if it's in there, it proves the book did belong to Gus, so I can just give it to you."

Chances were high that the book belonged to the Kelley family anyway, what with Jenna's fake appraisal and insurance fraud record.

Evelyn burst into tears. "I know you will. You're very kind."

Anne put her arm around Evelyn and led her to the little cement bench by the prayer garden. "What's wrong," she asked as she helped Evelyn sit beside her.

"I found out why my father-in-law has been so harsh about the whole thing," Evelyn said.

"What is it?" Anne asked.

"There's a chance there's an old copy of Gus's will tucked inside the book," Evelyn said.

Anne nodded, not understanding why this was so critical.

"It's an *old* will. One that leaves most of his estate to the Blue Hill Garden Club," Evelyn explained. "See, Gus was very disappointed in Jeff, my father-in-law, because—"

"Yes, I've heard all about Gus's threats to cut Jeff out of his will because Jeff wouldn't go into the medical profession," Anne interrupted.

"Right. Gus went back and forth on his threats, but in the end, he forgave Jeff and ended up leaving his estate to his son," Evelyn said.

"I'm with you so far," Anne said, having no clue where Evelyn was going with all this.

"Imagine the brouhaha that could happen if a copy of his old will turned up. A copy that left everything to the garden club. People might believe it was the most recent. They could contest the will," Evelyn's eyes filled with tears. "Even though we know what the last will decreed, we would have to go to court to defend the legitimate will. We don't have money for that. We could lose our house, everything we own." She began to sob again.

Anne hugged her. "*Shh*. I promised you I'd go to the bank first thing tomorrow and see if there are any documents in the book, and I still will. If there is anything in the book at all that belongs to Gus or Jeff or any indication it belongs to a member of the Kelley family, I'll bring it to you."

Evelyn stopped crying and hugged Anne. "Oh, thank you. I was right, you are very kind."

Anne hugged her back, then stood. "I have to get to my kids now. Don't worry, it's all going to be okay."

But as she walked toward the car, she couldn't help but wonder that she'd made the same assurance twice and what if she was wrong both times? After all, she'd been pretty wrong about Jenna. Maybe she was just as wrong about Evelyn and Rodney.

* * *

Later that afternoon, Anne was tidying up the house while Liddie played with her dolls in her room and Ben read on the laptop again. The ringing phone interrupted Anne's dishwashing.

Anne reached for a towel and dried off her hands, then grabbed the phone. "Hello," she said.

"Hello, Ms. Gibson," Ryan said.

"Hi, Ryan, did you want to talk to Ben?" Anne asked, positioning the phone into a more comfortable place on her shoulder.

"Actually, Uncle Alex says that if it's okay with you, we'd like for Ben to come over to play. We promise no football."

Anne chuckled. "Let me see if Ben's feeling up to it today. Hang on one second, okay?"

"Okay," he said.

She set the phone on the table and walked into Ben's room. "Sweetheart?"

"Yes, Mom?" Ben asked, looking up from the computer screen.

"Ryan is on the phone and wanted to know if you want to go over to his house to play," she said, smiling. "He promises no football, so I imagine you boys will play with your superhero figurines or something." This made her think about Rachel Winn again. She still was unsure about Rachel and her reclusive behavior.

"Um, not really," Ben said, shaking his head.

That was strange. Usually Ben jumped at the chance to go play at Alex's with Ryan. "Why not?" she asked. Had he and Ryan had an argument or disagreement of some kind?

He shrugged.

Anne headed back to the phone and picked up the receiver. Maybe Ben's ankle was still sore.

"Not today, Ryan. Maybe another day."

"Okay. Thank you, Mrs. Gibson." Ryan ended the call.

Anne set the phone back on the cradle then made her way back to Ben's bedroom.

He still sat with his gaze glued to the computer screen, reading that book again.

"Ben?" Anne asked, taking a seat near the end of his bed.

He looked up from the computer. "Yes?"

"I was just wondering why you didn't want to play with Ryan today? Did you two get in an argument?"

"No. Ryan and I are good."

He didn't make sense. "Is your ankle still sore?" she asked.

"It's fine. I should be able to play next weekend, just like Dr. Shields said I would. Coach already said I could start."

"Then why didn't you want to go over and play with Ryan?"

"I really want to read this book. I want to know what happens next," Ben said, his eyes lighting up, so like his father's used to when Eric had discovered a new author. "It's got me riveted," he added.

Anne chuckled. "Where'd you learn a word like *riveted?*"

"From my book," Ben answered. "And I like saying it because it sounds really cool." His smile spread from ear to ear.

Anne shook her head and stood. "Okay, but don't forget to clean up your room later. And take out the trash."

"I won't forget." Ben went straight back to using the laptop.

Anne walked out of the room, pulling the door closed behind her. She knew everyone got lost in a book from time to time — goodness knows she had more than a time or two, but still, this was somewhat concerning about his intense love of the series.

Chapter Twenty-One

Monday morning dawned bright and crisp, a perfect Pennsylvania October day. Anne swung by Coffee Joe's after dropping the kids off at school. After the week she'd had, she needed a treat. A nice cup of coffee to enjoy in the peace and quiet of the beautiful day.

Besides, she needed to kill a few minutes. Remi would open the library for her this morning while she waited for the bank to open.

"Hello, Anne," Coraline said as she crossed the coffee shop to join Anne at her little table. She set her coffee in front of her.

So much for her peace and quiet. Anne smiled, admonishing herself for her most uncharitable thoughts. "Good morning, Coraline. How are you this morning?"

"Enjoying the weather, of course. I do so love fall," Coraline said.

"I do as well."

"You know, Anne, dear, I've been thinking about our last conversation," Coraline said. "About Gus Kelley."

"Oh?" Anne asked, taking a sip of coffee. "What about him?"

"After I got back home, I remembered some of my friends in the garden club who talked about Jeff Kelley."

"What about him?" Anne had never met the man, but by the way Evelyn described the problems in her marriage because of her father-in-law, Anne couldn't imagine the man being much nicer than Gus, who everyone said was hard and mean.

"Well," Coraline began, "it seems like some in the garden club thought old Gus hadn't changed his will after all."

Anne narrowed her eyes. "What do you mean?"

Coraline lifted a shoulder. "It's just others talking, you understand. But a few of them think maybe Jeff altered his daddy's will after he realized he'd been cut out."

"Is there any proof of that?" Anne asked, remembering the panic in Evelyn's voice. Was it possible?

That would explain why Jeff was so hateful about Evelyn's mistake.

"I think it's just people talking is all." Coraline took another sip of her coffee. "I just thought I'd pass that information along to you, since we just talked about ole Gus and all."

Interesting.

Anne stood. "I see the bank's opening, so I'd better run. You have a good day, Coraline."

"You too, dear."

Anne walked briskly across the street to the bank. She didn't know whether to pray there was a copy of Gus's will in the book or not. All she knew is that she needed to check.

Inside, she was shown into the private area and left alone with her safety deposit box. She unlocked it and carefully pulled the book from the protective sleeve she'd slipped it in. Ever so carefully, she flipped pages.

No will plopped onto the table.

With great care, she fanned the pages again.

Nothing.

Just to be thorough, she went page by page, turning each one without pressure.

There wasn't anything stuck inside the book at all.

She let out a sigh—of relief or not, she couldn't tell—and returned the book to the sleeve, then secured it back inside the safety deposit box.

Well, at least she'd kept her promise. She could tell Evelyn with one hundred percent accuracy that there was no document in the book.

Which meant that she had even less of a clue who the book's rightful owner could be.

Back home, Anne walked into the library, intending to look up Evelyn Kelley's phone number and call her immediately. She didn't need to worry, however, as Evelyn and her husband stood at the front checkout counter, waiting on her.

"Well?" Evelyn asked, hope residing in her eyes.

"I'm sorry. There's nothing in the book. Nothing. Not even a slip of paper," she told them.

"Are you sure?" Evelyn asked.

"I'm positive," Anne answered. "I went through every single page. There's nothing there. I'm sorry."

"I don't believe you," Rodney said. His face twisted into something so ugly, so mean that if Anne wasn't seeing it for herself, she would never believe him capable.

Maybe he was more like his father and grandfather than Anne realized. And maybe Eric had been more than a little right about Anne.

"I want to see the book for myself," Rodney said, his voice rising a bit.

Anne glanced at Remi's wide eyes from across the library. She faced Evelyn and Rodney. "I'm sorry, but that's not going to happen." She crossed her arms over her chest. "Now, I need to ask you to either keep your voice down so you don't alarm other patrons or my staff, or you can leave," she said, her voice never wavering.

Rodney took a step closer to her. "I think you're lying. I think you found the—" He stopped as the door opened and Coraline came inside.

"I think you found some papers in there that belong to my family. I want them back. You can keep the book if it's so important to you, but I want those papers back," Rodney said.

"Hello, again, Anne, dear," Coraline said as she approached the threesome. "You accidently left your scarf at the coffeehouse. I tried to catch you at the bank, but you'd already gone, Rita said." She handed Anne her scarf.

Coraline turned to address Rodney Kelley. "Rita Sloan, that is, the bank manager. You know her, don't you Rodney? How are you?"

He opened his mouth, then shut it again. "Come on," he said to poor Evelyn, grabbing her arm and nearly dragging her out of the library.

"What was that all about?" Coraline asked Anne. "What papers was he carrying on about?"

Anne moved behind the counter and stored her purse. "Rodney claims the Poe book I found was part of his grandfather Gus's collection."

"Well, now, that could be true. Gus did have quite a rare book collection back in the day," Coraline said, leaning against the counter.

"That could be, but so far, there's no proof of anyone owning the book." Anne shrugged. "Anyway, Evelyn donated two boxes of books that belonged to Gus, without Rodney knowing. When he found out, he got angry because he claims some important papers were in the book."

"What kind of papers?" Coraline asked.

"According to Evelyn, Jeff and Rodney think it might be possible that a previous version of Gus's will, one that left everything to the garden club, might have been inside," Anne explained.

Coraline smoothed her old sweater. "I just wonder..."

"What?"

"What if it isn't a copy of an *old* will that was in there? What if it was the most recent will, and it left everything to the garden club. The way I hear it, old Gus swore Jeff wouldn't get a dime when he died."

Anne shrugged. "I don't know. What I *do* know is there are no papers in that book, will or otherwise. I checked between every single page."

"*Hmm.* Well, it is what it is," Coraline said.

"That it is." Anne smiled. "Thank you so much for bringing me my scarf. You didn't have to make a special trip just to bring it to me."

Coraline waved her off. "I needed the exercise. Besides, I enjoyed the walk. Now I'm ready to head on home. I have a sweater I need to finish knitting."

"Well, thank you again," Anne said.

After Coraline left, Anne decided she needed to e-mail her parents about the upcoming holiday schedules. The kids would so love to see their grandparents.

Anne opened the laptop Ben had left charging. Ben's book was still on the screen. Anne started to close the file, then stopped. That was odd. She hadn't noticed till now that the book was in a word-processing program format. When Ben had said he was reading on the computer, she'd assumed he'd downloaded an e-book.

When did Ben learn how to convert formats?

Anne stared at the header. As a librarian and an interested parent, she was aware of all the titles in the Coastal Club series, but she didn't recognize this title. And yet, it was oddly familiar.

A strange feeling knotted in the pit of Anne's stomach. Wait a minute. It was the title of the book coming out next that she and Grace had seen on the banner at the mall. This book wasn't even published yet!

How on earth did Ben get a copy of it?

Was it even possible? It was unethical if not illegal. Anne bit her lip as a wave of nausea rose up in her chest.

Dear God, please don't let him have pirated the manuscript from that fan fiction Web page.

* * *

"You will never believe this," Grace said as soon as Anne answered the phone.

"Hi, Grace," Anne teased.

"Hey. Now, guess what." Ever the journalist, that was Grace.

"I have no idea, so why don't you just tell me."

"I just got an anonymous tip that the Blue Hill Garden Club has retained Jessica Myer's law firm to look into Gus Kelley's final will." Grace spoke with the speed of lightning as she usually did when she was excited.

"Really?" The timing of the club's action was anything but coincidental, even if Anne believed in coincidences, which she didn't. She believed God had a master plan for everything.

"From what the caller said, the club's board met yesterday afternoon and voted unanimously to hire representation to look into the will. They'd received a tip that the will that ended up going through probate was a possible forgery and that Gus's real will is — are you ready for this? — hidden in an old book."

Anne gasped.

"What? Why the gasp?" Grace asked.

Anne quickly told Grace about Rodney and Evelyn Kelley's visit and about hers and Coraline's following conversation. "Could your anonymous tipster have been Coraline?" she asked Grace.

"Possibly. I didn't take the call, my receptionist did. She just said the caller was a woman."

"So it could have been Coraline," Anne said.

"I suppose it could've been her, but that doesn't seem like Coraline's style to me. She usually likes to...how do I say this? She likes to let people know she's the one in the know. Does that make sense?" Grace asked.

"Yes," Anne answered. Then again, Anne recalled the way Coraline had hemmed and hawed, avoiding Anne's questions about Rachel Winn. She'd thought that was out of character for Coraline as well. "Maybe we're wrong and Coraline can and does keep secrets."

Grace chuckled. "Now that would be front-page news for sure," she teased.

"It doesn't matter," Anne said. "I checked through every single page in the Poe book, and there isn't even a scrap of a will in there. Nothing. Nada. Nil."

"Too bad. I hate to see the Blue Hill Garden Club waste time and money on legal expenses."

"I don't know if it's a waste of time," Anne said. "Rodney Kelley and his dad sure seem intent about an old copy of a will. Who knows? Maybe Coraline's theory isn't so far-fetched. You never know."

"That's true. Anyway, how's Ben?" Grace asked, flipping subjects almost as fast as Liddie did.

"He's fine." Anne thought about the book she'd seen on the computer earlier. The more she thought about it, the more she considered it could be a fan-fiction type of thing. "Grace, do you know anything about fan fiction?"

"I do, actually. It's where rabid fans who love a series — movie series, books, even a couple of long-running television dramas — actually write installments to the series. For instance, the Narnia series. Fans are *still* writing adventures in Narnia, and that series was completed how many years ago?"

Anne had no idea about these rabid fanatics' habits. Maybe she should start paying more attention. "So the Coastal Club series that Ben and all the kids his age are so addicted to...do you think it has a fan fiction following?"

"Oh, most definitely. I'd bet they have all different types of fan fic going on."

"Do these fan fiction stories usually go by the title of the next real book in the series?" Anne asked.

"I'm not understanding. What do you mean?"

"Remember that banner we saw hanging in the Deshler mall?" Anne asked.

"Yeah. I remember. What about it?"

"Would it be common for one of these fan fiction stories to be named the same title of the next book coming out around Christmas?"

"Oh," Grace said. "I guess it happens. I just wouldn't think they'd want there to be confusion over it."

That was logical, but kids probably didn't know better. Or maybe they did. Anne sure didn't know. She thought about what she'd read over Ben's shoulder on the laptop. "Are these fan fiction installments usually any good?"

"Actually, most of them are," Grace said. "These people get so involved with the characters, the setting, the whole series that it's almost real to them. So they're really serious about what they write. There are forums all over the Internet for every fan fic group and they're fanatical about staying true to characters and the like."

That made sense. Anne herself had read books in a continuity series written by different authors, and sometimes the mannerisms and quirks of characters would fluctuate from book to book. That always annoyed Anne.

"As a librarian, shouldn't you know all this?" Grace asked in a teasing tone.

"Apparently I should learn," Anne replied. "Thanks for filling me in."

"Is there any particular reason you're asking?" Again, Grace's journalistic instincts were dead on target.

"Curious more than anything. I'd better run so I'm not late picking up the kids. Thanks again, Grace. I really appreciate you."

"Anytime, my friend. Bye."

Anne hung up the phone, thinking about the conversation. She'd just ask Ben about the book on the computer when he got home from school, plain and simple. They would deal with whatever it was.

Chapter Twenty-Two

What if there was another Edgar Allan Poe book?

The thought pulled Anne out of the shower later Monday night. The kids were already asleep by the time she wrapped the long terry cloth robe more tightly around her pajamas and crept down the stairs because the idea wouldn't let her rest, even though she was dead tired.

With all the focus on the rare Poe book, Anne hadn't even considered the possibility of there being another book by Edgar Allan Poe donated to the library for the book sale. It was entirely possible that there had been another Poe book, maybe not as old or rare as the one she'd found, and it was that book, not the one she found, that had the copy of the will tucked inside.

Now that she'd considered the possibility, there was no way she could ignore the boxes of books down in storage. Even though someone probably bought every title by Poe after Grace's write-up in the paper about the book Anne found, she had to check. Her sense of justice urged her downstairs and into the dark closet where the boxes of unsold books were stored.

She pushed the door open and reached for the light switch. Her toe slammed against something.

"Ouch!" Her cry was practically simultaneous with the cracking sound from her little pinky toe.

Hopping on one foot, she hit the switch and turned the light on. Tears stung her eyes. Oh, but that little stubbed toe hurt terribly!

She sat on one of the larger boxes holding some of Eric's belongings she was keeping for the kids and pulled the first box of leftover books to her. Anne carefully pulled off the packing tape. Thank goodness they hadn't layered the books but had packed them like they were shelved, spine side out.

Anne ran her finger over the spines as she read the title of each book. Plenty of great reads in the first box but no Poe titles.

She closed the box and re-stuck the packing tape as best she could, then slid the box out of the way. Grabbing the next box, she pulled it to her. This one wasn't as tall, so she had to bend farther over. Her glasses kept slipping down her nose as she yanked open the packing tape.

Through the Looking Glass, The Catcher in the Rye, The Scarlet Letter — all great books but not by Edgar Allan Poe.

After closing the box and moving on to the next one, Anne's back ached. And the strain on her eyes hurt. And the dust in the closet kept making her sneeze. And her toe still throbbed.

Yet she couldn't go to bed. She went through the third box.

The fourth.

Achoo!

Anne blew her nose and wiped her running eyes. She yawned.

Fifth box.

Her robe was officially filthy, its bottom hem sitting on the closet floor. Titles and more titles. Adult books. Children's books. Fiction. Nonfiction.

Sixth box.

This was getting seriously ridiculous. She ran her finger along the spines. *Third Edition of Roget's Thesaurus, Webster's Dictionary, College Edition, Tales of Edgar Allan Poe*...

Anne froze and backed up. The yawn that had been building evaporated. She pulled the book out of the box. A hardback, not very old and certainly not rare. The book-sale price tag on the cover read five dollars.

She slowly opened the book, flipping carefully through the pages. A yellowed envelope dropped into her lap. She held it up, and squinted to read the faded, flowery handwriting on the front. Finally, she made out the name of Gus Kelley.

Her heart hiccupped. She held what Evelyn and Rodney were so desperate to find.

She couldn't just give it to them. Not after hearing from Coraline. Not after learning about the Blue Hill Garden Club's retaining legal representation.

She'd call Michael. First thing in the morning. She closed the box, not even bothering with trying to get the packing tape to reattach. She'd deal with it later. Along with cleaning out the closet, which needed a through sweeping.

Anne stood and stretched. Yes, she'd call Michael in the morning, but now, sleep.

* * *

The clerk of court's office for Blue Hill's probate court was musty. It felt as if they'd already had the heater on this season, on high, and it worked well.

"Can I help you?" the older woman behind the counter asked, her gaze remaining fixated on the computer monitor in front of her. She popped her gum, then smacked it like a cow chewing on cud.

It took every ounce of Anne's self-control to grit her teeth and smile. "Yes, ma'am. I found a sealed envelope that I believe contains a copy of a will for someone who has passed," she said, pulling the envelope she'd found in the Poe book from her purse.

"Uh-huh." The woman popped her gum four times in rapid succession.

Anne had to remind herself not to ball the envelope by clenching her fist. "I spoke with someone in law enforcement and he advised me to bring it here."

"Uh-huh." She still didn't look up from her computer.

Anne coughed and slapped the envelope on the counter. "So I brought it here. Still sealed."

The woman stopped chewing her gum and finally looked at Anne. "You got it with you?"

"Yes, I do." She handed the woman the envelope. "Here."

The woman took it, shoved a rust-lined letter opener in the corner of the envelope, and ripped it open. Several folded pages fell out. The woman lifted it and read out loud. "Last will and testament of Gus Kelley." Her eyes widened and she locked stares with Anne. "This is Gus's will?"

"I just found it in a book," Anne said, suddenly ready to rid herself of the whole situation. Her stomach tightened.

"My sister's in the Blue Hill Garden Club. They've been talking about this will," the woman said with a nod. "How'd you come about it again?"

"My name is Anne Gibson. I'm the lib—"

"You're Edie's niece. The librarian, right?"

Anne nodded. "Yes. Anyway, we had a used-book sale and this envelope was found in one of the books donated."

"So you don't know if this is the most recent will of Gus's or not?" the woman asked.

"I don't. And honestly, I don't care. It's none of my business. I've done what any good citizen should do, and now I'm washing my hands of the matter."

The woman raised one of her eye brows. "Well, all righty then."

Anne gave a final nod, then turned and marched out of the stifling probate clerk of court's office. She gulped in the fresh, cool air once on the courthouse stairs.

In a way, she felt sorry for Evelyn. Maybe even Rodney. After all, they'd been right that there had been a copy of one of Gus's wills tucked between the pages of an Edgar Allan Poe title. They weren't lying about it, unlike Jenna Coleman.

The truly ironic part, Anne thought as she climbed into her car and started for home, was that they could've found the copy of the will themselves if they'd just browsed the books at the book sale. Or even if they'd thought to ask Anne if they could look through the leftover books. Surely there hadn't been that many Poe titles donated.

Maybe they'd like to have the actual book back?

It was a sad business, that was certain, when families couldn't get along and could only fuss and bicker all the time.

Anne remembered the minor little spats she and Eric used to have. Over the silly things like leaving the toilet seat up, not putting the cap back on the toothpaste, and forgetting to take the trash out. And now? Well, she'd give anything to be able to carry Eric's trash out or put the seat down after him or even cap the toothpaste for him.

People, families especially, should really take the time to realize how precious each loved one is and to tell them how much they're loved and appreciated. It was all too easy to take someone for granted.

Until they were gone.

Anne's mood had gone from melancholy to downright depressed by the time she made it home, but she'd made up her mind to return the Poe title back to the Kelley family. She collected the book, then drove over to Evelyn and Rodney's house.

She took a deep breath as she pressed the doorbell. The wait felt like forever until Evelyn, breathless, opened the door and pulled up short. "Anne. What are you doing here?"

Clutching the Edgar Allen Poe book to her chest, Anne offered a wavering smile. "May I come in, please?"

Evelyn glanced over her shoulder, then opened the door wider. "Sure. Come on in." She shut the front door behind them, then led Anne into the living room. "Would you like a glass of water? A cup of tea?"

Anne declined as she eased onto the couch. "No, thank you."

"So...," Evelyn sat on the chair across from Anne. "What can I help you with?"

"Well, I got to thinking last night. What if Gus's will *was* in an Edgar Allen Poe book, just not the one you thought?"

Evelyn sat up straight. "And?"

Before Anne could reply, Rodney walked into the room. "Well, Anne Gibson. What are you doing here?" he asked. Still well dressed, he wore his wariness like a suit jacket. That he was confused as to why Anne was in his living room was clearly evident on his face.

"As I was telling Evelyn, last night I thought perhaps Gus's will was hidden away in an Edgar Allen Poe book, just not the one you thought," Anne said.

His stare landed on the book she still clutched. "And?"

Anne licked her lips, suddenly feeling very foolish. "Well, I searched through all the boxes of books left over from the sale," she said.

"And?" Evelyn hurried her along.

"I found a Poe book. When I opened it, I found an envelope that implied Gus's will was inside," Anne said.

Evelyn shot to her feet, and Rodney took a step toward Anne. "You've brought it back to us?" he asked.

Anne nodded. "I know how important it is to have family belongings returned to you." She stood and handed over the book with shaking hands. "I hope that you'll treasure it as Gus must have."

Rodney flipped through the book, then held it by the cover and shook it. He stared back at Anne, his expression unreadable. "Where is it? Where's the will?" he demanded.

Anne's heart pounded. "Well…I called the police and was advised to turn it in to the clerk of court's office for due processing. That's what I did."

Rodney's eyes narrowed into slits. "What? Why would you do something so incredibly stupid?" He shook the book. "Why did you come here?"

Feeling as if her heart was ready to explode out of her chest, Anne took a step backward. "I—I'm sorry. I thought you would want to have the book back because it obviously meant a lot to Gus if he put a copy of his will inside," she stammered.

He threw the book onto the floor. It landed with a thud, open, pages to the floor.

Anne shook. How dare someone treat a book like that? She reached down and gently lifted the book. She smoothed the pages that had been bent in Rodney's tirade. "I thought you wanted the book for sentimental reasons. My apologies for such a mistake." She turned to leave.

"I'm sorry," Evelyn whispered as she followed her to the door.

Anne didn't reply, she just headed back to the library. Her downcast mood was even worse than before as she arrived and took the Poe book back into the library.

Bella's big smile that reached her eyes jerked Anne back into happier thoughts.

"Mrs. Gibson, Mrs. Farley called while you were out," Bella said.

Oh, so Mildred was back. Anne smiled. It was impossible not to smile when she thought about Mildred Farley.

Mildred was Aunt Edie's dear friend for many years, and as such, she had moved into somewhat of a stand-in role for Anne's great-aunt since Aunt Edie had passed away. Mildred was a combination of friend, great-aunt, grandmother, and confidante, and, as a longtime resident of Blue Hill, she had an in-depth knowledge of the town's history and people. But one of the things Anne loved most about Mildred was her gift of keeping secrets.

Anne checked the clock to see if she had time to run over to Mildred's and catch up. No such luck. She needed to leave to pick up Liddie in just a few minutes and then go directly to Ben's football team meeting. Grabbing her cell and running upstairs to get Liddie a book to read to keep her occupied during the football meeting, Anne quickly called Mildred.

"Hello, Anne. I've missed you and the kids," Mildred's comforting voice said over the line.

Anne smiled. "We've missed you. That's why I'm calling—to invite you to dinner tonight." She tucked Liddie's book into her bag and rushed into the kitchen. She checked the freezer and refrigerator. "Um, nothing fancy." Her mind flipped through quick recipes and the main ingredients she could pick up at the grocery store on her way home. "Just hamburgers or something."

"That sounds delightful. What time?" Mildred asked.

Anne shut the fridge and rushed down the stairs. Alex had said the meeting wouldn't last but maybe thirty minutes. She still had to run by the grocery store though. "How about five to five thirty?"

"Sounds great. What can I bring?"

"Just you."

Mildred's laugh warmed Anne all the way to her toes. "I'll bring some chips. See you about five."

Anne ended the call and headed out. She stopped at the checkout counter. "Bella, I'm making hamburgers for dinner. Would you and Remi like to join us? Mildred will be here."

Bella smiled. Everybody in Blue Hill loved Mildred to pieces. "Oh, we'd love that. I'll call Remi. What time?"

"As soon as we close the library at five. I've got Ben's team meeting after school, so I probably won't get back until a little before closing."

"Okay, Mrs. Gibson. We'll be here."

She rushed to the school and parked, thankful she didn't have to wait in the car-rider line since she had arrived about fifteen minutes later than usual. She made it to the school walkway just as the dismissal bell rang. She needed to catch Liddie before she started the walk down the ramp. Liddie would panic if she didn't see Anne's car.

"Anne! Anne!" Yvette called.

Midstep, Anne stopped and turned. "Hey, Yvette. How're you?" She waited until Yvette fell into step beside her to move forward.

"I'm fine. I'm glad I caught you here. I got another bracelet for Liddie to be able to give you as a replacement birthday present," Yvette said.

Anne frowned. "You didn't have to do that. She's probably forgotten all about it already."

"But *I* know." Yvette smiled. "Liddie did everything right. Becca was the one who went out of her way to be disobedient," Yvette said. "She's still grounded. I don't know when Greg will relent and let her off the hook."

Anne gave a little laugh. "I can only imagine."

"I knew it was expensive, being a Tiffany and all, but I had no idea just how much until he showed me the appraisal that he had to turn in to our insurance policy," Yvette said. "Wow, I'm glad the bracelet ended up safely with you. It could've been so much worse."

"Mommy, Mommy," Liddie ran straight at her and flung herself against Anne's legs.

Cindy and Becca ran right on Liddie's trail.

Anne hugged her daughter. "Hey there. How was school today?" She helped Liddie shrug off her backpack and held it for her.

"Good. Why aren't you in the car-rider line?" Liddie asked.

"Ben has a football meeting."

Liddie's smile fell off her face. "I'm gonna be so bored."

"I brought you your book from home," Anne said, pulling the book from her purse.

Liddie gave a half shrug.

"I have something for you too, Liddie," Yvette said. She reached into her pocket and pulled out a small little box.

"What is it?" Liddie asked, all smiles again.

Yvette leaned over and whispered in Liddie's ear. Liddie took the box, almost bouncing up and down with pure excitement. She held it out to Anne. "Here you go, Mommy. Your birthday present from me."

Anne smiled and took the box. She made a point to squat so she would be on Liddie's level as she opened the box.

Nestled inside against black velvet was a silver charm bracelet. It had a charm of a book dangling off the bracelet.

Anne gasped and looked at Yvette. "I can't accept this," she said.

"Mommy, it's my present to you," Liddie said, frowning.

Yvette leaned close to Anne. "It's not expensive. Trust me, the box probably is worth more than the bracelet."

Oh. Yvette must have used one of her boxes.

Face a little hot from embarrassment, Anne took the bracelet out of the box. "It's beautiful, Liddie. Thank you. I absolutely love it." She held out her arm and handed the bracelet to her daughter. "Will you put it on for me?"

While Liddie latched the bracelet, Anne's gaze sought out Yvette's. "Thank you," she mouthed silently.

Yvette smiled and nodded in silence.

"All done, Mommy. Look, the charm is a book 'cause you're a librarian and you love to read," Liddie said.

Anne kissed Liddie, then straightened. "So it is, Liddie. So it is. Thank you. I love it." She took Liddie's hand and headed to the gym, where the football team meeting would be held.

She did love the bracelet and the little book charm just as much as if it was a Tiffany's bracelet.

Actually, she loved it even more.

Chapter Twenty-Three

Hopefully five pounds of hamburger meat would be enough. Anne did a mental count: her family was three; Alex and Ryan, whom she'd invited since Ryan and Ben were acting like they were joined at the hip, so that made five; Mildred had called and asked if Coraline could come with her, so that made seven; Remi and Bella made it nine; and finally, Grace had called and said she needed to stop by to tell Anne something so Anne had invited her, which brought the total of people for dinner to ten.

Five pounds should be plenty, even if all the guys ate two large burgers. She'd gotten two packs of buns, so that would be enough for sixteen burgers. Definitely plenty.

"Ben, grab those two bags there," she said. She lifted the bag with the buns and handed it to Liddie. "Here, sweetie. You can carry this one."

"Did you hear what Coach Walden said about me, Mom?" Ben asked as he led the way up the back steps. He didn't even wait for her to respond before he continued. "He said I was one of the fastest runners he'd seen in a long time."

"I know. I heard that. I'm so proud of you," Anne commented as she unlocked their private entry door from the back stairs. "It's quite impressive."

"Yeah, and I'll get to start in the game this weekend." Ben set the two bags he'd carried in on the kitchen counter. "Ryan says we lost last week because I wasn't there."

"That's not a very nice thing to say, Ben. It could hurt the rest of the team's feelings," Anne said, pulling fresh lettuce and tomatoes out of the bags. "Just like with your baseball team, it's not about individual players, but the team as a whole."

"I know, Mom. Ryan was just trying to make me feel better about missing the game last weekend."

"Speaking of missing things, you need to get your homework done. We may be having company come over, but it is still a school night."

"Okay. I have to do some research on the Internet for English. Where's the laptop?" Ben asked.

In all the day's business, Anne had completely forgotten about the pirated book on the computer. At least she was pretty certain it was a pirated copy and not just fan fiction installments. It would be one pretty long installment if it were.

"Mommy, can I help you make the patties?" Liddie asked as she pulled a chair up to the counter. "I'm washing my hands first, just like I'm s'posed to."

She couldn't very well ask her son if he'd gotten one of the most sought-after books through ill-gotten gains with her daughter sitting right here. She'd have to talk with Ben later tonight after Liddie was in bed.

"The laptop's down in the library. And please tell Bella to lock up the library and come on up as soon as Remi gets here," Anne told Ben.

"Okay, Mom." Ben scrambled toward the stairs, sounding like a herd of buffalo.

"My hands are clean," Liddie announced.

"Good job." Anne tore off a paper towel and gave it to her. "You can start mixing the patties."

Anne opened the packages of hamburger meat and dumped all the ingredients on top in the big, plastic bowl. "Mix it up good," she told Liddie.

Liddie loved squishing everything together, which worked out well since Anne had always cringed over the task.

A knock sounded at the private entrance.

"Come in," Anne called out as she began washing the produce.

Alex and Ryan came in, grinning. "Where's Ben, Mrs. Gibson?" Ryan asked.

"Downstairs in the library, getting the laptop. Why don't you tell him to bring it up here?" Anne replied.

Ryan nodded and rushed out the door toward the stairs, grabbing the grand staircase's hand-carved mahogany banister. The top stair creaked as Ryan hit the wooden stair. "Don't run in the house—or the library," Alex called.

"It's okay. We did our fair share of running down those stairs when we were younger, remember?" Anne teased as she pulled out the knife and cutting board to slice the tomatoes.

"I remember your Aunt Edie hollered at me every single time I did too." Alex laughed.

Anne laughed as well. "She only did that for show. She was always partial to you. She let you get away with murder."

"She did not," Alex argued, but his eyes twinkled. He knew he'd always had a very special place in Edie Summers's heart.

"Mommy, the stuff's mixed," Liddie said.

"Okay, honey." Anne rinsed the knife and set it in the draining rack.

Alex stood in the doorway between the kitchen and the hallway. "What can I do to help?" he asked.

"Go light the grill," Anne said, turning to grab the lighter from the cabinet over the stove. She'd decided the weather was too beautiful and there were too many people to try and eat inside. They would eat in the backyard, on the picnic table. She'd added more lawn chairs to accommodate the growing guest list as well as laid some spare shawls and afghans on the back of the chairs. October evenings in Blue Hill could get a little chilly, and she wanted her guests to be comfortable and enjoy themselves.

Alex took the lighter and gave her a salute. "Yes, ma'am. One lit grill, coming right up."

Liddie laughed as he turned and headed out the door.

"Let me check the mixture," Anne said, looking over Liddie's shoulder. To be only five, Liddie did a pretty good job. "Okay, patty-making time."

Under Anne's direction, Liddie made a ball the size of her hand, then squashed it flat on top of the wax paper Anne had spread out over the baking sheets. She'd stack them three high to take down to the grill. They'd been making hamburger patties together for a year now, and Anne was proud to see how well Liddie did in the kitchen.

"Knock, knock," Bella called out. "Ben said we should come on up this way," she said, Remi right behind her, carrying a grocery bag.

"We brought some chips and dip and a pack of paper plates," Remi said.

"Thank you. I completely forgot to get paper plates at the store," Anne said, taking the bag and setting it on the counter.

"What can we do to help?" Bella asked.

"Well, if you really want, you can help Liddie finish making the patties," Anne said.

Bella and Remi both moved to the sink to wash their hands. "This is one of our favorite kitchen duties," Bella said.

"We always liked making puppy paw prints in the patties. It freaked Mom out," Remi said, grinning.

"Puppy paw prints?" Liddie asked, all ears.

"I'll show you," Bella said. "Maybe you can freak out Ben and Ryan."

"Speaking of Ben and Ryan, what are those two doing?" Anne asked.

"Looking at something on the laptop," Remi answered. "Is that okay?"

Anne nodded, but she wasn't really sure it was okay. If Ben had pirated a book, it definitely wasn't okay with her.

"Grill is lit and getting hot," Alex said, handing Anne back the lighter. "And Grace just pulled up. She has the makings for s'mores, so I told her just to put everything on the picnic table. Hope that's okay."

"That's perfect," Anne turned to Remi and Bella, even as she started shoving items to take outside in one of the grocery bags: spatula, a roll of paper towels, red-checkered plastic tablecloth, and the packages of hamburger buns. "Are you okay here?"

"We're good, Mrs. Gibson," Bella said.

"Yeah, we got this. Want us to take the burgers down when we're done?" Remi asked.

"Please. And the sliced cheese too, if you can," Anne said.

"You got it," Bella said.

Anne grabbed the lettuce and tomatoes and put them in a different grocery bag, then added in plastic cups before she threw in the squeeze bottles of ketchup, mustard, and mayonnaise.

"Here, let me carry those," Alex said, taking the bags from her.

From the fridge, she grabbed the jug of apple cider she'd bought at a roadside stand and followed Alex down the back stairs.

"Hey there," Grace called out.

"Hi." Anne let Alex dig out the tablecloth from the bag, and he and Grace smoothed it over the picnic table. She then began unpacking the grocery bags, with Grace's and Alex's help.

"So what did you have to tell me?" Anne asked Grace as soon as Alex headed back upstairs to see what the boys were getting into.

"You know that every afternoon, I send my receptionist to the courthouse to pick up the reports of everything going on in court, right?"

Anne nodded, anchoring the edge of the tablecloth with the stack of paper plates. Remi and Bella led the way down the back stairs, Liddie right behind them. "Can I swing, Mommy?" she asked.

"Sure, sweetie," Anne answered Liddie, then looked back at Grace.

"Well," Grace continued, "the probate judge put it on the docket to review a newly discovered will of one Gus Kelley."

"Really?" Anne asked.

Grace nodded. "Yep. I'm guessing that's the will you took in?"

"I guess." Boy, they sure were moving fast on this one. Anne felt even sorrier for Evelyn Kelley. Judging by the way Rodney had acted earlier, Anne couldn't help but be curious about what the will of Gus Kelley's that she found had to say. Rodney had unmistakably been upset she'd turned the will in to the clerk of courts instead of him. Just what was in that will?

Alex returned with Ben and Ryan on his heels. "I'm going to flip the burgers. They should be ready pretty quickly," Alex returned, heading to the grill.

"Mom, I'm letting Hershey out to play, okay?" Ben hollered.

Anne nodded, her attention still on the will situation.

Grace helped set out bags of chips and napkins. "I also learned that Jessica Myer's law firm had received notification of the review as well as Jeff Kelley's attorney."

"Well, I did what I had to do. From this point on, it's in the justice system's hands and not mine. Thank goodness," Anne said.

"If you don't mind, I'm going to run inside and wash my hands," Grace said as the sound of tires crunched on the drive.

Anne turned toward the private parking area. She smiled as Mildred and Coraline stepped from the car and headed to the backyard. Anne rushed to Mildred and gave her a big hug. The familiar scent of Chanel No. 5 tickled Anne's nostrils. Mildred had worn the same perfume since, well, ever since Anne could remember. The scent always made Anne feel like she was at home.

"I've missed you." Mildred smiled at Anne and they split apart just as Liddie led Remi and Bella down the stairs.

Liddie ran over and gave Mildred a big hug.

"Burgers are ready!" Alex announced, setting a platter on the picnic table.

The kids ran to the table, as did Hershey.

"Hershey, sit," Anne ordered. The beautiful chocolate Labrador dropped to his haunches.

Ben and Ryan stuck meat on buns and dumped potato chips on their plates. "Can we go sit by the tree to eat, Mom?" Ben asked. "We can pull up chairs and use some as tables too."

"Don't you want to put anything else on your burger?" Anne asked, then looked at Ryan. "Some ketchup, maybe?"

Both boys shook their heads.

"Okay." Anne shrugged. "You can eat by the tree."

The boys raced off, Hershey following like a bloodhound.

Anne turned to her daughter. "What do you want on your hamburger, Liddie?"

"I want it just like Ben's," Liddie said.

"Seriously?" Anne asked.

Liddie nodded. "And I want to sit by the tree to eat too."

"Okay." Anne walked Liddie over and got her situated near the boys, then returned back to the picnic table. She fixed her own plate and sat beside Mildred. "So tell me about your trip. How was it?" She took a bite of the burger.

"Simply amazing. The weather in Little Rock was wonderful. Warmer than here, but it did rain a little," Mildred said.

"Really? What was the scenery like? I've never been to Arkansas." Anne took another bite of her burger, then wiped her mouth as mustard oozed out the corner of her mouth.

Alex winked at her. Her face went red, but she threw him the thumbs-up sign.

Mildred set down her cup of cider. "The leaves were starting to fall off the trees and the grass was green. Arkansas is so open and spacious. My cousin's children had so much room to romp around. It was like a different world from here in Blue Hill."

"How enchanting," Coraline commented.

"The sky was so blue, and the clouds were as white as snow. It was nice to see such natural beauty that's so different from the beauty here. In my cousin's yard she had a little stream lining the end of her property. I found some beautiful rocks called quartz crystals. It's a very nice place to visit," Mildred said.

"Well, we might have to take a trip to Arkansas in the future," Anne said.

Mildred nodded. "Don't get me wrong, you all know how much I love Blue Hill, but it was a nice little vacation. I enjoyed visiting with my maternal side of the family. But enough about me," Mildred said, leaning closer to Anne and setting her wadded-up napkin on top of her plate. "Coraline filled me in on most of what's been going on at the library while I've been gone. I'm so sorry there was such a mystery about that Edgar Allan Poe book. If only I'd known…"

Anne's back went ramrod straight. "Wait a minute, Mildred. Are you saying you know who the rightful owner of the book is?"

Mildred nodded. "Of course, dear. You are."

Chapter Twenty-Four

Surprise stole Anne's ability to speak. Several moments of silence passed. The afternoon cool breeze flitted through the dried leaves on the old oak tree. Almost as if at a great distance, Hershey barked, followed by Liddie's excited squeals as Ben and Ryan pushed her high in the tire swing.

"What do you mean by that?" Anne finally asked Mildred.

"Well, dear, it's quite the tale," Mildred began.

Everyone seated around the table got very still and very quiet. The children played on the tree swing a few hundred feet away.

"Last year, before Edie passed away, she'd taken to reading some darker works than she usually read. She'd picked up a couple of Edgar Allan Poe pieces and found she truly enjoyed them." Mildred smiled and stared off in the distance, clearly remembering the past. "Edie said he was a burdened genius who'd been misunderstood."

Anne smiled. How many times had she and Aunt Edie had such discussions about J. D. Salinger's mindset when he'd written *The Catcher in the Rye*? Anne had so many happy memories of Aunt Edie that she would forever cherish.

"Anyway," Mildred continued, "on one of my trips, I visited a rare-book store. Imagine my surprise when I found a first edition of Edgar Allan Poe's *Tales of the Grotesque and Arabesque* sitting on the shelf for sell. Of course, the owner and shopkeeper was not a bibliophile at all and had no clue of the value of what he had." She shook her head. "He had it just sitting on the shelf. No protection, no nothing."

"So you bought it?" Anne asked.

Mildred nodded. "I bought it for Edie. For her birthday." She smiled. "I still have the receipt."

Everyone was quieter than quiet, except for Ben, Ryan, Liddie, and Hershey playing in the yard.

"What happened then?" Alex asked.

"Well, I bought her birthday card and set it on top of the present—in this case, the book, just like I always do for everybody, as soon as I buy them. Set it in the closet like I always do." Tears shimmered in Mildred's lively eyes.

Anne found herself blinking back her own tears.

Coraline cleared her throat. "Obviously, you never gave it to her," she prompted her friend from across the picnic table.

Mildred sniffed and shook her head. "*Mmm*. No. I didn't get the chance to give it to her." She gave a little cough. "I imagine it just sat in my guest bedroom closet, the envelope with her name sitting on top of it."

Anne squeezed Mildred's hand under the table.

"So how did the book get from your guest bedroom to the used-book sale?" Remi asked.

"I'm not positively sure how that happened, for certain, but I have an idea," Mildred said. "Edie and I passed books back and forth all the time."

Anne nodded. "Oh, I know you two did. Several times I'd start reading a book at Aunt Edie's then go home for a few days, and when I came back, the book would be gone. It had either been yours and Aunt Edie had given it back, or it was Aunt Edie's and she'd loaned it to you." That was the main reason it had taken Anne almost two months to finish *Gone With the Wind*.

Mildred's smile looked like she held the hint of a secret. "After Edie passed, I took time to grieve for my friend. I had a couple of boxes that just sat in the guest room, and whenever I'd find a book that belonged to Edie, I'd just put it in there." She smiled at Anne. "Even though by that time, you had already agreed to accept the appointment as librarian and oversee the renovations, I knew there was no hurry to collect books."

Anne met Alex's stare across the table and smiled at the memories. The bequest from Aunt Edie had come at the perfect time. Even though she'd been devastated to lose her beloved aunt not long after losing Eric, the chance for her and the kids to start over in her hometown was ideal. God had a good plan for her and her children. She just needed a little prompting to remember to trust Him all the time.

She'd had quite the adventures with Alex during the renovations. The strain in their friendship had begun to heal in her first weeks back in town. Now, Anne was delighted to think of Alex as close of a friend as ever before. Just like Wendy or Grace or Reverend Tom.

"That still doesn't explain how the book got from your house to the book sale," Bella gently prompted.

"Well, soon after Edie passed, my cousin Annabeth came for a visit. Sweet girl that she is, she understood that I was taking the time to grieve for my best friend. She came and did laundry. Cooked. Was just *there* in the house with me," Mildred explained.

Anne nodded. Her mother had come and stayed with her and Ben and Liddie after Eric died. Not that there was anything anybody could say or do to take away the pain or hurry the grieving process, there wasn't, but just having someone there to do normal things... it just helped.

"She saw me pick up a couple of books and take them to the boxes I had been compiling of Edie's books I wanted to bring to you, Anne. She inquired, and I explained."

"Mommy, look how high Ben swung me," Liddie called out.

Anne looked at her daughter and smiled, then turned her attention back to Mildred, although she was pretty sure that she and everyone else at the table could guess what happened.

"I don't know for sure, but I'm betting Annabeth saw the Edgar Allan Poe book in the closet with the envelope with Edie's name on it and thought it was Edie's, so she slipped it into the box with the other books." Mildred shook her head. "Once the boxes were filled, I didn't go through them again."

"Well, why would you?" Coraline asked. "You thought you'd been the only one to sort them to begin with."

"Right," Mildred said with a nod. "A few months later, I brought the boxes over here to you, Anne, dear. Do you remember?"

"Now that you've mentioned it, I do remember you bringing those boxes. It wasn't too long after the library first opened, right?" Anne nodded.

"You mean the ones you had us put in the attic? Right after we started volunteering at the library?" Bella asked.

"The ones that weighed as much as rocks?" Remi added on to Bella's question.

Anne smiled. "Yes, the ones that were as heavy as rocks. That's right, I had you two put them in the back alcove of the attic."

Mildred chuckled. "It was a good amount of books, now that I think about it. Two big boxes."

Remi grinned. "I remember. The bottoms were reinforced with pink duct tape."

"Just so you know, I loved the beautiful shade of pink of that duct tape that held everything together," Bella said.

Everybody laughed, but Anne's mind went to the Edgar Allan Poe book sitting in her safety deposit box at the bank.

Technically, the book belonged to Mildred.

Anne took a deep breath. "Mildred, I'll go to the bank first thing in the morning and get the book out of the safety deposit box and bring it to you."

"Whatever for?" Mildred asked.

Anne shook her head. "Maybe you didn't even realize its worth. The Poe book you bought Edie is worth twelve to forty thousand dollars."

"I realize that, dear. I did have it appraised." Mildred smiled. "I'm not as clueless as the man I bought it from."

Everybody chuckled.

"Actually," Mildred said, "I gave it a little thought on the drive over here. I want you to have it, Anne. Edie would want that, I think."

Anne's mouth went dry. "I can't accept such a valuable book, Mildred."

"Don't be a silly nincompoop. It's a gift. Of course you can."

Oh, she'd love it all right, but she just couldn't. It didn't feel right on so many levels. "I'm sorry, Mildred. I just wouldn't feel right about it."

Mildred tapped her chin. "Then how about this—how about I loan the library the book to display it here, in the library, in one of the cases. To honor Edie, and the poor burdened genius who'd been misunderstood, of course." Mildred smiled and winked at Anne. "What do you think? Would that be okay?"

Anne smiled, and nodded.

Coraline clapped. "I love happy endings."

"Perhaps you could put a picture of Mildred and Aunt Edie beside the book in the case." Grace said. "What do you think?"

"That sounds like a wonderful idea," Anne said. "And I have just the picture in mind of you two that will be perfect." It was a photo she'd snapped herself on her last visit to Blue Hill before Aunt Edie had passed silently in her sleep.

Mildred and Aunt Edie had been having a cup of coffee, both of them curled up on the loveseat in Edie's sitting room. An afghan covered both their legs, and both Mildred and Edie had books open in their laps. Anne had bounded into the room like she'd done since childhood, and happened to catch both ladies midlaugh.

It was one of Anne's favorite photos of the lifelong friends, perfectly depicting their love of coffee, books, and happiness over spending time together.

"Yes, I have the perfect picture to use." Anne smiled at Mildred. Mildred smiled back as she reached out to touch Anne's hand. "Edie would be proud of you, dear. As I am."

* * *

"I'm happy the mystery has been solved," Grace told Anne as she helped throw all the trash from the picnic table away in the oversized trash bag.

Remi and Bella had already taken the leftovers and condiments upstairs to put away in Anne's kitchen.

"Me too," Anne told Grace. It felt, well, still a little unsettled.

"I can't wait to write up the article. I can see the headline now: 'Rare Book Back Where It Belongs.'" Grace laughed.

Anne shook her head and reached for another dirty paper plate, almost tripping over Hershey. She started to holler for Ben. Speaking of books. "Grace, can you finish up here? I need to talk to Ben for a minute."

"Sure. I'll help Alex finish up," Grace answered.

Anne walked around to the big tire swing, where Ben, Ryan, and Liddie were all playing. The big old tractor tire hung on a thick nylon rope that suspended from a tall, strong oak. Hershey followed her from the table, finally realizing he wasn't going to get so much as a chip, and plopped down under the tree in the shade.

The grass underneath the tire was scarce where the kids had dragged their feet to stop the swing. Lots of long weeds and wildflowers grew on the slant down the back side of the hill. During spring, the front of the library's yard was filled with the bluebells, but the back side, with the wildflowers bending at random, always struck Anne as just as beautiful.

Anne stood off to the side of the tree. "Ben, can you come here?" Anne asked, motioning for Ben to come stand by her.

Ben stopped the swing and got off. Liddie hopped in the swing as soon as he stepped away. Ryan tickled Liddie, then gave her a big push.

"Is everything okay, Mom?" Ben asked as he joined Anne.

She took a deep breath, wishing she could just forego this entire discussion.

But she couldn't.

"Well, a few days ago I went to e-mail your grandparents about the upcoming holidays. Since you were the last one to use the laptop, I had to hunt down where—" Anne began.

"I'm sorry, Mom. I should've charged it, but I think I forgot. I'm sorry. It won't happen again," Ben apologized.

Anne held up her hand to stop him. "Let me finish, Ben. That's not what I wanted to discuss with you." She leaned against the tree, its bark digging into her side.

"Sorry."

She nodded. "Anyway, you left your book open on the screen. I was going to just close the tab so that you wouldn't lose your place, but I noticed it was in Word format."

Ben's face tightened and he paled a little. Did he realize he was busted?

Anne continued. "I looked at the header and didn't recognize the title. So I did some research. That book isn't due to be released for a couple of months!"

Ben's gaze fell to his old, beat-up sneakers. His eyes squinted in the setting sun, and he wouldn't make eye contact with Anne. He kept his stony silence.

"Ben, how did you get a copy of that book?" Anne asked, getting more than a little annoyed at her son's silence. Why wouldn't he just admit it was a pirated copy? That's what it had to be. There was no other logical explanation.

"It's just a book, Mom," Ben finally mumbled as he scratched the back of his neck, looking off towards the back of the hill.

So he wouldn't even admit it when there was no doubt he was busted. "No, Ben, it isn't *just a book*. This book hasn't been released yet. It's not available in stores." Couldn't he realize he was caught?

Anne was so disappointed she could barely speak. "Ben, tell me, where on earth did you get a copy of a book that isn't even due to be released for a few more months?"

He rolled a rock on the ground with the toe of his dusty sneaker. "It's not that big of a deal, Mom. I didn't break any rules or anything."

Anne let out a slow breath meant to calm her. It didn't do the trick.

She tried again. "This *is* a big deal, Ben. This is serious. So I will ask one more time. How did you get a copy of that book?" A red-hot heat rose from her chest and fanned across her face.

Ben looked away and set his jaw, just like Eric used to do when he would refuse to argue with Anne over something silly or petty.

Anne sighed in frustration. "Ben, tell me how you got that manuscript right now or you are grounded." Anne crossed her arms over her chest.

Out of the corner of her eye Anne caught Coraline and Mildred approaching. She groaned. This wasn't the time for Ben to pull his stubborn routine.

"Ben, it's okay. You can tell your mom," Coraline said as she reached out and put her hand on Ben's shoulder.

"What on earth are you talking about?" Anne asked, utterly confused.

"Okay, Mom, you were right. It is the soon-to-be published book in the Coastal Club series. When I was sitting in the Nonfiction Room reading the fan fiction sites and stuff, well..." He glanced at Coraline, who nodded. "Well, the author came up to me. I couldn't believe it!"

Anne looked from her son to Coraline. She didn't understand, but surely Coraline wasn't condoning this tall tale?

Ben kept on, as if he needed to purge the story from within him. "At first I thought she was joking, especially since I always thought the author was a guy. But she promised me she was the author of the Coastal Club series. She felt bad that I had to miss my first game. She saw me rereading the other books in the series and hanging out on the site's forum and stuff. She gave me the manuscript to read as long as I didn't show it to anybody else and I didn't reveal her real identity. How could I refuse?" Ben explained.

Anne pushed off the tree. What did Ben mean, *her real identity*? A best-selling author? Here? In Blue Hill?

Coraline nodded at Ben.

Anne's mind raced for the connection.

Who was always on a laptop in the library? Who always seemed to be lost in her own little world? Who would go swing on the swing set at night?

Who had a boy's superhero figurine in her sweater pocket?

"Rachel Winn is R. W. Winger?" Anne asked Coraline.

"Yup. You guessed it right. I wondered how long it would take you to figure it out," Coraline said as she shifted her balance from one foot to the other.

"Of course." Anne shook her head, then realized she had something else she needed to say to her son.

"Ben, I'm sorry for accusing you of stealing the manuscript and threatening to ground you," Anne apologized.

"It's okay, Mom. I guess it did look a bit odd," Ben said.

Anne smiled at her son, so grateful that he hadn't stolen anything or done anything bad. She was also amazed that he had kept such a secret, even under the threat of being grounded.

"Can I go play now?" Ben asked.

"Go ahead," Anne said.

As Ben ran back over to the tire swing with Ryan and Liddie, Anne turned to face Coraline.

"Rachel Winn. That's why you hemmed and hawed when I asked you about her," Anne said.

"I couldn't tell you. Rachel said if anyone found out, she'd have to leave. She's on a tight deadline and came to Blue Hill so her anonymity would allow her to finish the book on time," Coraline explained.

"How, exactly, did you know who she was?" Anne asked.

Coraline smiled. "Now, you know I like to protect our townsfolk, so when a stranger comes and stays, I make it my business to find out what they're up to." She smiled even wider. "Just for caution's sake, of course."

Just then Hershey started to lick Coraline's hand. Coraline bent down to pet Hershey. "I wouldn't have said anything, but poor Ben was truly between a rock and a hard place."

"Coraline told me just today when Rachel stopped by to give Coraline back one of the bird books she'd borrowed for research," Mildred said.

Anne shook her head. "I would have never guessed." But it sure made a lot of sense.

Finally!

Chapter Twenty-Five

As Anne sipped her coffee at the front counter at the library, she scanned the newspaper headlines. She liked to keep up with the current events. It helped to know a little bit so when someone needed to go through the library archives to find something, she could better help them.

The headline was printed in big bold black letters: "Jeff Kelley On Trial." Grace's byline was right underneath.

Anne took another sip of coffee and read the article.

A Blue Hill judge will soon oversee the trial of Jeff Kelley, who confessed to Blue Hill authorities that he forged his own father's will after the true and correct legal copy of the will unexpectedly surfaced. Kelley is charged with one count of felony forgery. He is released on his own recognizance pending a trial date. A few people spoke on Jeff Kelley's actions, using words such as shameless and wicked to describe his scheme, which cheated the Blue Hill Garden Club out of approximately forty-five thousand dollars.

Authorities estimate Kelley, if convicted, could face a seven- to ten-year sentence in federal prison. They had no comment when asked if they are investigating whether Jeff Kelley acted alone or if his son, Rodney, and/or Rodney's wife, Evelyn, were involved. Jeff Kelley confessed to acting alone, and neither Rodney nor Evelyn have yet been implicated in the crime.

Anne set down the paper, her heart heavy.

God, please give Rodney and Evelyn strength through this rough time. Even if they didn't commit any crime, I imagine it's hard enough to see a loved one put on trial.

At least Jeff had confessed. That had to account for something, didn't it? She couldn't even begin to imagine what Evelyn had to be feeling.

Just then Remi walked in, all smiles as usual. Just seeing the young woman's smile made Anne's day a little brighter. "Good morning, Remi," Anne greeted her.

"Same to you." Remi nodded. "Thanks again for the cookout last night. It was good, and Bella and I both enjoyed ourselves. You always include us and make us feel like part of your family. We really like that."

Anne reached out and hugged the bright girl. "So have you seen the newspaper today?"

"No, I was in a rush. What's going on?" Remi asked, taking a seat by Anne.

"Grace got a scoop."

"Really?" Remi asked.

Anne nodded. "It's good for her career that she got a scoop, but the information itself..." She shook her head. "Jeff Kelley confessed to forging his own father's will."

"How terrible." Remi frowned.

Anne nodded. "I know. They estimate that if he's convicted, he could face a seven- to ten-year sentence."

"That's sad, but what he did was wrong, and now justice must be served," Remi said, but her voice sounded like she was as heartbroken as Anne felt.

"I can't even imagine being in Evelyn's shoes right now," Anne said. Maybe she could call Evelyn later. Offer to help her.

"I will keep her in my prayers," Remi said.

"As will I." Anne stood and reached for her coffee cup. "Even though what he did was wrong, it's still got to be hard on the family. All of them."

"I bet so. I know she will get through it somehow. God doesn't abandon his children. Ever," Remi said.

Anne smiled at Remi's statement. It was so true.

* * *

Anne clutched Liddie's hand tightly as she led her up the silver metal bleachers. After Anne found a decent spot, she dusted off the few pine needles and sat down. The team was on the field doing warm-ups. The clock read five minutes until game time.

That familiar knot was back in Annie's stomach.

God, please give Ben everything he needs to do the best he can. I know he really wants to win. Since this is his first game, please ease any nerves.

"Mommy?" Liddie tugged on the sleeve of Anne's blue jacket.

"Yes, sweetie?" Anne glanced around for Alex. She spotted him, sitting higher and on the fifty-yard line.

"Which one is Ben?" Liddie asked. "They all kind of look alike."

Anne smiled at Liddie. "Ben is the one with the number nine on his shirt," Anne said as she pointed in Ben's direction.

"Oh, I see him!" Liddie smiled as she watched her brother stretch. She was too young to fully understand football, but she looked like she was just as excited as Ben was when he left for school this morning.

Anne checked the time left on the clock—one minute until the referees in their black-and-white stripes would blow the first whistle.

"Whew! I made it," Wendy said, plopping down on the bleacher beside Anne. "I was a little worried I wouldn't get here in time. Traffic. Who knew?"

"The game is going to start soon," Anne said, pulling Liddie closer.

Just Wendy's presence made Anne feel better.

The time ran out on the clock, and a foghorn sounded.

Liddie jumped. To be honest, so did Anne. She laughed and told Liddie, "That means the game is starting."

On the sidelines, all the cheerleaders stood in formation and chanted a loud cheer. Anne was impressed—she hadn't realized the flag football league had cheerleaders. Maybe Liddie would like to be one when she got a little older.

No, she wouldn't think about that just yet. Cheerleaders could fall off pyramids and get hurt…

The home team, Ben's team, had a lot of fans in the stands along with Anne, Wendy, and Alex. They clapped as the team got the ball first.

Christian, the quarterback, took a step off the line of scrimmage, looked downfield, then threw the ball at Ben. Anne held her breath. Ben caught the ball and began to run. After about a yard he ran faster.

And faster. Ben was halfway to the goal line and still running. One lone defender made a last-ditch dive to tackle Ben before he crossed the goal line. TOUCHDOWN! The fans cheered and cheerleaders did acrobatic tricks and jumps.

Anne stood up and screamed. Loudly.

Liddie looked at her as if she'd lost her mind while Wendy chuckled. Even Alex turned from his seat and grinned at her.

She didn't care. That was her baby on the field who had just made a touchdown!

The band launched into music and the cheerleaders danced around, their little skirts kicking up blue and white. Liddie watched in wonder as the cheerleaders performed a routine with flips and stretches that made Anne's back hurt just watching.

For the rest of the quarter, Christian didn't throw Ben the football and Ryan played great when he was in the game. He even got to pull the opposing team member's flag when he had the ball. The crowd went crazy over that one. Anne noticed that Tim Banks, Michael and Jennifer's son, also played on the team. He was good too, or so Anne figured. The crowd all exploded over something he did, so that had to be a good thing.

At halftime Ben, Ryan, Christian, Tim and the rest of the team went into the field house.

"Is it over, Mommy?" Liddie asked.

"No, honey, it's halfway over. Would you like some French fries or a hot dog?" Anne asked.

"I want a hot dog. With ketchup and mustard. Oh, and relish. Can I have that, please, Mommy?"

"Sure." Anne stood, wondering how she was going to juggle the drinks and hot dogs and keep up with Liddie too.

"Why don't I keep an eye on Liddie while you go to the refreshment hut?" Wendy asked.

"Thanks. Do you want something?" Anne asked.

"No thanks. Hannah's attempting to make chili tonight, so I'd better not."

The band played the Blue Hill high school's fight song as well as many other songs. The cheerleaders did a few dance routines as well, so the refreshment line wasn't terribly long.

Anne bought hot dogs and also a soda to share with Liddie. Turning to put condiments on the hot dogs, she felt someone staring at her.

"Hello, Anne," Donald Bell moved out from a crowd of people and snatched the soda just before it slipped from her hands.

"Hi, Donald. Thanks. I need another hand or two."

"What are you doing here?" he asked.

"My son, Ben, plays." She squirted ketchup and mustard on the dogs. Liddie would just have to get over the lack of relish. "What about you?"

"My nephew's on the team. First time."

Anne nodded. "It's Ben's first time too. He seems to be really enjoying it. Mike Walden seems like a great coach."

"Yeah, my nephew's crazy about him."

The awful, loud buzzer sounded again and the home team returned to the field.

"Well, I'd better get back to Liddie, my daughter," Anne said.

"Oh. Of course." He grabbed one of the carrying trays and shoved her soda in it before handing it to her. "It was nice to see you here, Anne. Enjoy the game."

"You too, Donald. Thanks." Anne might not be ready to date just yet, but Donald was a nice man. Who knew, maybe the day was approaching where she would be able to let go of the past.

But to dive back into the scene of dating? Anne didn't know if she ever would be ready to go back through that.

She headed to the bleachers and caught Alex's eye. He smiled and nodded at her as she passed.

Anne scooted along the bleacher next to Liddie, handing her daughter her hot dog just as Ben and the rest of the team finished doing a few warm-ups. The buzzer blasted the crisp October air again announcing that halftime was over.

The game carried on. Soon it was the fourth quarter with two minutes left. The score was tied. Ben was in his position to receive the ball from the quarterback.

Along with all the other parents, Anne was on her feet. Screaming. The ball was in play and the clock started to tick down precious seconds.

Six. Five.

Christian had the ball in his hands. He stepped back into the quarterback pocket and looked way, way downfield.

Ben, and only Ben stood midfield, his hands out.

Four.

Christian threw the ball. It seemed to hang in the air.

Three.

Ben caught the ball, then turned and ran toward the end zone.

Two.

Ben jumped into the air, holding the ball out in front of him.

One.

Just before the clock let out its loud buzz, the ball made it across the line, which put them in the lead.

Ben's team had won!

Anne and Liddie stood up and cheered with the rest of the fans. She would be hoarse tomorrow from all the yelling, but she didn't care.

Ben met Anne by the bleachers, grinning from ear to ear. "Did you see me? Did you see me make the winning touchdown?"

"Great job, Ben! That was awesome. I am so proud of you," Anne said as she hugged her sweaty son.

"Christian said he almost didn't throw it to me. He didn't think he could throw it that far, but he figured we had to do something, so he took the chance. And he got it all the way to me. We won!" Ben's face was flushed with excitement and exertion. A very healthy combination.

"Go, Ben. You caught the ball a lot," Liddie said, her own sweet voice filled with excitement.

"Thanks, Mom. Thanks, Liddie," Ben said.

"How about some milkshakes to celebrate? Does that sound good?" Anne asked as she looked at Ben and Liddie.

"Yeah." They both answered in unison.

Then they all got in Anne's Impala. They drove to the drugstore. Placing their order to go, Ben got a vanilla shake, Liddie got a chocolate shake, and Anne got a strawberry shake.

On the drive home, Anne remembered Whom to thank.

God, thank You for letting Ben play well – and not get hurt.

* * *

Anne checked in some books that had been dropped off in the basket while Remi shelved returns. After all the excitement, Anne enjoyed the normal "boring" work routine.

The library door whooshed open and Rachel Winn walked inside wearing her ever-present gray cardigan.

Anne studied her for a split second, then went back to checking in the books, realizing that she'd been staring. She didn't want to give away the fact that she knew who she was.

As was her habit, Rachel rushed into the History Room and set her laptop on the table.

Anne couldn't help but wonder if she'd made her deadline. There was no way she could ask, of course, but she did wonder. She turned to set the last couple of books she'd checked in on the cart for Remi when she caught sight of Rachel in the doorway.

Rachel stood there a minute, as if she wasn't sure what she was supposed to do. She looked around a bit and licked her lips. Then her eyes settled on Anne. "Do you have a moment?" she asked Anne.

"Of course." Anne pushed the cart to the end of the counter for Remi and looked at Rachel.

"I'm R. W. Winger, and I gave Ben the manuscript for the newest book in the Coastal Club series," Rachel blurted out. "I didn't mean any harm and didn't intend to get him in trouble, but Coraline said you threatened to ground him and he still wouldn't out me."

It wasn't Anne's proudest mothering moment. "Ben still didn't give me your name," Anne offered. "Once I had most of the information, I was finally able to put enough together to figure it out."

"I've been on a very tight deadline and wanted an opinion for the book. I needed a beta reader and, well, Ben had read all the other books in the series so I figured he could give great advice on this book. Besides, he was just so sad when he couldn't play the first football game of the season." Rachel moved her hands around as she talked.

"Well, it's an honor to officially meet you, R. W. Winger, and amazing that you wound up here in our little town of Blue Hill! You are quite the popular author among middle-school readers. Ben sure enjoyed getting to preview your next book. I basically had to pry him away from the laptop." Anne smiled, thinking of all the times she had found Ben wrapped up in the book, well, the story. "He loves the whole series," she said.

"I'm glad he does. I plan to dedicate this book to Ben. Would that be all right with you, Anne?" Rachel asked, smiling.

"I think Ben would like that. I think he would like it very much." Like it? He'd be over the moon about it.

"Well, that's all I wanted to say." Rachel hesitated, took two steps back toward the History Room, then came back to the counter. "Um, thank you."

"You're welcome Rachel. I'm glad we talked," Anne said. The woman was definitely better with kids than with adults.

Best-selling author or not, Rachel Winn was still an unusually odd person. Anne watched Rachel go back to her laptop. Rachel pulled the little Spider-Man figurine out of her pocket and set it beside the computer, setting it to stare at her while she wrote. *Fascinating indeed.*

* * *

The love of reading and friendship was perfectly depicted in the picture of Aunt Edie and Mildred that Anne had enlarged and framed. In the glass case beside their picture, in a safety sleeve, was the now famous-to-Blue-Hill copy of Edgar Allan Poe's *Tales of the Grotesque and Arabesque*.

Anne took a step back and stared at the display case. She hadn't realized Aunt Edie had begun to read, and apparently enjoy, some darker works of literature. Maybe Anne should start reading some of Poe's works.

She thought about "The Pit and the Pendulum," which had given her nightmares for days after she'd had to read it in college. *Hmm*, on second thought, maybe she'd stick more to the types of book in the front display.

Anne walked the length of the entire front counter, the whole display taken up with the books from the Coastal Club series. Rachel Winn, aka R. W. Winger, had donated and autographed a complete set of the books, which were the ones proudly displayed in the front case. Rachel had promised to send a couple of copies of the latest book as soon as it was released.

Even more exciting than that, Anne couldn't wait to see Ben's face when he realized that Rachel had dedicated the book to him. He was going to be a hit at school, that was for sure.

Gratitude warmed her heart as she smiled at the displays and at the bulletin board photos of the library's first Tea Time, which had been such a smashing success that Wendy was already planning another one.

Yes, Anne loved her family. Loved her friends. Loved her town.

The phone rang, and Anne rushed to answer it. And she most certainly loved her job. "Blue Hill Library, this is Anne speaking. How may I help you?"

About the Author

Emily Thomas is the pen name for a team of writers who have come together to create the series Secrets of the Blue Hill Library. *The Rightful Owner* was written by Robin Caroll. Born and raised in Louisiana, Robin is a Southerner through and through. Her passion has always been to tell stories to entertain others. Robin's mother, bless her heart, is a genealogist who instilled in Robin the deep love of family and pride of heritage—two aspects Robin has woven into each of her twenty-four published novels. When she isn't writing, Robin spends time with her husband of twenty-plus years, her three beautiful daughters and two handsome grandsons, and their character-filled pets at home…where else but in the South?

Robin gives back to the writing community by serving as executive/conference director for American Christian Fiction Writers. Her books have finaled/placed in such contests as the Carol Award, Holt Medallion, RT Reviewer's Choice Award, Bookseller's Best, Daphne du Maurier, and Book of the Year.

An avid reader herself, Robin loves hearing from and chatting with other readers. Although her favorite genre to read is mystery/suspense, she'll read just about any good story…except historicals! To learn more about this author of "Deep South mysteries and suspense to inspire your heart," visit Robin's Web site at robincaroll.com.

A Conversation with the Author

Q. *Aunt Edie has had a lot of adventures in her life. Can you tell us about the most exciting adventure you've experienced?*

A. Several years ago (okay, several decades ago), my husband took me to Jamaica for my birthday. We had a wonderful ten days, but on my actual birthday, we climbed Dunn's River Falls. Hiking up those falls was quite the adventure, and a memory for a lifetime.

Q. *Aunt Edie loved to travel. What's your favorite vacation destination?*

A. I love Jamaica, but I also truly loved Belize...it was so beautiful and peaceful. I also enjoyed Honduras and Cozumel for the quiet peace and beauty of the country.

Q. *Anne moves back to her hometown after years in New York City. What do/would you miss about your hometown?*

A. I always tell people I'm a Louisiana girl, born and raised, who has been transplanted to Little Rock. The things I miss most are my family and friends, because most of them are still in my hometown. I try to get back "home" as often as I can to visit. The one "thing" I miss most, though, is the food. There's just a special way we cook in Louisiana, and it's different from anywhere else. I can cook it myself, but going out to eat...well, it just isn't the same.

Q. Name the top three entries/things on your bucket list, and why did you choose them?

A. 1. I want to travel to Italy with my family because I love to travel and take in new cultures.
   2. I would love to learn to play the saxophone, because I can listen to that single instrument for hours on end.
   3. I want to spend the rest of my life never having to remove wallpaper again. Ever.

Q. What is the most memorable photograph you have on your wall?

A. Photographs are of my children and grandchildren, so they are all very special. But we have a painting, an authorized reproduction of Rene Magritte's 1964 "Son of Man," also known as "The Faceless Man" or "Man with Apple on His Face." My husband fell in love with it while watching the 1999 remake of "The Thomas Crown Affair" so for our anniversary, I commissioned the Magritte estate's authorized painter for a replica. My mother hates it, but we both love it.

Q. Which character in Secrets of the Blue Hill Library are you most like? Why?

A. I am probably most like Wendy, in her take-charge kind of way. I'm very organized and my mind tends to process the easiest way to create and manage events and such.

Recipes from the Library Guild

Wendy's Grandmother's Classic Chocolate Birthday Cake

2 cups all-purpose flour
2 cups sugar
¾ cup cocoa
2 teaspoons baking powder
1½ teaspoons baking soda
1 teaspoon salt

1 teaspoon espresso powder
1 cup milk
½ cup vegetable oil
2 eggs
2 teaspoons vanilla extract
1 cup boiling water

Preheat oven to 350 degrees. Prepare two nine-inch cake pans by spraying with baking spray or buttering and lightly flouring.

Add flour, sugar, cocoa, baking powder, baking soda, salt, and espresso powder to a large bowl or the bowl of a stand mixer. Whisk through to combine or, using your paddle attachment, stir through flour mixture until combined well.

Add milk, vegetable oil, eggs, and vanilla to flour mixture and mix together on medium speed until well combined. Reduce speed and carefully add boiling water to the cake batter. Beat on high speed for about one minute to add air to the batter.

Distribute cake batter evenly between the two prepared cake pans. Bake for thirty to thirty-five minutes, until a toothpick or cake tester inserted in the center comes out clean.

Remove from the oven and allow to cool for about ten minutes, remove from the pan, and cool completely.

Frost cake with favorite fudge chocolate frosting.

From the Guideposts Archives

This article by Kenny Warns originally appeared in *Guideposts* magazine.

I'm a New York City firefighter. I work out of Ladder Company 163/Engine 325 in Woodside, Queens. Proud? It comes with the job. Just like the danger. On Father's Day 2001, we lost our first firefighter in nearly forty years. It was a hardware store fire; the roof fell in. Then, on September 11, we lost two more guys. I was numb for a long time. I'm not a literary guy, but words from an old book kept running through my head: "It was the best of times, it was the worst of times." I'd always wondered what that meant. It never made sense to me. Until now. I remember going down to work at Ground Zero. The West Side Highway was lined with people holding up signs and cheering as we drove past. The cynical New Yorker in me thought, *They won't come back*. But they did, every day. This great, sprawling, diverse city became one big neighborhood. People connected. And then letters poured in. Thousands of them, from all over the country. I read many of them. People banded together in a way I'd never thought possible.

Like the folks in Akron, Ohio, who raised more than one million dollars for New York. The money helped pay for two new ambulances, three police vehicles and a new fire engine for Ladder

163. One day when I was feeling really down I opened a letter from a boy named Jackson. He'd written a few lines and drew a picture of a fire truck. I looked at the return address: Akron, Ohio. Well, I had to write back. "Dear Jackson, First, let me thank you for the brand-new fire truck. We've already used it. I'm one of the regular drivers and let me tell you it rides nice! I also want to thank you for your nice letter. It's been a very sad time for me. The cards and letters are helping me get through it." We exchanged more letters. When guys from our firehouse got invited to Akron I wanted to go to meet Jackson face to face.

Not much surprises a guy like me. Jackson did. Jackson is high-functioning autistic. You wouldn't know it just by looking at him or his letters. But like many autistic folks, Jackson can have trouble connecting with people. His mom, Vickie, said Jackson had seen a flattened fire truck in the World Trade Center rubble on TV. "What's New York going to do without its truck?" he asked. He emptied his piggy bank. Sixty dollars he'd been saving for vacation.

"Something changed," Vickie told me. "Jackson started giving more." He contributed to Toys for Tots, volunteered to help clean up trash around his school, and bowled to raise money for muscular dystrophy.

I went home renewed. Jackson gave me hope, hope that there is more good in the world than evil.

Last December I went back to Ohio to see my sister. I made a trip to see Jackson. "Kenny!" he shouted and jumped into my arms.

"I can't believe you're here," Vickie said. "Jackson has been so upset lately." This was right after the tsunami. Again Jackson saw tragic pictures on TV. He kept asking his mom, "What will all those people do? Where will they live?"

Jackson and I talked a lot. By the time I left he had a plan: He'd organize a bowl-a-thon for tsunami relief. Convinced that there was a way for him to help, he finally settled down. "Good things come back to you when you do good things," Jackson's mother told him. "That's why you're friends with Kenny."

I thought about that on the drive back to New York. Jackson did something good for me when I really needed it. In return I helped him when he needed it. All because I answered that letter. Thing is, that was the only letter I answered. Why that one? I guess God had it all figured out, how to make the worst of times...better.

Read on for a sneak peek of another exciting book in Secrets of the Blue Hill Library!

Cracking the Code

Anne Gibson tapped her pencil on the checkout desk as she studied the computer screen, which was opened to the budget spreadsheet for the Blue Hill Library. No matter how she tried to crunch the numbers, there was no room in this year's finances to pay for a major repair.

Wendy Pyle, a library volunteer and Anne's dear friend, leaned on the counter. "How's it going?"

"I just don't see how to squeeze in getting the elevator fixed without breaking the budget—let alone purchase a new one as Alex suggested. I'm going to have to appeal to the Library Guild or take out a loan. This is really bad timing with the county inspection coming up."

"They wouldn't shut us down for not having an elevator, would they?" Wendy asked, her blue eyes widening.

Anne pushed her glasses back up her nose and leaned back in her chair. "No, no, but they would write up a recommendation or sanction, depending on how you want to look at it. We would be listed in the directory as not being handicapped accessible. I really would like to avoid that."

"We'll just have to get it fixed by then," Wendy said with a determined nod that set her chin-length, dark hair bobbing. "God will provide. He always has."

"So true." Anne admired Wendy's steadfast faith and determined drive to get things done. Like the literacy program. In less than a month, Wendy had organized a whole new program, recruited a teacher to supervise, and enlisted volunteer tutors. This was in addition to her usual volunteer work at the library and duties involved in being a supportive wife to the local high school football coach and wonderful mother to seven children.

Anne glanced over at the back table, where her five-year-old daughter was busy coloring a picture for her kindergarten show-and-tell. "How's it going, Liddie?"

"I can't get Hershey's nose right." She held up her drawing. They were supposed to be drawing one of their pets or a friend's pet to share with the class in the morning. Since their only pet at the moment was a chocolate Labrador retriever they'd adopted from the shelter, Liddie concentrated on capturing his likeness in crayon.

"Maybe try drawing it a little bit longer, but I think you've done a great job already," Anne said sincerely. Liddie, with chocolate brown eyes and curly brown hair and blonde highlights, resembled her father so much at times that Anne's breath caught in her chest. Liddie had also inherited her father's talent for drawing.

Liddie's mouth pursed to a pout. "I want to start over."

"That's fine. We still have an hour until dinner." Anne appreciated Liddie's focus, although she hoped her daughter wouldn't get too stressed over getting the image perfect. Her original drawing was already well done for her age.

Wendy still lingered by the counter, straightening up some brochures for the local garden club.

"Did you need me for something?" Anne asked her.

"Not really. You already answered my question. I was going to ask if we had any more funds for advertising the literacy class, but I'm guessing that's out of the question right now."

"Unfortunately—"

"—the timing is terrible," Wendy finished for her. "I'm just concerned since we only have three people signed up. Surely there are more in need out there. Illiteracy is a national epidemic. I read someplace that thirty-two million adults in the United States can't read."

"Maybe word of mouth just didn't spread fast enough this time," Anne said. She was as excited as Wendy about the new literacy classes and had been praying that they would reach people who needed help the most. Teaching others to read had been a passion of her great-aunt Edie, who'd left her historic Victorian mansion to the town for a library. Anne wanted to make sure she made the most of her aunt's legacy to Blue Hill.

"But, again, there's no way around the need to get the elevator working again." Anne sighed. "That has to be our priority. Not only for the inspection, but we have patrons who can't climb the stairs. We're going to have to run up and down to get any books they want from the upstairs rooms. And it would have been terrible if one of them had gotten stuck in elevator like I did."

"Yes, it would've been." Wendy's lips twitched.

Anne raised her eyebrows. "Are you laughing at me?"

A giggle escaped Wendy. "I don't mean to. It's just you looked like a trapped bird, waving your arms under all those sheets."

Liddie looked up and giggled too. "Mommy must've looked funny."

"I was just surprised, that's all," Anne said with a laugh. That morning, Anne had been returning from the basement with a load of laundry to their private quarters on the third floor when there was a deafening boom of thunder. The elevator jerked to a stop, causing the sheets and pillowcases to fly out of the basket she was holding and land on top of her. She was stuck between the second and third floors without her cell phone and had to holler for Wendy who was downstairs shelving books.

"I'm just thankful you came in early and were there to get me out," Anne said with a shake of her head. Wendy had run out to the garage and brought in a ladder to rescue Anne.

Anne clicked the computer window shut on the budget and stood. "And I'm glad Alex could come over and take a look before he went to work."

When Anne had returned to her hometown of Blue Hill after the death of her husband and loss of her job in New York, she'd been glad to hire a familiar face, her high school buddy, Alex Ochs. He had done a marvelous job transforming the stately old house into a lovely library.

Alex was a contractor now, and Anne would forever be grateful for his skills and friendship. The library area now sprawled through the first two floors of the house with a portion of the second floor and entire third floor turned into living space for Anne and her two young children, Liddie and Ben. The house also contained an enormous attic and basement as well as a detached garage.

Alex had originally inspected the house's antique cage elevator and determined it was up to code. But when Anne got stuck, she called Alex over immediately after Wendy freed her and he'd taken a quick look. The lightning had fried the elevator motor and damaged the cab control mechanism. It was fortunate that Anne's hands had been full of the laundry basket and she hadn't been touching the metal sides or she might have been shocked. The magnitude of that lightning strike could have also set the house on fire along with taking out a circuit and the elevator. Anne kept thanking God for watching over the old Victorian and the people inside.

Alex was looking for replacement parts now but cautioned he may have to replace the entire motor. He also suggested that she compare the costs of a new elevator versus the repair and maintenance of the old one.

Anne loved the old elevator that she had used many times as a child. It was the jail when friends came over to play in the mansion on rainy days and a cage for her stuffed animals when she played zoo. She hated the idea of putting in a more modern one.

"I should know more when Alex gets back some estimates on the parts," Anne said. "Meanwhile, we could put up more flyers around town."

"I put one up in Coffee Joe's, Stella's Pizza, the diner, and the Senior Center. But I didn't get one at the market."

"I'll put up one there." Anne made a mental note to get a flyer over to the grocery store. "Word of mouth should eventually help too."

Liddie set her pencil down. "I wish Beth's daddy would go to the class."

"You do, sweetheart?" Anne asked. "Why?"

Liddie nodded. "I told my friend Beth at church about the storybook you are reading to me at bedtime, and she says her daddy doesn't read to her."

"How sad," Wendy said. "Maybe he just doesn't have time or maybe he doesn't like to read."

"Beth said he can't read very well," Liddie said. "Her mommy used to read to her every night before she went away. Her daddy tried, but then he stopped. It makes Beth sad she can't hear stories."

Wendy raised her eyebrows at Anne. "Maybe all he needs is a personal invitation. What's his name?"

"Her father is Luke Norris. He's a carpenter and works for Alex occasionally," Anne said.

"I'll see what I can do." Wendy's eyes gleamed with determination. "Right now, I think I'll go upstairs and check on the Children's Room. I saw little Charlie Barnes going up there with his mother, and you know how he loves to take books off the shelves."

As Wendy started up the stairs, the front door opened and an elderly woman with a cane stood in the entry. It was Betty Warring, which meant her sister Nellie couldn't be far behind.

"Hurry up, Betty," Nellie Brown said over her sister's shoulder. "I don't want to get wet."

"Stop fretting. We beat the storm." Betty shuffled forward, leaning heavily on her cane. "Besides, a little rain won't melt you."

"Easy for you to say." Nellie stepped inside, patting her short white hairdo. "You didn't just get your hair permed. I don't want to lose the curl."

"Be careful, your vanity is showing," Betty teased with a wink at Anne.

"Vanity, my foot. I don't want to lose the money it took to get looking this good." Nellie set her book bag on the counter.

Anne reached inside and pulled out two library books and proceeded to check them back in. The octogenarians lived together and visited the library at least once a week. They loved biographies and took turns reading the books out loud to each other. Despite their excessive bickering, everyone knew the sisters adored each other.

Betty looked out the window. "It looks like our April showers are now May showers. We've gotten enough rain to last the rest of the year. We're lucky we're not all getting washed away."

Anne agreed. They were making up for their lack of rain earlier in the spring. The forecasters were predicting a stormy week.

"Hurry along, Betty." Nellie headed for the biography section. "That storm will be here soon."

Nellie's prediction was correct. By the time the sisters had chosen a book on Winston Churchill and checked out, thunder grumbled in the distance. The remaining patrons hurried with their selections, and soon a line formed in front of the checkout desk. Anne hurried as fast as she could. In addition to the looming bad weather, it was almost five anyway, which was closing time.

A rumble sounded as the last patron left. Anne hoped Ben was on his way in from playing outside. She was headed for the door when it burst open and Ben ran in.

"Mom! Come quick! Hershey took a package off the porch, and he won't give it to me."

Anne ran outside with Liddie at her heels. Dark clouds rolled close overhead and the wind stung her face. Hershey stood in the middle of the lawn, a large brown package hanging from his jaws.

"Hershey, here boy!" Anne called, slapping her thighs to get his attention. "Come."

The dog stood stock-still, his dark eyes shining mischievously as he watched her.

Anne knew that look and changed tactics. She advanced slowly down the stairs. "Be a good boy. Stay there!"

Hershey wagged his tail. Anne was about a foot away from him, when he suddenly bounced up on his hind legs, danced backward, and bounded away.

"That's what he was doing when I tried to get the package," Ben said with his hands on his hips. "He thinks we're playing."

Thunder rumbled louder. The storm rolled closer. Anne could smell the rain in the air. They had to hurry.

"Hershey. Bad dog! Come here," Anne scolded, but it had no effect on the playful mutt as he raced around them. She turned to her children. "We're going to have to corner him by the fence. Liddie, you go that way." She pointed to her right. "And, Ben, try going around the other way."

Ben and Anne circled the dog that had now crouched down and watched them warily. They all edged in closer. Still Hershey didn't move a muscle, except for his wagging tail. Ben glanced at Anne and she nodded. He made a flying grab for the dog but only caught his tail. Hershey jerked away, evaded Anne's hands, bumped up against Liddie, and raced across the yard.

Anne shook her head watching their pet. At least he was having a great time. Normally she'd just wait until the dog realized they weren't playing a game, but she was worried about the package and impending storm. Could it be a delivery of new books? If they didn't get it soon, the rain would finish off any damage Hershey's teeth were doing.

"I'll go get a dog treat." Liddie sprinted back into the house.

"Hershey come. Now!" Anne was growing crankier with each passing moment. She looked at Ben. "Let's see if we can get him cornered again."

A flash of lightning illuminated the sky, and thunder boomed and shook the ground. Startled, Hershey twisted in midair and the package ripped. A cloud of green swirled into the wind.

Anne gasped.

The paper package was full of money!

A Note from the Editors

We hope you enjoy *Secrets of the Blue Hill Library*, created by the Books and Inspirational Media Division of Guideposts, a nonprofit organization that touches millions of lives every day through products and services that inspire, encourage, help you grow in your faith, and celebrate God's love in every aspect of your daily life.

Thank you for making a difference with your purchase of this book, which helps fund our many outreach programs to military personnel, prisons, hospitals, nursing homes, and educational institutions. To learn more, visit GuidepostsFoundation.org.

We also maintain many useful and uplifting online resources. Visit Guideposts.org to read true stories of hope and inspiration, access OurPrayer network, sign up for free newsletters, download free e-books, join our Facebook community, and follow our stimulating blogs.

To learn about other Guideposts publications, including the best-selling devotional *Daily Guideposts*, go to ShopGuideposts.org, call (800) 932-2145, or write to Guideposts, PO Box 5815, Harlan, Iowa 51593.

SIGN UP FOR THE
Guideposts Fiction e-Newsletter

and stay up-to-date on the Guideposts fiction you love!

You'll get sneak peeks of new releases, hear from authors of your favorite books, receive special offers just for you ...

AND IT'S FREE!

Just go to **Guideposts.org/newsletters** *today to sign up.*